PRAISE FOR SUSAN STOKER

FOR *JUSTICE FOR MACKENZIE*

"Daxton's desperation to find Mackenzie is rousing and believable, and readers will have a white-knuckle read until the end . . . pure entertainment."

—*Kirkus Reviews*

"Susan Stoker never disappoints. She delivers alpha males with heart and heroines with moxie."

—Jana Aston, *New York Times* bestselling author

"Susan does romantic suspense right! Edge of my seat + smokin' hot = read ALL of her books! Now."

—Carly Phillips, *New York Times* bestselling author

"Susan writes the perfect blend of tough, alpha heroes and strong yet vulnerable heroines. I always feel emotionally satisfied at the end of one of her stories!"

—Meghan March, *New York Times* bestselling author

"One thing I love about Susan Stoker's books is that she knows how to deliver a perfect HEA while still making sure the villain gets what he/ she deserves!"

—T.M. Frazier, *New York Times* bestselling author

FOR *RESCUING RAYNE*

DEFENDING
MORGAN

Rescuing Wendy

Rescuing Mary

Rescuing Macie

Badge of Honor: Texas Heroes Series

Justice for Mackenzie

Justice for Mickie

Justice for Corrie

Justice for Laine (novella)

Shelter for Elizabeth

Justice for Boone

Shelter for Adeline

Shelter for Sophie

Justice for Erin

Justice for Milena

Shelter for Blythe

Justice for Hope

Shelter for Quinn

Shelter for Koren (July 2019)

Shelter for Penelope (Oct. 2019)

SEAL of Protection Series

Protecting Caroline

Protecting Alabama

Protecting Fiona

Marrying Caroline (novella)

Protecting Summer

Protecting Cheyenne

Protecting Jessyka

Protecting Julie (novella)
Protecting Melody
Protecting the Future
Protecting Kiera (novella)
Protecting Dakota

SEAL of Protection: Legacy Series

Securing Caite
Securing Sidney
Securing Piper (Sept. 2019)
Securing Zoey (TBA)
Securing Avery (TBA)
Securing Kalee (TBA)

Beyond Reality Series

Outback Hearts
Flaming Hearts
Frozen Hearts

Stand-Alone Novels

The Guardian Mist
A Princess for Cale
A Moment in Time
Lambert's Lady

Writing as Annie George

Stepbrother Virgin (erotic novella)

DEFENDING MORGAN

Mountain Mercenaries, Book 3

Susan Stoker

Text copyright © 2019 by Susan Stoker
All rights reserved.

Published by Montlake Romance, Seattle

www.apub.com

Amazon, the Amazon logo, and Montlake Romance are trademarks of Amazon.com, Inc., or its affiliates.

ISBN-13: 9781542042253
ISBN-10: 1542042259

Cover design by Eileen Carey

Cover photography by Wander Aguiar

Printed in the United States of America

DEFENDING
MORGAN

Chapter One

Archer "Arrow" Kane couldn't believe the luck of the woman at his side. The Mountain Mercenaries had been sent to the Dominican Republic to rescue a kidnapped little girl, and had left the dilapidated home they'd found her in with an additional hostage. A woman. A very famous missing woman at that.

Arrow kept his hand on Morgan Byrd to keep her near him. At times he merely rested it on the small of her back; at others, he gripped her arm to help her over debris. She didn't look at him, didn't thank him, didn't acknowledge his touch in any way, but it seemed that she welcomed it. Whenever they stopped so Black could scope out the area to make sure they weren't being followed, she leaned toward Arrow. She was subtle about it, but since Arrow was hyperaware of her, he noticed.

Ball was carrying the little girl they'd come to the Dominican Republic to rescue. She was five years old, and her noncustodial father hadn't returned her after his court-approved visitation weekend. He'd fled to his home country with the child. That had been three months ago, and her mother had done everything possible to get her little girl back. When Rex had gotten wind of the situation, he'd immediately asked for volunteers to head to the small Caribbean island to bring Nina home.

Black, Ball, and Arrow had agreed to come. Ro was on his honeymoon, Meat was down and out with the flu, and Gray's girlfriend was dancing in a special performance in Denver, so he'd passed this time. It was supposed to be an easy job, especially since Rex had information on the general area where Nina's father was keeping her. But finding Morgan at the same location complicated things.

Arrow was still in shock. Morgan Byrd had been missing for a year or so. She'd disappeared from Atlanta one night, and despite several credible clues and surveillance video showing her dancing and having fun at a nightclub, there hadn't been any movement in the case. Until now.

How in the world she'd come to be in the run-down house in Santo Domingo, Arrow had no idea, and right this second wasn't the time to question her. But she'd obviously been through hell. She was covered in dirt, and her blonde hair was matted and filthy. She smelled like she hadn't showered in weeks—which was probably the case.

Regardless, there was something about her that drew Arrow. It wasn't her looks—because God knew she was looking rough right about now. It was her . . . resilience. Whatever she'd been through should've broken her.

Arrow had rescued his share of women and children from horrible situations, and many had been broken almost beyond repair. But when he'd entered the pitch-dark room, Morgan hadn't been cowering in a corner. She'd been protecting the little girl she'd taken under her wing with a crude knife. The weapon wouldn't have done much damage, but that didn't matter. She'd put herself between the child and whoever had entered the room.

She hadn't cried and begged to be taken away from her prison. Even now, she wasn't clinging to him. Wasn't hiding behind him. She was standing stoically next to him with one hand on Nina's back, trying to reassure and comfort her.

He was extremely impressed with Morgan. She was different from all the other women he'd saved over the years. It was as if he could sense her determination. He was proud of her. Proud of how she'd stuck up for Nina. Proud that she hadn't been broken. He also felt more protective toward this woman than anyone else he'd rescued. He couldn't identify all the reasons why, but the feeling was definitely there.

Arrow could've probably resisted the emotions he could feel bubbling under the surface if she weren't unconsciously leaning into him every chance she got. She might be tough and composed on the surface, but that slight telltale movement offered a very different story.

Underneath her bravado, she was scared to death. Arrow wanted to take her in his arms and reassure her. Tell her that he'd get her home to her father, to safety. But he knew from experience that showing even the slightest amount of sympathy right now could undo her. So he restricted himself to small touches, making sure he stayed by her side, giving her what comfort he could while still being on alert for the smallest signs of danger.

After what she'd been through, whatever that was, he wasn't going to let anyone or anything hurt her again before he got her home.

"All clear," Black said in a toneless whisper as he reappeared next to them without another sound. The man had been a Navy SEAL and could move silently through any kind of terrain. Arrow had long since gotten used to it, but next to him, he felt Morgan start violently as Black's presence surprised her.

But she didn't make a sound. She'd trained herself well to keep quiet. He'd noticed that in the room where she and Nina had been held captive. When he'd hit her arms to knock the knife out of her hand, she hadn't cried out. When the little girl had thrown herself at her, Morgan hadn't let out even the smallest umph as she'd landed on her ass. It had surprised him at the same time it impressed the hell out of him. He and his teammates had learned to move absolutely silently, but it had taken him years of training in the Marines and more dangerous missions than he could count. The mystery of how and why Morgan had learned to be silent, no matter what, bothered him.

"We need to move quickly," Black went on. "The safe house is roughly half a mile away, but we're about thirty minutes later than we'd planned. The city is waking up, and the last thing we want is for someone to see us and get curious."

Arrow pressed his lips together. Three Caucasian men wandering around the city wearing all black, with a woman and child in tow, would definitely attract attention. The kind they didn't need. He opened his mouth to speak, but Morgan beat him to it.

"We should split up," she said quietly. "We're slowing you guys down. If we split up, you can move faster with Nina," she told Ball, nodding at the child now sleeping in his arms.

Arrow could see how much the suggestion cost her. She was gripping Nina's shirt in her fist so hard her knuckles were white.

Black looked toward Arrow with one brow raised. From the second they'd stepped outside the hovel where they'd rescued the pair, Arrow's teammates had realized he had a connection with Morgan. It worked like that sometimes on their missions. They were trained to watch the reactions of the women and children, and if they showed the slightest inclination to trust one of the men over another, the team did what they could to encourage that. Trust was a huge issue when rescuing kidnapping victims. And having a victim trust even one of them made the mission that much easier.

They'd read Morgan's body language as easily as he had. Not to mention the way he'd been hovering over her. Black was asking, without words, for Arrow's opinion on splitting up. There was no doubt that he'd be the one going with Morgan.

Arrow turned to the woman at his side. He towered over her slight five feet three inches. At an inch over six feet, he was used to being taller than the people they rescued, but her diminutive height was one of the things that made his protective instincts rush to the surface more than usual.

He slowly moved his hand and lightly brushed his fingertips against her upper arm. It was covered with a ratty gray T-shirt, but he could feel the heat of her skin through it. "Are you sure?" he asked. "It would make things easier, but if you don't want to be separated from Nina, we can make it work."

She tilted her chin up to look him in the eyes, which Arrow loved. She was scared and nervous, but hadn't been beaten down to a point where she refused to meet his gaze.

"I want to do whatever will get Nina safe the fastest."

Arrow had known that was what she'd say. He turned to Ball. The former Coastie was standing patiently next to them. He was a foot taller than Morgan, and he held the child in his arms easily. "We'll meet you there."

The hair at the back of Arrow's neck stood on end, but he ignored it for the time being. He didn't like being separated from his teammates, but splitting up was the right thing to do at the moment. Once they were ensconced in the safe house, they could figure out their next steps. They needed to get in contact with Rex and let him know that Nina was safe, but also that they had a surprise addition.

They had the proper paperwork to get Nina out of the country, including her passport, among other legal items, but they had nothing for Morgan. They had chartered a jet to get home, but even so, they couldn't just plunk a mysterious, unidentified woman on the plane and expect authorities to be okay with it.

"Be careful," Ball said, his gaze intense.

Arrow knew what he meant. They had no idea about Morgan's story. Who took her. Why she was being held. What had happened to her. She was a total unknown in this scenario. Nina's father, they knew well enough. Rex had researched him and shared everything he'd learned before they'd left. But Morgan was a mystery.

He nodded at his friend.

"Got your radio?" Black asked.

Arrow nodded again. Each of them had a radio that they used to communicate with each other. They had a range of a couple of miles, but for anything beyond that, they had to use specialized satellite phones.

Morgan took a step toward Nina and Ball, but hesitated when Arrow's hand fell from her arm. Knowing she needed the reassurance, Arrow followed her and put his fingertips on the middle of her back. He could feel how tight her muscles were, but she merely approached Ball and stood up on tiptoe. She still couldn't reach the sleeping child's face, so Ball leaned down.

Morgan brushed her lips against Nina's cheek and stepped back. "Take care of her," she whispered. "She's been through a lot."

"Does she need a doctor?" Ball asked, putting one of his large hands on the back of Nina's head, holding her securely to him as he straightened.

Morgan shrugged. "Probably. She hasn't been eating too well, and she's been complaining that her tummy hurts. I figured it was probably just upset because of stress and not eating all that much, but I don't know."

Ball nodded. "Black's got medical training. He'll take a look at her, and I know her mom will have a doctor waiting for her when we get back to the States."

"What about you?" Black asked.

"Me?" Morgan asked.

"Do you need a doctor?"

Arrow saw the instant change in her demeanor—and blinked in surprise. All emotion disappeared from her face as she shook her head.

"Not right this second, no."

He wanted to argue. Wanted to reassure her that whatever had happened wasn't her fault. That he'd make sure she got all the medical attention she needed. But her closed-off expression and the blankness in her eyes, not to mention the fact that it was getting lighter and lighter the longer they stood around talking, kept him silent.

Black didn't look any happier with her answer than Arrow was, but his teammate didn't comment. He merely nodded and gestured to

Ball with his head. Within seconds they were gone, blending into the shadows of the extremely run-down neighborhood.

"Come on," Arrow said, reaching down and taking her hand in his. Once more, he was struck by the difference in their sizes. Her fingers were slender and dainty, while his were large and calloused. He'd removed the gloves he had on earlier, and he could feel how clammy her palm was. Another nonverbal sign of her nervousness, unease, and fright.

Without a word in protest, Morgan nodded and followed him as he headed in the opposite direction from where Black and Ball had gone. They'd circle around the neighborhood and get to the safe house from the north rather than the south, the direction his teammates were headed. It was the longer route, but he could move faster since he didn't have to worry about jostling a child.

Morgan stumbled a bit behind him. She couldn't see as well as he could since he'd pulled down his night-vision goggles, but once again, she didn't make a sound. She merely held on to his hand tighter and trusted him as he led her through dark alleyways and trash-filled streets.

He had no idea what had happened to her in the last year, but he made a mental vow right then and there to do everything in his power to make her feel safe once more . . . no matter what it took.

Chapter Two

Morgan held on to the soldier's hand as tightly as she could. The last thing she wanted to do was get lost in this godforsaken country. She had no idea who the men were who had shown up in the middle of the night like angels from heaven, but she didn't care. They could be drug dealers and terrorists, and it wouldn't matter—as long as they got Nina out of there and back to the States.

The fact that they knew who she was and agreed to take her too was a miracle as far as Morgan was concerned. They could've been Mafia henchmen, and she still would've gone with them. Anything was better than being where she was.

Morgan spared a second to wonder what had happened to the men who had been keeping her and Nina captive, but dismissed them a moment later. They were scum. Lowlifes of the highest order. She hoped they'd died horrible deaths.

She had no idea what the names of her saviors were, but it wasn't like they'd had time to stop and exchange niceties. She didn't care that they weren't there for *her*. When Nina had begged them to allow Morgan to come too, she'd wanted that with every fiber of her being. She probably should've been a bit more hesitant since she didn't know them. But with the way they were dressed, not to mention the expensive night-vision goggles they wore, there was no way they were in cahoots with the assholes who'd been holding her hostage.

Stumbling over a piece of trash in the alley, she mentally berated herself. She needed to pay attention. To not be so clumsy. She didn't want to irritate the man who was helping her. She had to do her best to not inconvenience him in any way. She couldn't afford for him to get annoyed and decide he couldn't take her with him, after all. If she were this close to rescue but then recaptured, it would crush her.

Her rescuer had hurt her when he'd made her drop the crude knife she'd threatened him with in the house, but compared to the last year, the bruises on her arms were nothing. And after that small, sharp pain, he'd gone out of his way *not* to hurt her. She'd felt his hands on her ever since they'd made their escape from the house, steadying her, letting her know that he was right there next to her. That he wasn't going to let anything happen to her.

She still remembered his words right before they'd left.

I've got you, Morgan. I'm going to get you home no matter what it takes.

He had her.

She wasn't sure she *wanted* to go home. Atlanta didn't exactly hold good memories for her. It had been a long time since she'd felt safe. But somehow, hearing this man's words and having him near made her feel as if she truly would get back to the United States.

"How're you holding up?" he asked quietly.

"I'm good," she said automatically.

He stopped abruptly, and Morgan immediately cut off the grunt she'd involuntarily made when she ran into his back. He turned and put his free hand on her shoulder. "No, really. How are you doing?"

"I'm fine," she repeated. "I just want to get out of here."

He stared down at her for the longest moment. Morgan had no idea what he was searching for or what he saw when he looked at her, but she did her best to look like she was strong and capable when inside she felt anything but.

"My name is Archer Kane. My friends call me Arrow," he said. "Archer . . . Arrow . . . not very original, but it's better than some nicknames I've heard."

Morgan blinked in surprise. She'd been sure he was about to call her on her lie. "Um . . . hi."

He grinned. "Hi."

She had no idea what he was grinning at, but she did her best to return his smile. It had been so long since she'd had something to smile about, she wasn't sure her lips even remembered how. But her attempt must've been adequate because he squeezed her hand and said, "It's not too much farther. We're going to circle around and come at the safe house from the north. Once we get settled, I'll get you something to eat, and we can see about getting you some medical care."

"I'm fine. I don't need a doctor," Morgan said urgently. The last thing she wanted was this man, or his friends, looking at her.

His eyes narrowed. "We'll discuss it when we're at the safe house."

She pressed her lips together. *Be agreeable. Be agreeable.* "Okay."

As if he knew she was only saying what he wanted to hear, Arrow's lips quirked upward, and he shook his head. "Come on."

She trudged on behind him, worrying more about what he was going to ask when they got to the safe house than their surroundings. Which was a mistake.

One second they were walking through a filthy alley, and the next they were surrounded by rough-looking men.

Once again, she bounced off Arrow's back, but this time his arm came up and wrapped around her waist. He spun them until her back was to the building on their right and he was standing in front of her. He'd dropped her hand and had both arms out, as if that could keep the men from getting to her.

The biggest man, the one with long, greasy hair, said something in Spanish. She'd been in the country for almost a year, but she still didn't understand much of the native language. The men who'd kept her captive hadn't exactly been willing to teach her, and besides, when they did interact with her, they didn't *ask* anything; they simply moved her where and how they wanted.

To her surprise, Arrow responded in very authentic-sounding Spanish. More words were said back and forth, but Arrow's protective stance in front of her never wavered. Morgan could feel herself trembling, but was determined to keep out of Arrow's way and let him do what he needed to do.

She felt horrible about the fact that she wasn't considering giving herself up to save Arrow. She wasn't going back to her previous existence. No way.

Another man ran down the alley toward them—and Morgan's stomach dropped. She knew this guy. He didn't have an ounce of compassion in him.

The second he arrived, he said something to his friends—and all four of them attacked Arrow at once.

Morgan didn't waste a breath on screaming. No one would come to their aid. She'd learned that the hard way. So she did the only thing she could—she fought. Arrow was good, but there was no way he'd be able to hold off all four of the men.

She picked up a metal pipe from the ground and, without an ounce of remorse, slammed it into the knee of the man nearest her.

He roared in pain and went down.

"Run!" Arrow yelled at her even as he punched one of the men in the face.

Morgan hesitated. She wanted to. Oh God, how she wanted to. But she had no idea where the safe house was or where to go. The last thing she wanted was to be on her own in the back alleys of Santo Domingo. She'd be recaptured in a heartbeat. She was safest with Arrow . . . and she could help him.

She swung the piece of metal and once again hit one of the men. This time she caught him in the arm. Before she had a chance to wind up again, he turned to her and swung his fist. She ducked, but he still managed to catch her on the side of her head. She went down to her knees, dropping the piece of metal in the process.

Immediately, she groped on the ground for her weapon, but it was too late. The fifth man, the one she knew, grabbed her by the hair and hauled her off the ground, holding her in front of him like a shield.

He said something to the others, and everyone stopped fighting immediately.

"Let me go," she spat, squirming in the man's grasp.

"Cállate, puta!" he said, and wrapped an arm around her neck.

Morgan knew *cállate* meant *shut up*, and she assumed *puta* was some sort of derogatory name, as she'd been called that many times over the last year. But she didn't know what the rest of the words that came spewing out of his mouth meant.

Arrow didn't hesitate, responding with words that sounded just as harsh. She didn't panic until the man holding her began backing down the alley.

He was taking her away from Arrow. Away from safety.

"No!" she yelled, suddenly sick of being hauled around against her will. She was shorter than the men and not as strong, but she was done being the victim. She wasn't going back to that house, or any others like it. She'd gotten lucky with Arrow and his friends. If she was taken away again, she wouldn't be so lucky the next time. She knew it as well as she knew her name.

She fought with all her strength, frantically, the events of the last year replaying over and over in her brain. She vaguely heard grunts and the sound of fighting, but nothing truly registered. The man dragged her farther down the alley toward a beat-up black car.

Knowing if she was put inside that car, her life would be even more of a living hell than it had been, Morgan felt determination rise up within her.

"Fuck you," she huffed out as the man struggled to rein her in and open the door at the same time. He managed to lift the handle, but Morgan kicked out with her foot and slammed it shut.

Her captor mumbled some words Morgan couldn't understand under his breath, but she didn't stop her struggles. Eventually, however, even though she was fighting with all her strength, the man got the upper hand. He clamped his hand over her nose and mouth and pressed down hard.

Morgan clawed at his hand, trying to remove it so she could get air into her lungs, but he was holding on too strongly. With his free hand, he reached over and opened the car door.

Just when she thought her luck had run out, she heard someone bark, "Down!"

Without thought, Morgan attempted to do as Arrow had ordered. Even though the guy was holding her up, she let every muscle in her body go limp.

At the sudden change of weight in his arms, the man swore and let go of her face long enough for Morgan to suck in some much-needed breath.

Her knees hit the pavement, and she winced at the pain that went through her body. Comparatively, however, it was nothing. Instinctively, Morgan fell the rest of the way to the ground, hunched over her bent knees, and covered her head.

The sound of a weapon discharging seemed obscenely loud in the quickly lightening alley. The weight of the man's body dropped down on her, and Morgan could feel wetness seep through the raggedy T-shirt she wore.

Almost as soon as the man's weight had crushed her beneath him, it was gone.

"Come on," Arrow said urgently.

Her lungs still burning, Morgan didn't hesitate. She stood with his help, and then they were running out of the alley, down the street, and between two buildings nearby. Arrow had grabbed her hand, and Morgan held on with all her strength. It felt as if he were her only lifeline in this terrifying world she'd been in for a full year. She knew she'd been two seconds away from disappearing once more. She had no idea how Arrow had gotten away from the other four men, but thank God he had.

She didn't even care that he'd shot—and hopefully killed—the merciless man who would've tortured her before passing her off to his friends and enemies alike. It didn't matter that she was a living, breathing human being with feelings and hopes and dreams. All that mattered to them was the fact that she was female.

Choking back the sob that threatened to escape, Morgan stared at the back of Arrow's head as they ran as fast as possible through the dangerous back alleys of Santo Domingo. She had no idea where they were, but Arrow had killed for her—and he was the only thing standing between certain death and freedom.

"Wait here," he said, pushing her back against a brick wall halfway down what seemed like the hundredth alley they'd fled through.

Shaking her head, Morgan hissed, "No! I'm staying with you."

As if he knew she was hanging on by a thread, Arrow paused. He put his hands on her shoulders and leaned down so their foreheads almost touched.

Morgan was panting heavily, finding it hard to pull oxygen into her lungs. Her hands came up to dig into his forearms. She wasn't letting go of him. No way.

"I need to check out this building and see if we can lie low without disturbing anyone."

"I'll come with you."

"I'm not going to let anything happen to you," he said.

"Right. Because I'm going to be right by your side." She knew she should be more compliant. Should be doing anything and everything he said without a word so he wouldn't come up with a reason to pawn her off on someone else or leave her. But she couldn't. Not with something this important.

Arrow huffed out a sigh and turned his head to look back the way they'd come. Then, just as quickly, he looked back down at her. "Fine. But don't make a sound. Step where I step. And if I tell you to do something, you do it immediately and without question. Got it?"

Morgan nodded quickly, feeling almost lightheaded with relief.

"Come on," Arrow said. He grabbed one of her hands and tucked it into the waistband of his pants. "I need both hands free," he said by way of explanation.

Morgan would've preferred to hold his hand, but this was almost as good. His shirt was tucked in, so she couldn't feel his skin, but she *could* feel the heat from his body against her fingers. The morning was warm and humid, just like most mornings in the tropical country. It would only get hotter as the sun rose above the horizon.

Following behind Arrow, Morgan did her best not to make a sound as she clung to him. They entered the dilapidated two-story building without a sound. It was obviously abandoned. There was junk everywhere. Discarded pieces of wood and metal, trash, and even rotting food. It smelled horrendous, but Morgan barely noticed the smells of the city anymore.

Gingerly stepping over the trash and debris, trying to put her feet exactly where Arrow did, she once again ran into his back when she didn't notice he'd stopped walking.

He turned and put his hands on her shoulders. "We need to hide here for a while," he told her.

Eyes wide, Morgan stared up at him. "But I thought we were going to the safe house with your friends and Nina."

"We were. But after what happened in that alley, we need to hole up instead. I don't think the guys I fought will stick around to talk to the cops, but that gunshot will definitely bring the authorities running.

And the last thing I want is to have to deal with the local police. Not with you having no identification."

Morgan wanted to ask him for more details about how she was going to get out of the country, but she only cared about one thing at the moment. She hated herself for being so fixated on not being left behind, but she couldn't help it. "Will your friends leave us here?"

"No," Arrow answered immediately. "But even if they did, it wouldn't matter. I've got ways of communicating with them and the others back in the States. They might need to get Nina out of here, but they'll come back for us."

The thought of Nina getting home to her mom made the panic Morgan felt at the idea of staying behind manageable. "Okay," she whispered.

"We need to hide, though," Arrow said, looking around. "There's no way to get to the second floor, not with those stairs half-missing. Not that we'd want to be up there in the heat with no roof, anyway. We're going to have to make us a hidey-hole down here. Something that looks natural if someone happens to peer inside, but not so stifling that we'll suffocate."

Morgan took a deep breath and looked around. There was a ton of debris on the floor. Nothing that looked like it could hide two full-size adults . . . well, one medium-size and one big one.

"Are you okay?" Arrow asked gently.

Morgan looked up at him and automatically nodded.

He shook his head in exasperation. "I think you'd say that even if you had a knife sticking out of your side, wouldn't you?" Without waiting for her to respond, he took her hand in his and led her over to a corner of the room. "Stay here."

Morgan clutched at him. "Where are you going?"

He immediately paused and turned to reassure her. "Nowhere. I'll be right here in the room with you. You'll be able to see me the whole time. I'm just going to see what I can do about making us a shelter."

Ashamed of herself for her neediness, Morgan forced herself to let go of his hand and nodded. "Okay. You'll let me know if I can do anything to help?"

"Of course." He reached up to her face and used his thumb to wipe something off her cheek. Morgan had no idea what it was . . . dirt, blood, or something else she didn't want to think about. Ultimately, it didn't matter. It was one of the few kind touches she'd had in a year.

Then he turned and quietly began stacking wood and metal in what looked like a haphazard way, but was actually very precise. Morgan stood against the wall and watched, not taking her eyes off him. She was starving, but the feeling wasn't anything new. Most of the time her captors forgot to feed her, and it wasn't until they wanted to be entertained that they'd give her something like a bowl of beans, without any utensils. She'd long since gotten over any pickiness she might've had when it came to food. She ate anything and everything, even things she never would've touched in her old life.

Water had never been an issue, as the room she'd been kept in had a sink in the corner. She didn't know how clean the water was, but it had kept her alive—that was all that mattered.

She would've killed to have that sink at the moment. After everything that had happened, she was extremely thirsty. But she was free. Well, sort of free, and she'd made a promise to herself not to be a bother or annoyance to Arrow.

"I think that'll do it," he said, more to himself than her, after about half an hour.

Morgan looked at the pile he'd made and couldn't help but be impressed. It looked totally inconspicuous, and he'd done a good job of keeping the dirtiest boards on top. She could see a fairly big space underneath where they could stay hidden.

Arrow smiled at her then, and Morgan felt her heart leap in her chest, but she squashed it. He was here doing a job. That was all. It wouldn't do for her to get attached to her rescuer. She didn't think she'd ever be able to be in a normal relationship again. Not after everything she'd been through.

"Looks good."

The words had no sooner left her mouth than they heard loud voices from the alleyway. Arrow was by her side before she could think. He swung her up into his arms and stepped quickly and silently over the boards to the hidey-hole. He put her feet on the ground and gestured for her to get inside.

Without hesitation, Morgan sat and scooted as far under the debris as she could, lying down on her side in the process. Arrow was hot on her heels. He lay down and scooted backward, forcing her to do the same, pressing her back against the wall of their makeshift shelter. He turned so he was facing the entrance to their hidey-hole, and she was completely hidden from view behind him. She rested her forehead against his broad back, but not before she saw the pistol Arrow held in his hand.

Her heart beating almost as hard as it had when they'd been running from the thugs in the alley, Morgan did her best to slow her breathing and not make a sound. The room was hot, and it was uncomfortable being this close to Arrow and sharing his body heat, but she didn't move a muscle.

Within seconds, the door they'd come through merely half an hour before was kicked open with a loud bang.

Chapter Three

Arrow pressed his lips together and concentrated on the opening to their hiding spot. He hadn't had enough time to make it as authentically random looking as he'd wanted, but he hoped it would do. If whoever had just kicked in the door walked around the room, they'd definitely be discovered.

Behind him, Morgan didn't move. He could barely tell she was breathing. When the guy in the alley had grabbed her, he'd seen red. What made it worse was the fact that the man knew who she was. From what he'd been saying to Morgan, their time together hadn't been pleasant. He could only imagine what she had gone through over the past year, but hearing the man say he couldn't wait to get her on her back for him and his friends again had made Arrow lose it.

He'd fought like a man possessed, and had barely made it to her before the guy would have shoved her into his car and disappeared, probably forever.

He hadn't planned on killing him, but when he'd seen the absolute terror and despair on Morgan's face as the man had tried to cut off her air, he'd acted without thinking. She'd done exactly what he'd needed her to do, which had made killing the asshole easier . . . and faster. She was covered in blood and grime, but he couldn't help but admire her and feel a tug of . . . something.

Arrow honestly had no idea how in the world he could be attracted to her. This wasn't the time or the place, and she definitely wasn't the kind of woman he usually went for, but he couldn't deny there was something about Morgan Byrd that made him want to kill every motherfucker who dared put his hand on her.

Mentally shaking his head, he concentrated on translating what the men at the door were saying. He wasn't sure how many there were, as their voices sounded muffled from his spot under the debris.

"No one's here. Let's keep going."

"Wait. We need to search. They could be hiding."

"They aren't. Look around—this place is disgusting. No one is here. We need to keep looking before they disappear."

"Who is the man with her?"

"I have no idea. But if we lose her, we don't get our money. We're getting paid to keep her here and alive."

"What about the kid?"

"Screw the kid! She doesn't matter. She's José's problem. The woman is who we need."

"They can't have gotten far."

"We'll talk to the others and make sure everyone has their eyes open. They won't be able to get out of this part of town without someone seeing them. We'll find them."

"The man is an issue. He needs to be taken care of."

"Oh, he will be. He'll regret interfering."

Arrow heard faint shouting from outside the room.

"Come on!" someone yelled from what sounded like the alleyway. *"They're down this way!"*

The silence in the room was thick and heavy when the men abruptly left. Arrow could feel Morgan's heart beating wildly against his back, and he hoped she didn't decide to suddenly protest their close quarters. But he needn't have bothered worrying. She wasn't moving an inch. She was frozen in place. Every muscle locked tight. He didn't think she understood what the men were saying, as she hadn't flinched when they'd talked about someone paying to make sure she was kept alive.

What Arrow didn't understand was *why*. Why had someone wanted her brought down here to the Dominican Republic and held captive? It made no sense. The person behind her kidnapping had to know she'd be treated badly, but whoever it was obviously didn't care.

It was no surprise that the locals were doing what was asked of them. Santo Domingo was a poor city in a poor country. The money they were getting was probably at least ten times what they could make in a regular nine-to-five job. It was no wonder they were so desperate to find Morgan and haul her to whatever hellhole they'd stash her in next. Losing her meant their paycheck would disappear . . . not to mention whatever else they'd been doing with her.

"Are they—"

Arrow quickly turned and covered her mouth to cut off Morgan's quiet words. She didn't fight him but simply flinched, then sagged into him. He hadn't meant to scare her, but he had no idea if someone was still there, waiting to see if they would slip up and show themselves. The stakes were obviously much higher than he'd first believed. She wasn't just a kidnapping victim—there was much more going on here.

He'd known people to pay others to kill someone. To kidnap them and make them disappear. But to pay someone to snatch her and keep her alive out of the country, and in the process make her life a living hell for months on end, took a special kind of crazy. It made no sense, and Arrow didn't like things that didn't make sense.

He removed his hand from her mouth and lightly caressed her cheek in apology. As if understanding what he didn't dare say out loud, Morgan silently buried her face into his chest, clutching his vest with its myriad pockets. She didn't make another sound.

Once more, the admiration Arrow had for this woman tore through him. She hadn't panicked; not really. The only time he'd seen her lose her cool was when she'd thought he was going to leave her in the alley.

He understood. After what she'd been through and being unexpectedly rescued, he wouldn't want to let his savior out of his sight either.

She hadn't cried. Hadn't asked for anything to eat or drink. Hadn't freaked out when he'd shot a man mere inches from her. Didn't make a sound when blood had sprayed over her or when the dead man had fallen on top of her. She hadn't complained when he'd started running, and she'd done everything right by being absolutely silent when they'd almost been discovered. It was unnatural how well she was dealing with everything.

Morgan almost acted as if she'd had military training, but he didn't think she had. He didn't remember any of the newscasts talking about her being a veteran. No, it was more that she was acting out of a sense of self-preservation. Had been since she'd been kidnapped, most likely. Arrow had seen the bruises on her arms and neck. He'd seen signs of the physical and mental abuse she'd endured. Not making a sound could've been the difference between drawing the attention of whoever was holding her captive and having them ignore her . . . the preference, of course, being the latter.

It broke his heart.

And *that* Arrow didn't understand.

He'd been on hundreds of rescues. Had seen hundreds of women and children in much worse shape than Morgan. Why should her situation make him more emotional than he'd ever been in the past? Why did the thought of someone abusing *this* woman make him want to burst out of his hiding spot and track down the men who had just been there talking about Morgan as if she were a piece of property and kill them all? That wasn't his way. Hell, that wasn't the Mountain Mercenary way. But he couldn't deny the feeling was there.

He waited for another ten minutes before daring to speak, and when he did, his words were barely above a whisper. "I think they're gone."

She immediately nodded but didn't speak.

"We can't move yet. We need to wait until tonight."

"Okay," she whispered.

"Did you understand what they were saying?" He needed to be sure. She shook her head.

"The bottom line is that they're looking for you . . . for us. They've got all their friends on alert too. It's too dangerous to walk around during the day. We'll stick out like a sore thumb. We need to lie low until it's dark."

"Okay," she said again.

Arrow frowned. He didn't like her immediate compliance, even though it was pretty much what he needed from her and what he expected. Kidnapping victims generally had a hard time thinking for themselves. They were happy to put the responsibility for their safety on someone else. There were times Morgan acted stereotypically, but then she did something like pick up a piece of metal and jump into the fight back in the alley. It was his experience that, when given the chance, kidnapping victims would either run, trying to keep themselves safe, or they'd completely shut down, being absolutely no help when the shit hit the fan.

Morgan had done neither. He was a little surprised she was being so complacent now. Especially when he'd just told her they were being hunted.

As he struggled to come up with the words that would reassure her, a strange sound emanated from where she had tucked her head against him. Alarmed, Arrow pulled back—and looked down at Morgan in disbelief.

She was snoring.

She'd actually fallen asleep against him. The heat was oppressive, they could be caught by men who wanted to kill him and most certainly continue to abuse her in the worst ways, she had to be hungry and thirsty, and yet, she was asleep.

Arrow stared at her and tried to figure her out. Her blonde hair was streaked with dirt, looking almost brown instead of the bright yellow he knew it to be from photos that had been on television. She had bruises all over in various stages of healing, her lips were dry and cracked, and there was a funky smell wafting from her clothes . . . and he'd never been more impressed with a woman before in his life.

He shook his head in disbelief. Arrow couldn't believe she was *sleeping*. In all the missions he'd been on, this had never happened. Not once. The women were always super hyped up. Aware of their surroundings and skittish. Not one had unwound enough to sleep, especially not before they were safe.

Arrow forced his muscles to loosen and listened to his surroundings. As the minutes passed, he cataloged each slight noise and dismissed them as sounds of the city waking up.

He had no idea how long he'd been lying there holding Morgan as she slept, but eventually the warm air and the woman curled into him did their thing . . . and he fell into a light sleep himself.

The next thing he knew, he was on his back, and the knife he always carried on his belt was against his throat. His eyes opened and looked into Morgan's panicked, confused green gaze.

"It's me," he said in a calm whisper. "Arrow. You're safe, Morgan. We got away last night." He could've easily disarmed her, but he stayed completely still and willed her to remember who he was.

Comprehension came immediately, and she moved the knife away from his neck. "I'm so sorry," she apologized. "I woke up and didn't know where I was." She scooted away from him, but stayed on her side, watching him warily.

"It's fine," Arrow soothed. He didn't tell her that she was only the second person to ever get the drop on him. He prided himself on always being aware, but obviously he'd dropped his guard a little too much while sleeping next to her. He filed that fact away for the future. "I can't say that I'm all that thrilled to be here either."

She frowned in question.

"I don't like small spaces," he told her, surprising himself, as he hadn't admitted that to anyone in a long time. His team knew, but that was about it.

She didn't immediately respond, but eventually took a deep breath and said, "Can't say I blame you. I'm not too fond of them myself. But there's a difference between being in a small space because I put myself there, and being shoved somewhere I don't want to be."

It was Arrow's turn to frown. Was she talking about him making her crawl into this makeshift hidey-hole?

As if she could read his mind, she put a hand on his arm and said, "Not you and not here. Besides, this one is open on one side. Night and day, Arrow. Night and day."

Swallowing hard and mentally reprimanding himself for jumping to conclusions while at the same time tamping down his anger at who- ever had abused her, he asked, "How are you doing?" Shifting until he was sitting with his legs crossed in the small space, Arrow picked up the knife she'd dropped and returned it to the holster at his hip. He had to hunch over, but it felt good to sit.

"I'm fine."

"Hungry?" Arrow watched as her nostrils flared momentarily before she shrugged nonchalantly.

"I'm okay."

"We need to get something straight right now," Arrow said sternly, not looking away from her. "You need to stop lying to me. I'm not a mind reader. If you're hurt, I need to know. If you're hungry or thirsty, I need to know so I can do something about it. If you don't talk to me, this entire mission could go down the toilet. Help me to help you, Morgan."

Instead of getting upset, her eyes seemed to shoot green sparks as she said, "I don't care about food. Or water. Or about getting clean or bumps and bruises. All I want is to get out of here. That's it. If that means I go hungry, fine. If that means I have to wait a bit to get some water, no problem. But the last thing I want is for you to take unnecessary risks to try to provide for me and get caught. I know as well as you do that without you, I'm fucked. So I'm fine. Peachy. Golden."

Arrow couldn't help but smile. This was the woman he'd come to know in such a short period of time. The practical, no-nonsense Morgan Byrd he admired so much. "So if I told you I had some protein bars in my pocket, you wouldn't be interested then?"

She swallowed hard and licked her dry lips. "I'm interested," she said simply.

Leaning over, Arrow pulled one of the meal-replacement bars from his pocket. There were hundreds of them on the market now, but no matter how many he'd tried, they all seemed to taste like cardboard to him. But he couldn't deny they were healthy as all get-out. He never went on a mission without a few stuffed into his pockets. They'd literally saved his life in the past.

Before handing one over to her, he said, "I'm not planning to leave your side until you're safe, Morgan. I'm going to do my best to avoid going anywhere without you—even to find food or water. I don't feel comfortable leaving you alone, not until we're on US soil. Besides, tonight we'll get out of these lovely accommodations and find my teammates. If I have anything to say about it, you'll be neck deep in a bubble bath before another twenty-four hours go by."

Instead of looking excited about the prospect, Morgan seemed more contemplative than anything else.

"What?" Arrow asked.

She raised her eyes to his, and Arrow couldn't help but think of the term *old soul*. She looked like she'd lived a thousand lifetimes.

"I've had a lot of time to think about everything that's happened to me, and I'm not sure I'll be safe even when I'm back in the States. I mean, that's where I was taken from. What if it happens again?"

Arrow frowned. "It's unlikely." He said the words automatically, but the fact of the matter was that it *could* be likely. He had no idea who'd taken her in the first place, or why. And knowing someone was paying the thugs down here to prevent Morgan from escaping meant someone was incredibly invested in keeping her exactly where she was.

He thought about Allye, one of his teammates' women. She'd been kidnapped not once, but twice. Someone who was determined to control and/or abuse another person could definitely make it happen if they wanted to.

Morgan didn't comment, but simply continued to stare at him.

"It's not that I don't want to talk about this. My team and I need to know every little detail about what happened a year ago. Anything you can remember can help us track down who was behind your kidnapping. But, unfortunately, now is not the time or place. We're as safe as we're going to get for the time being, but it's better if we're as quiet as possible just in case."

Morgan nodded and brought the protein bar up to her mouth. He watched her nibble on it for several minutes, as if she had to make it last a very long time.

Arrow couldn't help but say, "I've got more. You don't have to conserve it."

She sighed and looked away, not meeting his eyes. "I know I'm not in a position to be picky. And what I'm about to say is going to make me sound ungrateful and bitchy . . . but it doesn't taste that good."

Arrow did his best to smother the chuckle at her words. "Can't argue. I know some people love them, and I've tried just about every flavor under the sun, but I haven't found one that I really enjoy eating. I only choke those things down when there's no other alternative."

She scrunched up her nose. "And I guess now's one of those times, huh?"

"Looks like it. You need the calories and nutrients. But that's not the worst news."

"What?" she asked, finally looking up at him.

"I don't have any water for you to wash it down with."

She grimaced again, but gave him a small smile. "That's okay. I'll manage."

Arrow blinked. He'd seen her smile earlier, but he'd paid little attention to it at the time. He liked seeing the genuine humor in her eyes. Even the small quirk of her lips changed her entire countenance. The dirt and grime seemed to disappear.

The thoughts going through his head were as close to an epiphany as Arrow had ever had.

He wanted to do everything in his power to keep that smile on her face. To make her laugh. To see her relaxed with no worries. He didn't want her to have to worry about whether whoever had kidnapped her in the first place would manage to do it a second time when she got home. If the thugs in Santo Domingo were going to track her down and drag her back to her own version of hell.

Why her?

Why now?

Arrow had no answers—only a gut feeling that he was meant to be here at this moment. Not Black. Not Ball. Not anyone else on the team. *Him.*

"I know you will," he finally said softly. "I'll do my best to get you some drinkable water as soon as it's safe to leave."

"Okay," she agreed. "I'd appreciate it." She lifted the partially eaten bar. "With this thing, I'll need it," she teased with another small smile.

Without thinking, Arrow reached up and brushed the back of his hand down her cheek.

She froze, the smile fading from her face and her eyes wide.

Kicking himself for scaring her, Arrow immediately dropped his hand. "When you finish that, I recommend you sleep again if you can. It's going to get even hotter in here, and I'm not sure what we'll face tonight."

She nodded agreeably.

An hour later, Arrow was back on his side, Morgan tucked against his chest. After she'd eaten half the protein bar and declared herself full, he'd eaten what was left of it and settled them under their hideaway. Within minutes, despite saying she wasn't tired, Morgan was snoring once again.

Arrow didn't sleep this time. He stayed awake watching over the woman in his arms. No one was going to hurt her. Not on his watch.

Chapter Four

Morgan held her breath and stopped when Arrow held up his hand with his fist clenched. He'd briefly explained before they'd left their hideout what his hand signals meant. Most were self-explanatory, or she remembered them from some of her favorite TV shows that she used to watch before she'd been kidnapped.

She'd woken up disoriented again, but this time Arrow had been awake when she'd opened her eyes. He quickly reassured her, making the fear fade faster than it had the last time. Morgan didn't think the dread upon waking would ever be something she got rid of. She'd lived in terror every day for the last . . . however many days it had been. Somewhere along the line, she'd lost track of time. Between being moved from shack to shack and being held in windowless rooms, it had been impossible to keep the days straight.

From what Arrow and his friends had said, it had been at least a year.

A *year*.

Fifty-two weeks.

Three hundred and sixty-five days.

It was hard to believe because it felt like *so* much longer. An eternity.

She felt as if she'd aged a decade.

Nina had been thrown into her room a week ago. It was the first time the men who were holding her hostage had put someone else in her room. Morgan was relieved that they didn't seem interested in Nina . . . in *that* way.

Morgan had tried to take care of her from the moment Nina's terrified eyes met hers. The little girl had been so relieved to hear someone else speak English that Nina had latched on to Morgan as sort of a surrogate mom. From what Morgan could understand from the little girl, she'd been brought into the country by her father, then mostly left alone. She'd been put inside a room with some toys, only allowed out to use the bathroom, and then, like Morgan, she had been shuffled from one house to another, unable to communicate with anyone.

Morgan had met Nina's father once. He'd come by to talk to his daughter, and it was more than obvious the man didn't care about her well-being. He'd told the little girl that her mom didn't want her anymore and she was going to live in the Dominican Republic from now on. He was going to dump Nina with her grandmother on the other side of the country, while he lived in the capital and earned money for her upkeep.

Nina hadn't been happy and had begun sobbing. Her father had smacked her, telling her to quit crying. Morgan had jumped to the little girl's defense and received her own beating for her trouble.

Based on the little Morgan had pieced together, Nina's father was acquainted with some of the men who were keeping Morgan hostage, and he'd planned to leave the girl in their care while he earned money so they could travel to the city where his mother lived.

Morgan let Nina have most of the food and water they'd been given, as it was obvious she'd either not been given enough previously, or she'd been too traumatized to eat or drink much. Morgan also went with the men who came for her without a fight, to try to minimize the physical violence the little girl had to witness, and she slept with her body between Nina's and the door. The little girl was upset about being separated from her mother, but she hadn't been sexually abused. At least not from what Morgan had been able to ascertain, thank God.

Arrow and his friends appearing in the middle of the night had been the miracle she'd prayed for since she'd been taken. It had taken a year, but *finally* someone had come. They weren't there for her, but ultimately it didn't matter. She was free now . . . and she'd do whatever it took to stay that way.

Creeping around the streets of Santo Domingo at night should have been terrifying. But with Arrow, it wasn't quite as scary. There was something about the man that reached inside her battered and bruised psyche and made her feel safe.

He stood almost a foot taller than her five-three, and his light-brown eyes and dark hair didn't stand out as much as her blonde did. The fact that it was cropped close to his skull did make him unique, as there weren't that many people she'd seen in the country so far who wore their hair in the military style that Arrow did. But it was probably the black pants, black shirt, black vest, and pockets bulging with who knew what that stood out most. He was obviously way more badass than the few people they'd encountered so far on the streets.

Morgan didn't know how old he was, but she estimated quite a bit older than her twenty-six . . . no . . . twenty-*seven* years. Maybe in his midthirties. She guessed he was prior military of some type simply by his mannerisms and his silent, competent way of sneaking around. She wouldn't be surprised to find out he'd seen combat at one time or another.

But the bottom line was that she felt safe with him. When her hand wasn't tucked into the waistband of his pants, he was holding it tightly in his own. Morgan had no idea where they were or where they were going, but she was content to let him lead. He'd put on his night-vision goggles again, and every time she tripped over her own feet, he was there to keep her upright.

Arrow turned to her and pushed the goggles up on his forehead. "I need you to stay here while I go make a distraction."

Morgan's hand immediately tightened in his. She wanted to shake her head. Wanted to cry out and beg him not to leave her, but she forced herself to let go of him and nod.

She obviously hadn't hidden her distress as well as she'd hoped because his hands came up and cradled her face. "I'm not leaving you for long, Morgan. But I need to do this. From what I can tell, we're pretty much surrounded. They aren't as stupid as I'd hoped. They obviously suspected we'd try to slip around them when it got dark. Not only that, but they're desperate."

"Why?" Morgan whispered.

"Money."

"Money?"

"Unfortunately, yes. Someone is paying them to keep you here."

Morgan shook her head in confusion and frustration. "I'm no one," she said. "I'm a beekeeper, for God's sake!"

Arrow blinked. "A beekeeper? Really?"

She nodded. "Yes. I have a bunch of hives, and I collect honey. I sell it online and to local stores . . ." Her voice trailed off, and she looked at the filthy ground at her feet. "At least I used to. I've been gone so long my bees probably died or flew off, and all my contacts have certainly moved on by now."

She felt his finger under her chin, and she looked up.

"That's cool," he said with a small smile.

Morgan couldn't help but return it. It *was* kind of cool. She'd never been afraid of the insects growing up. She'd been more fascinated with them. And when she found out how valuable and necessary they were to society and the food chain, she'd decided to do what she could to help in a small way.

"I don't know who's behind your kidnapping, but I promise I'm going to figure it out."

She wanted to ask why. Why would he care? But she wasn't going to look a gift horse in the mouth. The truth was that she was petrified to go home. If someone was paying these thugs in the Dominican Republic to keep her here, they could certainly have her snatched the second she arrived home. She had no idea who she could trust . . . except for Arrow and his team.

"We need to talk," he went on. "I'll need to know everything about your family, boyfriends, girlfriends, people you work with, vendors . . . hell, even the guy at the grocery store who bags your stuff. My team and I will narrow down who might want you out of the way and why. But first we need to get out of this alley and out of this country."

Morgan nodded. "And in order to do that, you need to go do your invisible-man routine, and you can't do that with me hanging on to your pants like a three-year-old, huh?" She joked about the situation to cover her nervousness and reluctance to let him leave.

"If it makes you feel any better," Arrow said, "I want to leave you here about as much as you want to be left. But I swear on my honor that I'm coming back for you. Nothing will keep me away."

"You can't promise that," she told him.

"I can. And I am," he vowed.

Taking a deep breath, Morgan nodded. "Okay, where should I hide?"

Arrow grimaced. "It's not exactly the Ritz."

Morgan looked around and saw a few large, dark shapes, but she couldn't make anything out. It was amazing how little light there was in Santo Domingo. She supposed it was because of the poverty level. She was used to streetlights, and even lights on the outside of buildings, but here, everything was just so dark.

Arrow put his hand on her arm and guided her next to a plastic container. The smell emanating from it was horrendous, but Morgan didn't care. In fact, the stinkier it was, the better for her because some- one would be less inclined to check it out. Obviously, Arrow thought the same thing.

"I know it's gross, but the fact that this restaurant specializes in fresh seafood and therefore has a lot of smelly trash will work in our favor. I haven't forgotten that I've promised you a nice long bubble bath. I owe you double after this."

She could tell he felt awful for her having to hide with rotting fish guts, but she shook her head vehemently. "You don't owe me, Arrow. If anything, I owe *you*."

"We don't have time for this discussion right now, but trust me when I say you don't owe me a damn thing. You didn't ask to be here. You didn't ask to be kidnapped and abused. You didn't ask for this."

Morgan thought about his words for a heartbeat. Then a part of her old self surfaced. He was right. She'd had a lot of time to think about it, and even if she'd done something stupid that last night she'd been in Atlanta, she didn't deserve what had happened to her. "You're right. I didn't ask to be here. So you *do* owe me. My favorite bubble bath is chamomile. If you can get your hands on some, I'd appreciate it."

When Arrow chuckled, Morgan was amazed that she felt a hundred percent better. Their situation still wasn't good, but somehow, laughing in the middle of a run-down alley in the Caribbean made everything better. Laughing with *Arrow* made it better.

"Deal," he said. Then he surprised the shit out of her by leaning down and kissing her forehead. Before she could respond, he pulled back and turned to the trash overflowing from the bin. "Let's see how to make this as bearable as possible for you."

There wasn't much to work with, and it only took a few minutes for her to shimmy herself under a trash heap. She was short, so she could easily lie behind the wide plastic bin and hide herself under the news-papers, fish guts, and other miscellaneous trash. Arrow made a cover for her head out of a cardboard box, keeping the trash off her face. She was lying on her back, and she knew as soon as Arrow put the box over her head, it would be pitch-dark, even darker than it had been walking around the back alleys of the city, and she'd be alone. She didn't want him to leave, but at the same time, she wanted him to go so he could hurry up and come back.

"Do not leave from here, no matter what you hear. Understand? I can't see you, and I'm wearing night-vision goggles. If you stay quiet and don't move, anyone walking down this alley will go right by you. So don't panic."

Morgan nodded. He made it sound so easy, but she knew if someone did happen to come by her hiding place, it would be extremely difficult to remain still. "What are you going to do?"

"I'm not sure. I'll figure it out as I go."

She didn't know how to respond to that, so she simply stared up at him.

"You're killin' me, beautiful."

"I'm not doing anything," she protested, surprised that he'd called her beautiful. She figured he must call every woman that, because she was anything but beautiful right now. She hadn't seen herself in a mirror in weeks, but she could feel how badly her hair was matted and could see how grimy her skin was. But the fact that Arrow had used the term of endearment still felt good, comforting. It had been a long time since she'd been around a *nice* man. And Arrow was definitely nice.

"I know," he said. "You don't have to do a damn thing. That's why you're killin' me. If you were crying, protesting, or arguing with me, this would somehow be easier."

Morgan looked up at him and said with a straight face, "I can yell at you, if you want."

He smiled. "Probably not a good idea. I'm going to cover you up now," he warned. "I'll be back as soon as I can. Don't move from here, no matter what. Got it?"

"Yup. I'll just lie here and dream about eating a huge steak. I'm not sure I'm ever going to want seafood again."

Arrow stared at her with a look she couldn't decipher before nodding. He placed the cardboard box over her head, immediately making her feel claustrophobic. She heard the thud of garbage being piled on top of it, burying her completely.

Morgan shut her eyes and thought about anything but where she was and what was happening. She thought about her bees. Wondered, not for the first time, if they were still alive, if anyone had bothered to empty the honey in their hives. She thought about her mom. She had to be so worried about her. Morgan hated that her mother had been put through the agony of her only child being kidnapped.

It had been a surprise to hear that her *father* was the one who'd urged the press to keep her case active.

Morgan had tried to get her dad's approval her entire life. Her parents had divorced when she was young, and despite the fact she didn't live with him, he'd never been satisfied with anything she did. Her grades, her choice of extracurricular activities, her friends, even her current job. He lived in the Atlanta area, so she saw him fairly often, but she still hadn't figured out how to get his approval.

Her parents were *very* divorced. She'd learned from an early age not to talk about her father to her mom, and vice versa. She didn't think they'd said even one word to each other since she was little.

Morgan wondered if her disappearance had brought her parents together enough to at least speak. Wondered if they'd done any press conferences together, pleading for information about her whereabouts.

Shaking her head, Morgan dismissed the idea. She couldn't see either of her parents bending enough to tolerate being around their ex . . . not even for her.

Changing gears, for the first time in months she thought about the other people who'd been in her life before she'd been kidnapped. She'd been dating a nice guy. Lane Buswell was a few years older than her. He was a mortgage broker and her complete opposite; maybe that's why they'd hit it off. He had dark-red hair and green eyes and wasn't too tall for her taste . . . at least, what her taste used to be.

Morgan had thought about the night her life had changed over and over again, examining her actions and trying to decide if she could've done anything to cause a different outcome. It was stupid to play the what-if game, but she'd had a lot of time to think about it.

She'd been out with Lane and a group of their friends that night. They'd gone to a nightclub, and she'd left early. She'd walked to her car, which had been parked in a public garage, and someone had snatched her from there.

Morgan figured that by now Lane had probably moved on, assuming she was dead. Not that she could blame him. Even the small house she'd rented was probably home to someone else by now. She'd been thrilled to find it. It was on five acres, perfect for her beehives. But by now, her stuff was probably in storage or had been sold off.

Thinking about her old life was extremely depressing, and Morgan forced herself to turn her attention back to her current situation. She was hidden, yes, but that didn't mean she was safe. All it would take was one person in cahoots with her jailers and she'd be right back where she came from . . . or worse. Money made the world go round, and it also made desperate people even more desperate.

"Please hurry," she whispered almost tonelessly.

Chapter Five

Arrow silently slunk between two run-down buildings, sticking to the shadows and going undetected by the two men standing nearby. In the twenty minutes since he'd left Morgan, he'd counted fifteen men lurking around the streets and alleys with no discernable purpose, other than possibly being on the lookout for them.

He'd overheard a few conversations too. Around half the men thought that Morgan was long gone and they were on a wild-goose chase, and the other half were convinced the *puta* was still in the area and was just hiding.

The latter made him nervous, because the last thing he wanted was for the men to start a concentrated search. She was well hidden, but when it came to desperate men, there was no such thing as completely hidden. He knew from his time in the Marines, and from working for the Mountain Mercenaries, that no plan was one hundred percent foolproof. He wasn't willing to risk Morgan's life to find out.

He'd scoped out the lay of the land; it was time to put his plan into motion.

Arrow had briefly touched base with Black and Ball throughout the day. They'd gotten out of the poor area of the city where Nina and Morgan had been kept. They were in a hotel on the other side of the bay, where cruise ships typically docked. It wasn't exactly an economically rich area, but it was night and day compared to where he and Morgan had spent their time hiding.

Rex had been in touch as well, and he and Meat were working on the logistics to get Morgan out of the country. The plan was for Arrow and Morgan to meet up with his teammates tonight, but if that wasn't possible, they'd reserved a room for Mr. and Mrs. Coldwater at a mid-level motel. Their cover would be that they were newlyweds. It would give them an excuse not to leave the room and to wait for Rex to do his thing. Arrow hadn't told Morgan the details, hoping they'd be able to join his teammates and Nina.

Apparently Nina wasn't doing well. While Black and Ball were being as gentle as possible, the child was traumatized and kept crying for Morgan. Arrow was determined to do whatever he could to reunite Morgan with Nina . . . for both their sakes.

Arrow smiled, remembering one of his conversations with Morgan earlier that day. They'd been lying under the debris in the building, and after Morgan had mentioned how miserable the heat was, he'd pulled out a small folding hand fan. She'd looked at him incredulously and jokingly asked what in the world else he had in his pockets. He had laughed it off but managed to give her another protein bar, a pair of nail clippers when she'd lamented about the shape of her fingernails, and had even unearthed an extra shoelace to replace the broken one in her shoe.

The truth of the matter was, he had all sorts of goodies in his pockets. Items he'd learned over the years could be invaluable during a mission. As well as food, water purification tablets, needle and thread—which could be used to sew both fabric and human flesh, if necessary—and a stash of cash just in case, he also had things he could use to both kill and maim, as well as to distract.

It took another twenty minutes for Arrow to put everything in place, but when he was finished, he felt satisfied that he'd done what he could to give him and Morgan a window of opportunity to get the hell out of this part of the city undetected.

Crouching down between two buildings, Arrow waited for the first detonator to go off.

When it did, he was pleased to see the two men lurking nearby take off running toward the sound.

As he made his way back toward Morgan, he heard the other explosions he'd set. They went off right on time, hopefully leading the assholes away from his and Morgan's escape route.

The second he entered the alley where he'd left Morgan, he could feel his body relaxing. He could see the mound of trash looked exactly as he'd left it earlier. Crouching, he whispered, "Morgan? It's me, Arrow. It's time to go."

He brushed off the fish heads and bones and picked up the box he'd put around her head. She peered up at him, her pupils huge in her face and the dark alley.

"Come on, beautiful. Time to go."

She awkwardly scooted out from under the debris, and when he brushed his fingers against hers, she grabbed hold of his hand as if she'd never let go.

Just then, a louder boom sounded to the west. That was the last explosion he'd rigged, and hopefully the one that would take all attention off where they might be as the thugs tried to figure out what was going on. Arrow had chosen the placements for the explosions carefully. He wasn't opposed to killing, if it had to be done, but there was no way he was going to hurt someone indiscriminately. He'd used a bit of C-4 next to abandoned buildings, making sure there weren't any squatters inside, and had used a timer to set them.

They should hopefully bring the police and fire department, and draw the attention of anyone looking for Morgan.

"I take it that's your handiwork?" Morgan asked.

He could hear the fright, and relief, in her words. He'd been gone longer than he'd planned, but it had been necessary. He'd had to set the small flashbangs and explosions a bit farther out than he'd initially assumed. "Don't know what you're talking about, beautiful. I was just out for a nightly stroll."

Her teeth flashed white when she smiled.

"Come on. Stay right by me and don't talk. I'm pretty sure we should be in the clear, but I'm not going to take any chances."

Morgan nodded and took a deep breath. She looked down at their clasped hands, then he felt her fingers loosening. He was about to protest, but she moved her hand to his waistband once more. Even through his shirt he could feel that her fingers were cool against him. He reached down and moved her hand so it was at the small of his back.

"Hang on, beautiful. There's a bubble bath calling your name."

Then, without another word, he set off out of the alley toward the east and safety.

∼

It took two hours, as Arrow was being extremely careful about the route he was taking, but eventually they were standing outside the motel where Rex had made reservations for them. If it was up to Arrow, he would've gone the rest of the way to the hotel Black and Ball were staying in, but he could tell Morgan was dead on her feet. She was stumbling more and gripping his pants so tightly he could feel the material digging into his skin.

He was impressed with how well she'd held up as it was. He'd stopped several dozen times simply to listen, to take in his surroundings, and she hadn't said a word. Hadn't questioned him. She'd let him do what he needed to do without interruption. He didn't know many people, other than the men on his team, who could've done the same thing.

With every minute that passed, Arrow became more and more intrigued by the woman at his side. But he couldn't afford to let down his guard until they were back on US soil. There was no telling who was in on the plot to keep Morgan in Santo Domingo.

It was still dark out, but as they walked through the city, it began to stir. It had to be close to sunrise, but when he looked at Morgan, her eyes were wide open, and she didn't look tired in the least. He knew it was a ruse, though. The dark circles under her eyes and the way her shoulders drooped gave her away.

A rush of feelings swept through him. Anger at whoever had put her in this position in the first place. Remorse at having to push her so hard tonight. And regret that he hadn't stopped earlier.

"Hold on just a bit longer, beautiful, and you'll be chin deep in hot water."

She smiled at him, which made Arrow's breath hitch. Even covered in grime and smelling like a fish factory, her smile lit up her face and made her the most beautiful woman he'd ever seen.

"How are we going to play this? I'm not sure even the stupidest desk clerk will be able to overlook the eau de fish I'm wearing. He's never going to believe we're on our honeymoon."

Arrow had told her the plan while they were walking, about how a room was waiting for them, courtesy of his handler. He'd explained how they were supposed to be Mr. and Mrs. Coldwater from California.

"Trust me?" His words came out more a question than a statement.

She didn't look away from him as she nodded.

Arrow's heart constricted once more at her immediate response. He put his arm around her shoulders and drew her into his side. "Keep your eyes down and look defeated," he told her.

Morgan chuckled. "That won't be hard."

He resisted the urge to return her humor. "Come on. Here goes nothin'."

They walked into the somewhat run-down motel lobby, and a bell tinkled above their heads as the door closed behind them. Morgan's arm snaked around his waist as she clung to him. She kept her head down, and he felt her stumble as they walked toward the desk.

Arrow tightened his arm around her and ground his teeth together because he knew she wasn't acting.

A scruffy, sleepy-looking man appeared from a back room. *"Hola."*

"Hola," Arrow said. Then, still speaking in Spanish, he added, *"We have a reservation for Mr. and Mrs. Coldwater."*

Without a word, the man turned to the computer and clicked a few times on the mouse sitting next to the keyboard. Then he looked up, and his eyes went from Morgan back to Arrow before he asked in Spanish, *"Cash or credit?"*

Without letting go of Morgan, Arrow reached into his pocket and pulled out the wad of American dollars he'd stashed there before heading inside. He knew money spoke volumes in this part of the world. *"Cash."*

The clerk's eyes lit up, and he couldn't take his gaze off the money.

Launching into the story he'd concocted, Arrow told him that he and his newly wedded wife had run into problems on their way to the motel. They'd taken a taxi and gotten more than they'd bargained for when the driver had taken them on a joy ride of Santo Domingo, demanding more and more money. When he finally let them out, he'd taken their suitcases with him and they'd had to walk for miles to the motel. Arrow further explained they'd had to hide behind trash bins to keep away from the roving bands of thugs that came out after dark.

The clerk didn't seem moved in the least. All he cared about was the money in Arrow's hand, and Arrow realized his entire spiel was completely unnecessary. The man just didn't give a shit. Arrow wanted to roll his eyes in disgust, wanted to demand a little compassion for their plight, but instead, he simply handed over the money. It was a hundred dollars more than the room cost, and the clerk took it without a word.

He handed over an old-fashioned key and told them where their room was. *"Gracias,"* Arrow said with a nod. But the man had already disappeared into the room behind the counter—with the extra cash stashed deep in his pocket.

When the door closed behind him, Morgan asked, "Did he suspect anything?"

He'd forgotten that she didn't understand Spanish, and explained, "No. He was only concerned with the money."

"Good."

Arrow could tell that Morgan was flagging. He'd managed to steal a bottle of water for her earlier, but he knew he needed to get some real food in her as well as several glasses of water. It was hot, and they'd both sweated more than their fair share. They needed to replace the lost fluids pronto.

They walked to the end of the row of rooms, and he used the key to enter the second-to-last one. Pushing open the door, Arrow winced at the condition of the room. It looked fairly clean, although the decor was straight out of the eighties, right down to the cheesy art on the walls and the threadbare comforter on the double bed.

He stared at it for a moment before realizing the clerk had definitely believed their cover story. Rex had told Arrow that he'd reserved a room with two beds, but unless the beat-up old couch in the corner was a pullout, the clerk hadn't seen any reason to give them more than one bed, since they were supposed to be newlyweds.

Expecting Morgan to protest the accommodations, he was somewhat surprised when she dropped her arm from around his waist and walked toward the bathroom. She turned when she reached it and asked, "Do you need to use the bathroom before I hog it?"

He smiled and shook his head. "No, beautiful. It's all yours."

"Thanks." Then, without another word, she entered the small room and shut the door. He heard the water in the sink turn on almost immediately, and he suddenly wished he could've stopped and gotten her some basic toiletries, like a toothbrush, toothpaste, shampoo . . . chamomile bubble bath . . .

Shaking off the ridiculous thoughts—they'd been trying to stay one step ahead of the men who wanted to force her back into captivity; they hadn't had time to shop, for God's sake—Arrow pulled out the tiny radio he'd been using to communicate with Black and Ball. He sent a short, encrypted message letting them know they were at the motel and they'd catch up with them the next day. Then he paced.

Being fidgety wasn't like Arrow. He was generally very calm. He could wait for hours for the exact right time to make his move in combat situations. So why he was wearing a path in the old carpet was beyond him.

He heard the water in the shower come on—and instantly pictured Morgan standing under the spray without a stitch of clothing on.

He shook his head in disgust. He had to get his shit together. The last thing the poor woman needed was him hitting on her. Lord knew what she'd been through; it might be years before she'd be comfortable letting any man near her . . . not that he could blame her.

Focused on his hatred for men who exploited and abused women and children, Arrow was startled when he heard a loud crash from the bathroom. He was moving before he'd even thought about what he was doing. He had his pistol in his hand and was inside the bathroom in seconds, ready to blow away anyone who dared try to take Morgan.

He froze at what he saw.

Without hesitation, he put his weapon on the countertop and stripped off his vest with its myriad pockets. His shirt came off next, but he left on his undershirt. He stripped out of his cargo pants; luckily he had on a pair of baggy boxers, so he hoped she wouldn't be unduly alarmed.

Morgan didn't say a word, simply stared up at him with huge eyes and tears coursing down her cheeks. She looked exhausted—and broken. And Arrow hated it.

She'd obviously slipped in the tub and landed on her ass. The shower curtain was askew, giving him a clear view of her huddled form at the bottom of the tub. Arrow quickly switched the water from the showerhead to the tap and twisted the drain, keeping the water from escaping. He was surprised the water was still hot, but he wasn't going to look a gift horse in the mouth.

"Scoot forward, beautiful," he said softly.

She did as he asked, pulling her knees up to her chest in the process. Arrow stepped into the tub behind her and sat. His legs stretched out beside her hips, and he waited.

It took a while, but finally, when the water in the tub had covered their hips and was lapping at their bellies, she slowly sat back, resting against his chest.

"That's it," he murmured. "Relax, Morgan. I've got you."

She sighed and closed her eyes. Her arms were still crossed over her chest, and he couldn't miss the way they trembled as she wept.

Taking a risk, Arrow pulled her hands down, then wrapped an arm around her chest, covering her with his large forearm.

That did it. He could feel her relax completely against him, her hands coming to rest on his knees at her sides. Her chest heaved with sobs, and her breath hitched as she continued to cry. Not commenting on her tears, he simply held her and waited until the water was almost flowing over the edge of the small tub before using his feet to turn off the taps.

Eventually, she stopped crying and simply lay limp in his arms. They stayed that way in silence for several minutes before he asked gently, "Are you okay? You didn't hurt yourself when you fell, did you?"

She shook her head against him but didn't speak.

Arrow sighed. He wanted to urge her to talk, but despite the fact she was lying in the bathtub with him, they were essentially still strangers. He didn't like the additional bruises all over her body in various stages of healing. He didn't like the way he could see her ribs. And he *definitely* didn't like the way her knees were scraped and bruised. But the last thing he was going to do was demand she talk to him. He wanted her trust more than he wanted his next breath, but she had to give it freely; he couldn't wrest it away from her unwillingly.

The water cooled off, and Arrow used his foot to turn on the hot water, warming it up once more. He did this twice more, letting out water before turning on the tap each time.

Finally, Morgan said, "I'm ready to get out now."

Arrow's body was stiff from lying in the cramped tub, but he didn't let one groan escape his mouth as he stood. He grabbed a towel and held it out for Morgan. He turned his back, giving her privacy, and pulled off his soaked undershirt. He dried himself as best as he could and waited for her to indicate she was dressed once more before looking in her direction.

"I'm decent," she said softly.

Arrow turned—and his breath caught in his throat.

She was beautiful dirty and disheveled, but clean, and with her skin pink from the warm water, she was gorgeous. Her hair still needed a lot of work. He could tell Morgan had done her best to shampoo it with the small bottle provided by the motel, but some of the mats would have to either be cut out, or very carefully and slowly dealt with.

She looked up at him with her big green eyes and waited for him to say, or do, something. The towel was wrapped around her torso, and she was holding it closed with one hand. He could see the space where it didn't quite meet along her side.

Reaching down, Arrow picked up his other shirt. It wasn't exactly clean, but it smelled a hell of a lot better than her clothes did. "You can wear this if you want. I'll wash our things in here while you go get settled in bed."

When she didn't move, but simply continued to stare at him, Arrow said, "I know there's only one bed, but trust me, there were supposed to be two. I guess the clerk really bought our newlywed story. I'm sorry. I can sleep on the floor, or I can go down and ask for a different room if that would make you feel more comfortable. I—"

"The room is perfect," Morgan interrupted. "I don't want you on the floor. I'd feel safer if you were on the bed with me."

"Then that's where I'll be," Arrow told her.

"I . . ." She paused, then licked her lips uncertainly. "I can wash my own things."

"I know you can, beautiful. But let me do this for you. I want to take care of you."

"You are. You have," she told him. "But I'm not weak and helpless, regardless of what just happened." She gestured to the tub behind her, but didn't take her eyes from his.

Arrow couldn't help it. He chuckled. At the confused look on her face, he quickly explained, "I'm not laughing at you. I'm laughing at the fact you could believe for one second that I'd think you were weak or helpless. Morgan, please believe me when I tell you that you are amazing. I've seen more than my fair share of women who have been in your shoes, and most of them didn't handle things well. I don't blame them for their reactions, not at all, but many were hysterical. Crying, shaking, not listening to what we asked them to do for their own safety. And, God forbid, if something went wrong in their rescue, they completely broke down. You've done everything right. You haven't panicked, you've kept a cool head on your shoulders, and even when you were scared, you still held it together. The last thirty minutes has actually made me feel much better about your mental state."

"How does me breaking down make you feel better?" she asked, clutching the towel harder.

"Because you're reacting. You're feeling. I hate what happened to you, and I don't even *know* what happened to you. But suppressing all feelings about it won't help in the long run. If you need to cry, you cry. If you want to rage against the unfairness of what has happened, I'm here for you to smack around. If you want to talk about it, I'll listen. But shutting down all your feelings isn't the best way to get through it."

"It sounds like you have personal experience with this kind of thing."

"I was a Marine, beautiful. I saw some shit and *did* some shit that has fundamentally changed who I am. It took a long time, but I learned that if I talked about it, unloaded the feelings that were festering inside me, I felt lighter. Talking doesn't change what happened, but somehow it made me realize that the things that happened to me and the things I did don't make me a bad person."

"I'm not ready to talk about it. I don't know if I'll *ever* be ready," she admitted.

"Give it time," Arrow said gently. "Now's not the time or the place, but eventually I think you'll come to a point where you need to purge it from your system. But I don't ever want you to think that you aren't strong or that you aren't handling things well. You are. You've been amazing. I'm so fucking proud of you, I can't even put it adequately into words. And the fact that you let me comfort you, in even that small way, goes a long way toward helping me deal with what I do for a living as well."

"What do you mean?"

"I didn't go through what you did, but I see the aftermath all the time. Broken women and children who have been abused beyond anything the average person can imagine. I've experienced them pulling away from a simple touch of my hand. I've seen them shrink from me when I tried to meet their eyes. Me and my teammates are often treated with distrust and disdain. We don't blame the victims, not in the least, but it's tough, especially when we have the utmost respect and sympathy for those we're helping."

"I hadn't thought about it that way," Morgan admitted.

"It's not your issue to think about," Arrow told her. "But letting me comfort you just now was a gift. Thank you. So no more talk about you being weak or helpless. Okay?"

"I'll try."

"Good. Now . . . go on. Climb under the sheets, and I'll be there as soon as I finish in here."

"Thank you."

"You're welcome." Arrow watched Morgan walk out of the bathroom, and he took a moment to collect himself. He was pissed beyond belief. Not at Morgan, but at the assholes who'd damaged her psyche. She was strong, there was no doubt, but she was definitely hurting.

Working quickly, he washed her panties, T-shirt, and jeans. He did the same with his underclothes, but not his cargo pants. They would take forever to dry, and he wanted to make Morgan as comfortable as possible as they slept. That meant not being naked when they were in the same bed together.

When he had hung their clothes to dry, he went back out into the other room. He strode to the door and made sure it was locked up tight. He pulled a chair in front of it, just in case, before looking over at the bed.

Morgan was under the sheet and thin comforter; he could see just her head sticking out. Smiling, Arrow went over and picked up the towel she'd discarded on the floor. He hung it up in the bathroom before heading to the other side of the bed. He lay down on top of the covers and turned to face Morgan. "Is this okay? I really can sleep on the floor if you prefer."

"I told you, it's fine," she replied, then turned to face him.

"You get enough water to drink?" Arrow asked.

Morgan nodded. "I sucked enough down in the shower to make me feel bloated and uncomfortable before I had my little freak-out."

Frowning at her description of what had happened, Arrow merely nodded. "And food? Do you need another protein bar? We'll get real food later, but I don't want you to go to sleep hungry."

"I'm fine."

Arrow studied her for a heartbeat. Her hair was spread over the pillow, and just looking at it made him want to both cry and rage over what had happened to her. He kept himself together, though.

"Will you . . ." Her words trailed off.

"Will I what?" he asked. "I'll do anything you want or need." He wasn't the least surprised to realize what he said was one hundred percent true. Anything she needed, he'd move heaven and earth to give her.

"Can we sleep like we did in that building?" she asked.

He must've looked confused, because she elaborated by saying, "You holding me but with my back to you this time?"

Arrow was surprised at her request, and he must've taken too long to answer, because she said, "Never mind. That's too much. Forget it."

Before the last word was out of her mouth, he'd scooted over so he was right next to her. He helped her turn on her side, and he curled his body around hers. She fit against him perfectly. She felt even tinier in his arms. Her personality and strength had somehow kept her from seeming quite so small when they were sneaking through the city.

She sighed in contentment and snuggled farther into him.

Arrow was having a hard time staying disconnected from this woman. He wanted her to trust him. The entire team of Mountain Mercenaries had been taught to be on the lookout for victims who seemed to be latching on too tightly to their rescuer, but for once, Arrow didn't think about his training at all.

For the first time in his professional career, he felt his objectiveness disappearing.

Morgan felt too good in his arms.

Her ass cradled against his groin.

The feel of her belly under his hand.

Her head resting in the hollow of his throat.

Several minutes went by, and Arrow realized that she wasn't sleeping. She should be. They'd been on edge for hours, and it had been a hard, stressful journey through the streets of Santo Domingo to the motel.

"What's up?" Arrow asked quietly.

"I don't know what's going to happen later today, or tomorrow, or next week. For the last year, I've thought that what happened to me was just a bad coincidence. That I was in the wrong place at the wrong time. But . . . after hearing some of the things you've said since you saved me, both to me and to your friends, I know it wasn't a coincidence, after all. That someone wanted me gone, but apparently not dead. That scares the shit out of me . . . and I want to figure out who hates me that badly. Will you help me?"

"Yes." There was no other answer Arrow could give her.

"Now?"

"No. You need to sleep, beautiful. You're safe. I won't let anything happen to you. But I also want to wait and have this discussion when my team can be there. I know you don't know them, but they really are the best of the best. And if anyone can figure it out, it's them."

"Okay."

Arrow didn't like her distant tone. "The other reason I don't want to talk about your life in Georgia right now is because I'm being selfish. I like having you in my arms, and I know if you start talking about the people in your life who may or may not want you gone, it'll piss me off, and it'll stress you out. I don't want you to have to repeat anything distressing twice, so I'd rather enjoy having you relaxed and not stressed. If that's okay with you."

"I just want to make sure someone has the info about my life . . . just in case," she said.

"I get it. But, Morgan, I'm not blowing smoke up your ass. I'm going to get you out of this country safe and sound. I swear on my life, I'm not leaving without you."

His words seemed to be exactly what she needed to hear, because he felt every muscle in her body relax. Finally. She melted into his arms and let out a long relieved breath.

"Believe me, I want to hear about everyone you've ever met, no matter how inconsequential you think they are, simply so we have a good snapshot of anyone who might have a beef with you. But right now, I want you to sleep knowing that I'm here watching over you."

"What if it *was* a stranger abduction?" she asked.

"It's possible, but unlikely," Arrow told her honestly. "A stranger wouldn't be going to the lengths he has to keep you here . . . and alive. I promise we'll talk about this soon. Will you try to sleep now?"

"Okay."

"Okay," Arrow agreed.

And between one breath and the next, Morgan was out. She began to snore in the cute way she had almost immediately.

But Arrow didn't sleep. Not one wink. He took his responsibilities, and his promises, seriously. No one would touch another hair on this woman's head if he had anything to say about it. He and his teammates could figure out who the asshole was who wanted to crush this beautiful woman beneath his shoe . . . and they'd crush *him*.

Morgan Byrd was going to be free to live her life however and wherever she wanted. He'd make that happen, or die trying.

Chapter Six

Hours later, Morgan went from being asleep to being immediately awake, just like she'd done for the last year. She couldn't afford to wake up slowly. She had to be fully aware at all times.

Sitting up in bed, keeping the covers pulled over her, she sighed in relief when she saw Arrow sitting at the crappy desk in the corner. He was fiddling with the clock radio and had pieces of it all over the desk in front of him.

"What are you doing?" she asked quietly.

He looked up, and Morgan was amazed to see a slight blush spread across his unshaven cheeks. "You're awake," he said.

"I am."

Arrow smiled. "I couldn't sleep, and didn't want to disturb you or leave you here alone. I needed to think, and I do that best when my hands are busy."

"So you decided to kill the clock radio?"

He smiled. "I'm an electrician back in Colorado Springs. I love tinkering with things. I turned on the radio to try to mask the noises from outside so you'd be able to sleep longer, and couldn't get any stations to come in clearly. I thought maybe I could fix it." He shrugged. "One thing led to another . . . and here I am."

Morgan looked from the sheepish expression on his face to the mess of wires and plastic on the desk in front of him. She could just imagine him as a little kid, constantly taking things apart to see how they worked. "Did you figure out why the stations were fuzzy?"

"Nope," he said with a grin.

Morgan returned his smile. The muscles in her face felt stiff, as if it had been so long since she'd smiled, she'd forgotten how to use them.

"I was going to wake you up in about ten minutes anyway," Arrow said, pushing the pieces of the radio to the side and standing. "We need to get going and meet up with the others."

Morgan nodded.

"Your clothes are almost dry. You can take another shower and get dressed. Then we'll head out, get something to eat, something better than protein bars, and go to the other hotel. Black said he's got toiletries for you, including an entire bottle of conditioner. If you trust me, I can try to help you untangle your hair before we resort to using scissors on it."

One of her hands went up to her hair protectively, as if that would keep it safe from having to be cut. Last night in the shower, she'd known it was going to be iffy. It had been too long since it had seen a brush or comb, and she wasn't sure it could be saved. She shouldn't be upset about that—she was alive, her hair would grow back—but somehow, losing her long blonde hair seemed like the ultimate fuck you by the universe. As if she hadn't been through enough.

Forcing herself to drop her hand and swing her legs off the side of the bed, she mumbled, "Okay."

Before she could stand, Arrow was there, crouched at her feet. He wasn't touching her, but the earnest look on his face made her stop and look him in the eyes.

"If it's more comfortable, we can find a hairdresser to work on it."

She blinked in surprise. "A hairdresser? Here?"

"Yup. I have no idea where we'll find one, but I can ask Meat to find one for you. He's one of my teammates back home. He's a computer genius, and I have no doubt he'd be able to do it. We could get her to come to the hotel. In fact, that's probably a better idea anyway. I'll contact him as soon as—"

Morgan put her hand on Arrow's arm when he started to stand up, stopping his words midsentence. "I trust you to do it," she said. "There's no need to call in a professional. I just want to leave here as soon as possible. Besides, I'm not sure I trust anyone other than you and your friends."

Arrow had settled back on his haunches at the first touch of her hand. "Okay, although I'd rather cut off my own hand than do anything to hurt you, beautiful. And that includes anything that might emotionally disturb you."

"I know. It's fine. It's just hair. It'll grow back."

"Don't," he ordered. "Don't pretend this doesn't bother you. You have every right to be worried about your hair."

Morgan looked at him for a long moment before giving herself permission to nod. "Thanks."

"Don't thank me. You don't thank me for anything I do to help you. One, it's technically my job, but two, me helping you actually has *nothing* to do with my job. Now, come on, go get a shower. And be careful, it's slippery in there."

He smiled at the last bit, and Morgan couldn't help but grin wryly at his reminder of last night, when she'd had her little breakdown. She wanted to ask him what he meant about helping her having nothing to do with his job. Did he mean that he didn't usually help other women he rescued as much as he was helping her? But she couldn't see that. Even knowing him just the short time she had, Morgan had a feeling he went out of his way to make every woman feel comfortable in his presence.

So she didn't know what he meant . . . but she wasn't sure she was ready for the answer. She hadn't been free for two full days yet. She wasn't feeling anything for her rescuer other than gratitude . . . was she?

Arrow respectfully turned his back once she was standing, giving her privacy. His shirt covered her down to her thighs, but it was still a thoughtful thing to do. She scooted into the bathroom and shut the door.

She avoided looking at herself in the mirror and quickly stripped and stepped into the shower. She knew she spent too long under the hot water, but it felt so good, and it had been a year since she'd been able to get clean without having to worry about who might burst into the room and catch her unawares.

Within twenty minutes, they were dressed and leaving the motel behind. Arrow hadn't bothered to inform the clerk they were checking out, but he did leave a twenty-dollar bill under the remnants of the clock radio he'd taken apart. He'd told her he could've put it back together, but it would've taken more time than they had.

After several minutes, when Arrow didn't say another word, Morgan asked, "Where are we going?"

He used his chin to point ahead of them. "Across the bay there. But first . . . lunch."

Morgan knew it was past noon. They'd gotten to the motel in the early hours of the morning, and he'd let her sleep in. She was hungry, but she'd honestly blocked it out because she felt as if she'd been hungry for the last year. Her captors had given her enough food to keep her alive, but that was about it. She hadn't even thought to ask Arrow for food because she'd gotten so used to being turned down or laughed at when she begged for something to eat.

Determined to break that habit, and to ask for what she needed when she needed it, Morgan said, "Tell me it isn't seafood."

Arrow stopped in his tracks and stared at her.

Feeling uncomfortable with his sudden scrutiny, Morgan did her best to meet his eyes and not apologize for the somewhat inappropriate joke.

Then his lips moved upward in a smile. His white teeth seemed brighter in the light of day. He said, "You got it, beautiful." Then he squeezed her hand and started walking again. "While you showered, I got in touch with Meat. He did a search of the area and the route we'd be taking to get to Ball and Black, and he took it upon himself to order our food for us. It'll be ready by the time we get there."

"Seriously?" she asked. "Is that even possible?"

Arrow chuckled. "Anything's possible with Meat. He's a genius with that computer of his . . . not as good as Rex is, but then again, I'm convinced Rex has more clandestine contacts than the Russians do."

"Rex?" Morgan was trying to keep the names of his friends straight, but it was tough.

"Yeah. Rex is our . . . leader, for lack of a better word. He's the one who decides which cases we go on."

"So he decided that you guys should come after Nina?"

"Exactly. Nina and her mom are from Colorado Springs. She'd heard of what we do and was desperate enough to contact him. He listened to her case, did some research, and agreed to help."

"Wow. So she just called him up?"

"Nope. That's not how it works. She got the detective investigating her missing daughter's case to contact him. Rex is very well known in police and private-investigator circles. He doesn't take every case. He only chooses the ones with the most solid information and the highest chances of success."

Morgan let that sink in for a moment, then said, "You knew who I was the second I said my name. You said that my dad has been pushing to find me since I disappeared. Did he contact this Rex person? Was I deemed a bad risk, and that's why no one came for me?"

Arrow stopped again so suddenly, Morgan would've run into him if he hadn't turned and caught her shoulders. "No, Morgan. Absolutely not."

She shook her head. "You don't know that."

"I do."

He said the two words with such conviction, Morgan wanted to believe him, but couldn't. "I'm so confused. My dad and I don't really get along all that well. He cheated on my mom when I was little, and that's why they got divorced. I saw him while I was growing up, but he was definitely a weekend kind of dad. He wasn't really there for me. I don't understand why he was the one who was on the news and pushing to find me when most of the time I wasn't sure he really even *liked* me. But if he was as desperate to find me as you say he was, then wouldn't he have explored every option? Wouldn't the cops have told him about Rex? Was he lying the whole time, and didn't really want me found but pretended he did?"

"I don't have answers for you, beautiful," Arrow said. "But I'm gonna get them. I do know without a doubt, however, that if Rex had been approached about your case, he would've taken it and would've done everything in his power to find you."

"Why?"

Arrow pressed his lips together for a second, as if he was struggling with something, before saying, "I'm going to tell you something that none of my other friends know. For now, I need you to keep this between the two of us. Can you do that?"

She nodded immediately.

"I'm a member of a group called the Mountain Mercenaries. Rex is in charge. He sends me and my teammates on cases to rescue women and children in precarious situations. Abuse, kidnappings, terrorism— you name it. But what my friends don't know is why he started the group. Why he's so passionate about helping women. It's because his own wife disappeared. He did everything he could to find her, but the police said they had no leads. The private detectives he hired lost her trail when she was taken out of the United States. He ran into a brick wall and couldn't find anyone to help him."

"Oh my God," Morgan breathed. "Did he find her?"

Arrow shook his head slowly. "Not that I know of. He learned a lot in his search for her, about what the laws can and cannot protect people from. He learned how to fly under the radar and how to get information from people without leaving a trace. He uses this information to help others. He was devastated when he couldn't find anyone with the skills and knowledge to find his wife, so he *became* that person. But unfortunately, he still hasn't been able to find *her*."

"How do you know this? Did he tell you?"

"He doesn't talk much about himself at all. In fact, me and my teammates have never met him in person. He brought us all together for a job interview, and when he never showed, we all thought we'd been set up. But he'd obviously been watching us the whole time, because hours later, he contacted us and offered us jobs with the Mountain Mercenaries if we wanted them."

"But you're not really a mercenary," Morgan said. "You're a rescuer. A savior."

For some reason, Arrow smiled at that.

"What?"

"It's just that both Allye and Chloe said the same thing to Gray and Ro."

"Who?"

He waved his hand dismissively. "I'll tell you about them later. Anyway, so we've never met Rex. He disguises his voice when he calls to give us assignments. But one night, he called me after a mission. We'd gone down to Venezuela to rescue a group of women who'd been taken after answering online ads for housekeeping help. They were mostly Hispanic, but we'd told Rex that one of them said there was an American woman who'd been there when they'd arrived. We searched but couldn't find her.

"Rex called me and asked all sorts of questions about the missing American. What she looked like, how tall she was, things like that. When I admitted I didn't know, he kind of lost it. He tore me a new asshole, which was completely out of character for him. So I asked why this woman was so important. Surprisingly, he told me about his missing wife. How he was constantly on the lookout for her. How, with every case he took on, he wondered if he'd find some link to his own missing woman."

"God, that's awful," Morgan breathed. "How long has she been missing?"

"I'm not sure. We've been working for him for a few years. So I'd say it has to be at least another couple of years before that."

"Do you think she's still alive?"

Arrow looked her in the eye and said, "Do you think anyone thought *you* were still alive after a year had passed with no clues?"

Morgan swallowed hard. He had an excellent point. Her father may have been trying to keep the kidnapping in everyone's minds, but it didn't sound like anyone else had. She thought about her friends, about her ex, about her mom . . . had they all written her off as dead? It was a depressing thought.

"Anyway, to bring this conversation full circle, Meat helps us out with the computer shit. Looking through surveillance videos, hacking into email accounts if we need it . . . and going online and finding a safe place thousands of miles away from Colorado Springs to order lunch for you and me."

Morgan wanted to talk more about Rex and his missing wife. Wanted to talk about her own case. But she recognized Arrow's need to change the subject. So she nodded. "Okay. What are we having?"

"No clue. I've just got an address. But I promise it's not seafood."

"Honestly? I'd eat anything. I've learned not to be picky since I've been here. I would've starved if I was. But I have to admit I'm relieved not to have to eat fish."

Arrow leaned forward then and rested his lips on the top of her head. He didn't put his arms around her. Didn't unnecessarily crowd her. Morgan knew she could've ducked away, and he would've allowed it. But having him this close to her felt good. Right.

She tried to tell herself that as soon as they were back in the States, he'd be leaving, but she knew she was lying to herself. Arrow wasn't treating her the same way he'd treated other victims he'd rescued. She felt it deep down. She had no idea what was in store for them. All she knew was that he made her feel more like herself than she had in a very long time.

"You amaze me, Morgan," he whispered against her hair. Then he pulled back and took her hand in his once more. "Come on. Let's go see what Meat found us to eat. Then we'll get you back to Nina. She needs you. She's not adjusting well."

Twenty minutes later, Morgan stared up at the neon lights of the building in disbelief.

"The Hard Rock Cafe?" she asked with a laugh.

Arrow shrugged. "Told you it wasn't fish."

Morgan felt as if she'd fallen down a rabbit hole. This was so not her life, was it?

Without another word, Arrow tugged on her hand and headed for the door.

She pulled back, refusing to take another step.

"What?" Arrow asked, alarmed, looking around for danger.

"I'm not going in there!" Morgan hissed.

"Why not?"

"Because! Look at me! I'm disgusting. I still smell like fish. I think that stench is stuck in my hair for good."

"Are you hungry?" Arrow asked.

She stared up at him and bit the inside of her cheek before admitting, "Yes."

"Then we're going in. I'm not going to leave you outside, Morgan, so don't even suggest it. No one is going to say anything. Meat has already ordered food for us. All we have to do is go up to the counter and tell them we're here to pick it up. I'll pay, and we'll be out of there. Ten minutes, tops."

She wanted to keep refusing, but the delicious scents wafting from the building were too much to resist. "I don't like this," she told him.

"I'm aware. And I wish I could take you inside as if we're on a date. With you wearing a slinky black dress that shows off too much leg and too much cleavage that I could stare at all night. I wish I could be a different man at the moment, who wasn't armed with eight different ways to kill a man, not including my bare hands. But if I *was* a different man, then I'd probably leave you to stand here while I went inside to pick up our food, and that would leave you open and vulnerable to anyone who might be walking by—or might be scoping out the joint for a wayward American woman who someone desperately wants to keep in their clutches. So we're going inside, together. I'll protect you from anyone who dares think they can take you from me. We'll get the lunch Meat ordered for us and get to the hotel, where you can see Nina, we can start figuring out who's been behind the last year of hell you've endured, and we can get that beautiful hair of yours all fixed up. Okay?"

"I don't think I've ever owned a slinky black dress," she blurted.

And just like that, the scowl on his face was replaced with a look she couldn't interpret. She took a deep breath at seeing it. It was intense, and somehow it seemed like he could see right into her brain to her insecurities and doubts.

"Then I'll make sure you have one in your closet when I *do* ask you out. Now, come on. I'm starving."

And with that, Morgan followed him into the iconic American restaurant.

Exactly ten minutes later, they exited through the same door. Morgan carried a giant bag of food. Arrow had apologized, said he'd carry it, but he wanted both hands free, just in case. She had hurried to reach for the handles, happy to let him be in charge of protecting them. She'd gladly carry the food.

Her mouth watered as they walked down the sidewalk, trying to blend in with the other tourists who were milling about. She wondered why Arrow's friends hadn't holed up in the Marriott Hotel near the Hard Rock, but she didn't ask. He had his reasons for everything, and so far things had worked out, so she wasn't going to second-guess him. This was a very different area from the one she'd been held in. Touristy in comparison, and thus it felt a bit safer.

But she knew that even one block away, things could change very rapidly. One second they could be surrounded by foreigners on vacation or businessmen, and the next they could be in the slums.

They walked for several blocks toward the waterfront before they took a left and headed for a building that looked completely out of place in the poor country.

"A casino?" she asked incredulously.

"Yup," Arrow responded. "It's a perfect place to blend in."

"Hide in plain sight, huh?"

"Exactly."

Arrow looked down at her with such pride, she felt herself blushing. They walked under the brightly lit sign proclaiming the building a hotel and casino and headed straight for the elevator. Morgan assumed Arrow knew what room his friends were in, and was surprised when he hit the button for the top floor.

"I figured you'd want a room on a lower floor, for an easier escape route if needed."

"Good thinking, but the higher the floor, the harder it is for anyone to surprise us. Black installed wireless cameras in the stairwells and elevators. No one is going to sneak up on us."

"And if they don't sneak, but make a blitz attack?" Morgan asked.

Again, Arrow looked pleased at her perception. "Then they'll regret it. Believe me, between me, a former Marine; Black, a Navy SEAL; and Ball, a badass former Coast Guard officer . . . no one will be getting their hands on you or Nina anytime soon."

Morgan knew he meant his words to be reassuring, and they were. Knowing that the other two men were just as capable of protecting her and Nina as Arrow was went a long way toward helping her relax . . . just a bit.

As they walked down the hall, a door opened, and a little girl came running out. She ran toward Morgan as fast as her legs could carry her.

Dropping the bag, Morgan opened her arms and caught Nina. Luckily, Arrow was there to steady her, keeping her from falling back on her ass.

Nina didn't say a word, but Morgan could feel her shaking in her arms.

"Come on, beautiful. Let's get you guys into the room," Arrow said in her ear.

Morgan nodded and stood, with his help, and put her arms under Nina's butt, holding her to her chest as she walked down the hall in the direction the little girl had come.

An extremely tall man, even taller than Arrow, stood in the doorway of room seven forty-eight. He had blond hair, and his eyes were ice blue. Morgan shivered after looking at them for even two seconds. He was almost scary, but she could see Arrow was relaxed at her side, so she knew she had nothing to fear from the guy.

The other man in the room wasn't as tall as his teammates. He had black hair and brown eyes and was staring at her with an intense gaze. He wasn't as muscular as his friends either, but she had a feeling he was the most dangerous of the bunch. How she knew that, Morgan had no idea, but she made a mental note never to piss him off.

"Good to see you," the tall man said to Arrow.

"You too, Ball. Things go okay here?" Arrow asked.

Morgan followed their movements with her eyes, even as she sat at the end of one of the beds with Nina still in her arms.

"She's been . . . upset," the other man said. Morgan assumed this was Black by process of elimination.

"Did she need any medical treatment?" Arrow asked, crouching down in front of Morgan and Nina.

Morgan met his eyes as Black answered. "Not that I could see. But I wasn't about to freak her out even more by checking her over as closely as I wanted."

Morgan read between the lines. Nina had probably taken one look at the two deadly men and shut down. Black wouldn't have wanted to take off her clothes to examine her and scar her even more than she probably already was.

Nina whimpered, and Morgan shifted her higher up on her chest. "Shhhh, baby. You're okay. These are the good guys. They won't hurt you."

The little girl moved her head until she could see Morgan's eyes. "Not like the bad men did to you?"

"No, baby. They saved us from the bad men. See? I'm here and I'm fine. I even got to shower. Wouldn't you like to get clean too?"

She felt Arrow's hand on her knee, and even that small touch bolstered her. Gave her the strength to try to help deal with Nina's demons.

The little girl nodded.

"How about some food first?" Arrow suggested. "I know Morgan is hungry, and I am too. Would you like to see what we got for lunch?"

Nina rested her cheek on Morgan's shoulder and stared at Arrow with big eyes.

Morgan sighed. "It's okay, Nina. He's not like your father. He won't hurt you if you spill anything."

"Will he make you do anything if you want to eat? Like the other men did?" the little girl asked quietly, in a way that made it more than obvious Morgan had done whatever was necessary to keep their kidnappers away from Nina.

She ignored the sharp inhalations from the men in the room and concentrated on the little girl in her arms. "No. You're safe here. *I'm* safe. These are the good guys," she said again. She gestured to Arrow. "And this is Arrow. His first name is Archer. That's how he got his nickname. An archer is someone who shoots with a bow and arrow."

"Like Princess Merida?"

Morgan smiled. "Exactly like Princess Merida." She glanced at Arrow, who looked amused, but confused. "She's the heroine in the animated movie *Brave*," she informed him.

"I've never seen it," Arrow confessed. "Is it good?" he asked Nina.

She bobbed her head up and down quickly. "She's really brave."

Morgan grinned when Nina stated the obvious.

"So she's a lot like you, huh?" Arrow asked. "I bet she'd be super proud of how brave *you've* been."

Nina didn't answer, but Morgan could see that she was thinking about what Arrow had said. She continued, "Black and Ball are also good guys. They won't hurt you. They're doing everything they can to get you back to your mommy."

"I miss Mommy," Nina whined.

"I know you do, baby. But in order to get back to her, we have to do what Black, Ball, and Arrow tell us. They'll keep the bad guys away. We also have to take care of ourselves, though, too. That means staying clean and eating the food they bring us."

"I'm hungry," Nina whispered.

"Me too. Want to see what we brought for lunch?"

Nina nodded.

Morgan looked up to see Arrow staring at her with a weird look in his eyes. "What?"

He merely shook his head and reached for the Hard Rock Cafe bag. He pulled out carton after carton until they were practically covering the bed.

"Holy cow," Morgan breathed. "I guess your friend Meat thought we were really hungry, huh?" she asked.

Black chuckled. "He just knows what it's like to be in a foreign country and to be craving good ol' American junk food."

"Well, he got that right for sure," Morgan observed. There were french fries, a hamburger, chicken fingers, potato skins, a chicken Caesar salad, mac and cheese, three steaks, a hot dog, and three pieces of chocolate cake for dessert. "There's enough food here to last a week!"

"Not with three full-grown men plus you two," Arrow told her. "Go on," he said as he nudged her knee with his own. "Pick what you want. We'll take whatever you two don't eat."

Truthfully, Morgan wanted all of it. Seeing the food laid out in front of her made her salivate. "What do you want, Nina?"

The little girl chose the hot dog, some fries, and a chicken finger. Morgan picked the hamburger, fries, half of the salad, and half of a piece of cake. She knew she'd never be able to finish it all, but simply having it in front of her was heaven.

Thirty minutes later, all that was left of the food were a few fries and a couple bites of chocolate cake. Nina had fallen asleep halfway through her lunch. Black said she'd hardly slept at all the night before because she was so scared of him and Ball.

Morgan felt as if she were going to burst, she was so full, but she couldn't remember ever being more content. Two days earlier she never would've thought she'd be sitting in a hotel room in a casino in the country that had become her prison and worst nightmare. Not only that, but she felt safe and protected. That was almost a miracle.

Her eyes felt heavy, and she was even a bit chilly in the air-conditioned room.

Just when she'd decided to lie down next to Nina and take her own nap, Black said, "Rex wants to know where we're taking you after we get Nina home to her mom."

Chapter Seven

Arrow glared at his friend for ruining Morgan's relaxed mood. It was the first time he'd seen her completely let down her guard, but Black's words made her stiffen, and the worry lines in her forehead had returned.

Without thought, he reached out and put a hand on her knee. Nina was sleeping soundly on the bed next to her, she was sitting in the middle of the queen-size bed with her back against the headboard, and he was sitting on the edge of the bed near her hip.

"I . . . I guess I'm going home to Atlanta," Morgan said hesitantly.

"Before you make a decision, maybe we should have a discussion about the people in your life so we can see if we can figure out who might be behind your kidnapping," Arrow said gently.

Morgan nodded, but he noticed she was chewing on her lip in agitation.

He wanted to reach over and pull it out, then rub his finger over the abused piece of flesh, but he refrained . . . barely.

"Morgan, would it be all right if we called the rest of the team and had them listen in while we have this discussion?" Black asked. "We've found that we work best when we all brainstorm together."

She nodded, but didn't stop gnawing on her lip.

Arrow couldn't stand it any longer. He reached up and used his thumb to pull her lip out of her teeth. "If you're still hungry, I could get you something else to eat," he teased.

She brought startled eyes up to his and shook her head. "No, I'm stuffed. I just ate more in one sitting than I usually got in a week."

That made Arrow want to go back into the city and hunt down the assholes who'd held her and Nina. "You can trust the others as much as you do me," he told her quietly. "I'd trust them with my life. *Have* trusted them with my life on more than one occasion."

"How many more are there?" Morgan asked.

Arrow blinked in surprise, then realized that he'd never really told her about the others. "Three. Four if you include Rex. There's Gray, Ro, and Meat. I've told you a little about Meat already. He's our computer guru, but he also makes the most amazing furniture you've ever seen. Gray is an accountant when he's not squiring his girlfriend, Allye, to her various dance recitals. And Ro is a mechanic. He and Chloe met not too long ago when we helped take down her asshole brother."

She stared at him for a beat. Then she said, "Oh . . . um . . . okay. I can handle three or four people listening in. I was afraid you were going to say there were like ten more guys who would be hearing my humiliating experience."

Ball had been leaning against the far wall, but at her words, he pushed off the wall and came toward them. Arrow noticed that Morgan flinched at the quick movement, but she swiftly hid it and raised her chin in an almost defiant manner. He was proud of her for not cowering, but hated that she felt she needed to protect herself from his friends.

"Nothing about what happened to you is humiliating," Ball said, his voice low. "You didn't ask to be kidnapped. You didn't ask to be brought down here. You didn't ask for anything that happened to you while you were here. Frankly, I'm more than sick of men taking advantage of their superior size and strength to hurt women and kids. Especially someone who looks like you."

"Looks like me?" Morgan asked.

"Yeah. Like a Disney princess. If someone is able to hurt *you*, there's literally no hope for them. None."

Arrow wanted to chuckle at the look on Morgan's face, but he refrained. Ball was right. She *did* look like a character straight out of a Disney movie. Small and delicate . . . but he knew firsthand that she had nerves of steel.

"I'll call Rex first," Black said. "He'll connect with the others."

"I'll clean up this mess," Ball offered as he began to collect the empty food containers and trash.

Arrow twisted so he was facing Morgan. His knee brushed against her, and he was grateful when she didn't flinch. "If anything gets to be too much, you can take a break," he told her.

"I'm fine," Morgan replied immediately.

"Okay, but as long as you know this isn't an interrogation," Arrow insisted.

She took a deep breath, looked over at Nina, who was still out like a light, then back at him. "I know. I want to figure this out more than you do, Arrow. To tell you the truth, I'm scared to death to go home. I can't help but think the person who did this is there waiting for me. He obviously never expected me to escape my captors, but now that I have, he'll probably be even more determined to send me back. Without you and your friends, I know I won't figure it out until it's too late. So while I'm not all fired up to tell you about the mistakes I've made in my life and the stupid stuff I've done, I know I need to. I have to."

"Morgan, I—"

"I wasn't done," she said, interrupting him. "Every day for the last year, I've wanted to give up. Wanted to find a way to kill myself so I wouldn't have to deal with what I was going through. But then I realized that if I did, no one would *ever* know what had happened to me. My mom, my friends, Lane, and even my dad would always wonder. I didn't want to put that kind of burden on them. So I did what I could to fight through the depression. I lived one day at a time. One hour at a time. Sometimes even one *minute* at a time.

"I know part of my feelings are because of the situation, but . . . I've never trusted anyone quite like I do you. If you think it's best I don't go back to Atlanta, I'll actually be relieved, and I'll go wherever you tell me to if it'll keep me safe. You and your friends have all the expertise here. I'm willing to do whatever it takes to get to the bottom of this so I can get back to my life."

Arrow had never been so impressed with anyone. He'd told her as much before, but every time she opened her mouth, he was that much more awestruck by her. He suspected he was falling head over heels already, but it was way too early to be muddying the waters with his feelings. "We're going to figure this out so you can go wherever you want to go and do whatever you want to do."

"Thank you."

"You don't ever have to thank me," he told her, picking up her hand and kissing the palm before closing her fingers, as if helping her to hold on to the kiss. "You living your life is thanks enough. I'm so relieved you didn't give up."

"You ready?" Ball asked.

Arrow raised an eyebrow at Morgan.

She took a deep breath and didn't look away from his gaze as she said, "I'm ready."

"Morgan?" a disembodied, digitally altered voice asked from the super-fancy phone Ball put on the foot of the bed. He'd explained earlier that it was some sort of satellite phone that couldn't be hacked.

"Yeah. I'm here."

"I'm Rex. And first, I'd like to say how happy we are that we found you."

"Thanks. But I'd venture a guess that I'm happier than you are," Morgan said.

The sounds of several men chuckling came through the phone line and echoed around the hotel room.

"I'm Gray," a deep voice said. "I apologize for me and the rest of the guys not being there with you right now."

"It's okay," Morgan told him.

"I'm Ro," a man with a British accent said. "Anything you need, all you have to do is ask and we'll get it for you."

"And I'm Meat," another man said. "If it's okay with you, I'll be doing some searches as we talk. So if I ask seemingly random questions, bear with me. I'm trying to verify information that I'm pulling up on my computer as we talk."

"I appreciate it," Morgan told them. "But seriously, I'm not that interesting. I lived a really normal life. I don't understand why anyone would want to do this to me."

"Let us worry about that," Rex told her. "Your job is to tell us everything, no matter how silly or inconsequential you think it is."

Arrow hated how stressed Morgan looked but knew there wasn't much he could do about it. They needed information. Information only she had. Until they had it, they were shooting in the dark. He slowly reached out and covered her hand, which was resting on her belly, with his own. Everything inside him melted when she visibly relaxed. *He'd* done that for her. He vowed to do whatever was necessary to make this easier on her.

"Tell us about the day you were taken," Rex ordered.

"Jeez," Morgan said under her breath. "I see we aren't going to start out with something easy, huh?"

"It's better to get the hard stuff over with," Rex responded, obviously having heard her.

Morgan took a deep breath, then began to speak. "It was a normal night, at least I thought it was. I went out with a group of friends and we—"

"Who?" Meat asked. "And where?"

"Sarah Ellsworth and her boyfriend, Thomas Huntington. Karen Garver and her boyfriend, Lance Buswell. And my boyfriend at the time, Lane Buswell. We were at a dance club downtown called Harlem Nights."

"So Lance and Lane are brothers?" Black asked.

Morgan nodded. "Yeah, Lance is four years younger than Lane, but they're still pretty close."

"What do they do for a living?" Meat asked.

"Um . . . Lane is a mortgage broker, and his brother works with some sort of construction company, I think. I don't remember the name, sorry."

"No worries. I can find it," Meat reassured her. "And their girlfriends? What can you tell us about the girls?"

"Karen is my age and owns her own boutique store. She sells environmentally friendly specialty foods and cosmetics and candles and stuff. She was one of my first customers when I started selling my bees' honey. We've been friends for a few years, and I was the one who introduced her to Lance. Sarah is a few years younger than me. I met her one night when me and Lane were out. She was a bartender at the bar and we hit it off. Her boyfriend, Thomas, I don't know as well. They recently started dating, and if I'm being honest, he was always pretty standoffish. He never acted like he enjoyed hanging out with us. Like we were beneath him or something." Morgan shrugged. "But I can't imagine any of them wanting to hurt me."

"Sometimes the last person you think might have it out for you is the one who hates you the most," Rex said without any emotion in his tone. "So what happened that night? How'd they get you?"

"So, as I said, we were at Harlem Nights. It was a Thursday, and we figured it would be less crowded since it wasn't the weekend, but we were wrong. The place was packed. We could barely move. We managed to get a small table in a back corner, but the music was so loud, I had the worst headache. I wanted to leave early, but the others were having a good time. I didn't want to be a party pooper, so I told them to stay, and I'd catch up with them some other time."

"Your boyfriend let you leave by yourself?" Arrow asked, feeling extremely pissed off. He was even more upset when Morgan looked surprised by his question.

"Of course. We arrived in separate cars."

"Please tell me he at least walked you to your car," Arrow asked.

Morgan shook her head. "He offered, but I told him to stay and enjoy himself."

"Asshole," someone on the other end of the phone said.

"Go on," Black suggested. "Ignore the comments from the peanut gallery."

"It wasn't his fault," Morgan said, defending Lane. "We'd been growing apart, and by that time, we were pretty much just friends, even though we hadn't officially broken up. I had a feeling he had his eye on one of the servers in the nightclub, and I think he was just as relieved as I was when I left. Anyway, so I headed out of the club and made my way to my car. I had parked in a public garage not too far from the bar. There were several people around, and I didn't notice anyone that made me feel nervous about walking by myself. I got to my car and had my keys in my hand. I clicked open the locks and sat down. That's . . . that's the last thing I remember. Someone either rushed me from the side or they were inside my car in the back, and as soon as I sat down, they did something to knock me out."

Arrow felt her hand begin to shake, so he picked it up and sandwiched it between his own. He held on tightly and was rewarded with a small smile before she continued talking.

"I was in and out of it for a while. I have no idea how long. I thought I was dreaming. I remember voices around me and people arguing, but not who or what they were saying. My kidnapper must've kept me completely knocked out, because when I finally woke up, I was sweating my ass off in the back of a moving vehicle. I think it was one of those moving vans. It was pitch-dark, and I was in a cage of some sort. I have no idea how long we traveled, but when the door was finally opened, a man wearing a police uniform came toward me. I begged him to help me, but he didn't say a word—he just lifted a gun and shot me."

Arrow jolted, and Ball asked what had been on the tip of his tongue. "What the fuck? *Shot* you?"

"With a dart gun of some sort," Morgan told them quickly. "I pulled it out as fast as I could, but it was too late. Whatever drug was in it worked fast, and I was once again knocked out. Anyway, this happened several times. I was kept in that cage for what I estimated to be days. I wasn't even allowed out to use the bathroom."

Her eyes dropped to her lap, and once again, Arrow felt the urge to go back to the house where they'd found Nina and Morgan and kill everyone.

"They treated me worse than a dog," she continued. "I was allowed one bottle of water a day, and only occasionally did they bother to feed me. At some point, I must've been loaded onto a plane, but by then, I was so out of it and so depressed that I didn't pay much attention. I was brought here to Santo Domingo . . . and eventually, you guys showed up."

Arrow frowned. There was a lot she was leaving out . . . like a year's worth of details. And as much as he didn't want her to have to relive it, they needed to know everything. Not only to help figure out who might've been behind her kidnapping, but to emotionally help her as well.

"Were you held at the same house the whole time?" Ro asked.

"No. I was . . . passed around . . . for lack of a better word. I was kept in one house for a while, drugged, put back into the cage, loaded into a truck, and moved to another house. I have no idea what was said between the people who had me because I don't know Spanish. I wish I'd at least taken it in high school—I might've been able to pick up *something*. Some of the men who had me were nicer than others. Some fed me more often than others and they didn't . . . you know. But like clockwork, I'd be moved every couple weeks, until I started recognizing the men who had me."

"What do you mean?" Gray asked.

"They were on some sort of rotating schedule," Morgan told them. "I counted ten of them. I even recognized the rooms they were keeping me in after a while."

"Hmmm. Okay, so there was a core group of ten men who were responsible for keeping you, then transporting you to the next person on the list. Smart," Gray commented. "So these ten men are probably the ones who were sharing the money they were being paid to keep you down here."

"We need to get you to a hospital," Rex said. "Get you checked out, especially considering what you went through at the hands of the men who kept you captive."

"No!" Morgan said forcefully. "I just want to get out of Santo Domingo."

"Morgan—" Rex started, sympathy easy to hear, even in the mechanically altered voice.

"Look. I'm not an idiot," Morgan said firmly. "I know I need to be checked for any diseases they might've given me, but anything that's wrong with me today isn't going to go away even if I see a doctor tonight. I have no objection to seeing one, but not tonight. And not *here*."

There was silence in the room for a beat. Arrow felt anger tightening his chest. Morgan hadn't told them anything he hadn't already assumed had happened, but all of a sudden it seemed way more personal. He regretted not running into more of her captors during the rescue. He wanted them all dead. Every last one.

"I understand your reluctance, but we could have Rex vet any doctor you see, to make sure he or she is on the up and up. And you're right, seeing a doctor tonight won't make any issues suddenly disappear, but it *could* stop anything from getting worse," Arrow said as gently as he could.

"Please," she whispered. "I can't. Not here."

Sighing, Arrow nodded. He wasn't happy about her decision, but he couldn't force her to see a doctor.

"Tell us about your parents," Rex conceded, changing the subject.

Arrow was relieved. Morgan was not doing well talking about her time in captivity. No one asked for details about what she'd been through at the hands of those ten men. They knew. He made a mental note to urge her to see a therapist as soon as possible after returning to the States . . . but not before seeing a doctor.

"My parents?" Morgan asked, blinking in confusion. It was quite a jump in topic, but Arrow knew Rex had done it to jar her out of the bad memories that had to be swirling in her mind.

"Yeah. They're divorced, right?"

"Yeah. *Very* divorced. My mom hates my dad, and my dad isn't that fond of my mom either. They got married somewhat young, and I guess things were good for a while, but then after I was born and things got tough, they drifted apart. My dad cheated on my mom, and she cheated on him right back. The divorce took forever to be finalized because they fought over every little thing. In the end, my dad had to pay my mom alimony, which pissed him off, and my mom was mad that he was able to request to see me as much as he wanted since he was paying child support.

"I wasn't that close to my dad because I'd grown up listening to the awful stories Mom told me about him. I'd go and stay with him on weekends, but when I was really young, I'd cry for my mom the whole time. It wasn't until I was in college that I realized how much my mom's bitter attitude toward him had affected me. I made an effort to try to get to know him better after that."

"And did it work?" Arrow asked gently.

Morgan shrugged. "Somewhat. I mean, we still weren't that close. But we were both making an effort. He was busy with his job as the CFO of a Fortune 500 company, and I was busy with college and friends and then getting my bee business up and running."

"Where did your relationship stand when you were kidnapped?" Meat asked.

"It was cordial. I didn't exactly call him up to chitchat all the time, but when we *did* have lunch or something, it didn't seem like there were any hard feelings," Morgan said.

"What about your mom?" Meat asked.

"What about her?"

"What did she think about you trying to have a better relationship with your dad?" Meat clarified.

"She was fine with it. I mean, I'm an adult. She didn't want to know when I saw him or what we talked about, but she eventually admitted since he was my father and always would be, it was a good thing if I had some sort of relationship with him."

"What does your mom do for a living?" Ball asked.

"She's a dental assistant."

"You and her don't have the same last name, do you?" Meat asked.

"No. She went back to her maiden name, Jernigan, after the divorce was final. She wanted to officially change my name, but my dad put his foot down and refused to let her," Morgan said.

"Do you know where your dad was the night you were kidnapped?" Meat asked.

Morgan's brow furrowed, and she shook her head. "No. I have no idea. We weren't close enough to keep tabs on each other like that. I had lunch with him the week before, but that's about it."

"According to the police reports, he doesn't have an alibi. At least not one that can be corroborated," Rex said. "He left work around six, which was verified by his employee swipe card, and his car was seen on a surveillance camera leaving the parking garage. He says he went straight home and was alone all night, but again, there's no one to vouch for him that he's telling the truth."

"You think my *dad* did this?" Morgan asked in disbelief. "There's no way."

"Why not? Nina's dad snatched her from the only home she's known and didn't plan on returning her," Black said. "It happens, Morgan. All the time."

"Not *my* dad," she insisted.

"You said yourself that you don't know him all that well," Rex said without a hint of sympathy in his tone. "Maybe he did it to get back at you for snubbing him all those years. Or he did it to get back at your mom for cheating on him. Humans can hold a grudge for a very long time, Morgan. We can't rule anyone out."

"Fine," Morgan spat, her eyes shooting sparks at the phone lying on the end of the bed. "In that case, maybe Lane did it because he didn't want me seeing anyone else, even though he didn't love me anymore. Maybe Lance had a crush on me and wanted me all to himself, or he was mad I was going to break up with his brother. No, I have it—maybe Karen and Sarah were in this together, and they just wanted someone to scare me, and it got out of hand. Or someone that night saw me in the club and figured he'd just take me."

She was breathing hard, as if she'd run a mile at full speed.

Arrow murmured, "Easy, beautiful."

Morgan turned on him then. "No! This is crazy."

"Just because we bring up a name doesn't mean we necessarily think they were the ones who did it," Meat said soothingly.

"Then why mention them in the first place?" Morgan shot back agitatedly. "I mean, you might as well accuse every single person I've sold honey to, or the homeless man I give money to when I go downtown to meet my dad, or my seventh grade teacher who I had a crush on when I was twelve. You might as well accuse my mom, or my postman, or the bouncer at the club that night. Where does it stop? When does the list start getting smaller? If you're going to accuse my own father of having me kidnapped, it could literally be anyone I've ever spoken to in my life."

"That's exactly right," Rex said sternly. "It *could* be anyone, Morgan. The sooner you understand that, the sooner you'll be able to think clearly and help us figure this out. People can be evil. Some just hide it a hell of a lot better than others. We aren't pointing the finger at anyone yet. We're just talking. Trying to get information on the people closest to you so we can eliminate them. We wouldn't be doing our jobs if we dismissed someone simply because *you* don't think they could be behind it. We're good at what we do because we're not emotionally connected to the primary players."

Arrow kept his eyes on Morgan. He couldn't look away if his life depended on it. He wanted to take her in his arms and reassure her that they'd figure this out. That she was safe. But he couldn't. He didn't have the right. He had to sit there and watch as her world was torn apart once more.

But he should've known she would reach down deep inside herself and find the same strength she'd used to get through the ordeal thus far. She closed her eyes and took a deep breath. Then another.

Arrow would've sat back, given her some space, but she turned her hand in his and gripped him so tightly, he knew her nails were leaving half-moon marks in the back of his hand.

"You're right. I'm sorry. I just . . . this is just so overwhelming."

"I know it is," Rex said. "You're doing amazing. And again, we are so relieved and happy to have found you. I won't bore you with statistics, but I imagine you have an idea that generally people who disappear for as long as you did aren't found, and if they are, they aren't walking and talking, if you know what I mean."

"I do. Thank you," Morgan told him.

Nina jerked on the bed and began to moan in distress. Morgan immediately turned to her and brushed her hand over her head. "You're okay," she said quietly. "You're safe. Go back to sleep, baby. I'm here."

Her words did the trick. Nina settled back down without ever having woken up completely.

"How's she doing?" Gray asked quietly.

"I'm not sure," Morgan said.

"She had a tough night," Black informed everyone. "Woke up screaming every hour or so. Nothing we did worked, and she was scared to death of us."

"Morgan being here has really helped," Ball added. "I think the fact that she's female is working in her favor."

"It's more than that," Arrow countered. "It's Morgan. She protected Nina when they were in that hell house together. Nina knows deep down that Morgan was the only thing standing between her and extreme danger. It's going to take a while for that feeling of vulnerability to fade."

"Which brings us to another point," Rex said. "And full circle in this conversation. Where are we bringing Morgan when you all get back to the States?"

No one said a word for a beat.

"While we were talking, I looked up Ellie Jernigan," Meat said.

"My mom? Why? What's wrong? Is she okay?" Morgan asked.

"She's fine," Meat soothed quickly. "But she doesn't live in Atlanta anymore. She moved."

"She did?" Morgan asked. "To where?"

"Albuquerque, New Mexico," Meat said. "It looks like she moved there a few months after you were kidnapped. Seems she wanted to get away from the city, from your dad, and from the constant news coverage of your disappearance. She's been calling the detectives in charge every week, though, wanting to know what new information they might have, whether they have any leads on your disappearance. She told a newspaper reporter that she'd only stayed in Atlanta because you were there. She took a job with an Albuquerque dentist and has been living a quiet life."

"Wow. I never thought she'd move," Morgan said.

"Albuquerque isn't that far from Colorado Springs," Arrow said quietly. "Only five, five and a half hours."

She stared at him, and he saw that she understood exactly why he'd mentioned that. Eventually, she asked, "Has anyone told my parents that I'm alive?"

"Not yet," Rex answered.

"After our discussion today, about how any one of my friends could be behind my kidnapping, I'm not that comfortable going back to Atlanta," Morgan said. "I have a feeling I'd always be looking over my shoulder, wondering if someone was following me. Every time I talked to Lane or Karen or anyone I used to work with, I'd wonder if they were plotting to get me back down here. I kind of like the idea of starting over in a new city like Albuquerque. I've never been there."

"It's a dry heat," Black said with a grin.

Morgan chuckled, and Arrow was relieved. It was a strained laugh, but she was making the effort. He was so proud of her. "Would your mom object to you living with her while you got back on your feet?" he asked Morgan.

She shook her head slowly. "I don't think so. I mean, she cried the day I left for college. Even after I graduated, she wanted me to move back in with her. She loved visiting me, and we'd talk about my bees and my business for hours. I can't imagine she'd object to me moving in with her now. Especially not when I've basically come back from the dead."

"I'll call and talk to her," Gray volunteered. "I'll tell her as much as I can about how you're doing and where you've been. Then I'll ask if it's okay if you stay with her while you're getting back on your feet."

"I should probably go back to Atlanta, though," Morgan said. "At least for a bit. I need to check on my bees. And my business. I should also probably see Lane. And my dad. I need to—"

"We'll take care of as much of the business side of things as we can," Rex told her. "Obviously, you'll want to see your father and your friends, but don't worry about your belongings and the legal stuff. We'll arrange to get your belongings sent to New Mexico. And if anything was sold or given away, we'll get you new things."

Arrow hated the look of sorrow that crossed her face when she thought about her stuff being sold, but she rallied enough to thank Rex.

"Thank you. I'll probably have to figure out taxes for the business, but I just hope my bees are okay."

"I'll help you get new bees," Arrow said. He hated the damn things. Ever since he'd watched a show about killer bees when he was little, he couldn't stand any kind of flying, stinging insect—bees, wasps, hornets, yellow jackets . . . even bumblebees gave him the creeps. But for Morgan, he'd overcome his aversion.

"Thanks," she whispered, and stared at him with gratitude in her eyes. Arrow could tell she was at the end of her rope.

"I think this conversation is done," he told their handler. "Morgan is beat, and it's been a long day."

"Understood," Rex said. "So, Morgan, one more question . . . are you okay with coming back to Colorado Springs briefly? I'm going to look over what you've told me, and I'm sure I'll have more questions. Once you meet with the team, we can escort you to Albuquerque and to your mom."

"Yeah, I'm okay with that," Morgan said. "But how are you going to get me out of the country? I don't have any identification."

"I've been working with Rex, and we've got it covered," Meat said. "And if anyone asks . . . you were the one who signed the form to get a copy of your passport from the American embassy in Santo Domingo."

Arrow was relieved to see the slight grin on Morgan's face.

"Gotcha. Thank you, Meat."

"You don't have to thank me, darlin'. You just take care of yourself and get your butt back home. I can't wait to meet you."

"Same here," she said.

After a few more pleasantries, Rex ended the connection. They had a flight planned for the next day. They'd leave Santo Domingo and fly straight to Colorado Springs, where Nina's mother would be waiting. Arrow made a mental note to have a talk with Morgan about what to expect and how to deal with the press, but for now he wanted her to relax, secure in the knowledge that she was safe. Safe with him.

"Feel like a short nap?" Arrow asked her.

"I could nap," she responded.

"Good. Black and Ball are going to head out and find some other things for both you and Nina. More toiletries, a few pieces of clothing—things like that. Anything or any brands you'd like to specifically request?" Arrow had spoken with his teammates briefly before they'd called Rex, and they'd agreed not only to go back to the neighborhood where he and Morgan had been hunted and see what information they could gather but also to do the shopping.

"That's not necessary—" Morgan started, but Black interrupted her.

"I am not a shopper," he told her. "I'm lucky to get to my local grocery store once every couple weeks. I much prefer shopping online, but for you, I'll gladly go to the store to get what you need to make you feel more human. Let us do this for you, Morgan. Let us help you."

"Well, jeez, when you put it that way, how can I refuse?" she joked.

"You can't," Black stated. "But don't get used it. I can guarantee when we get back to the Springs, Allye and Chloe will take over shopping duty."

"They're Gray's and Ro's girlfriends, right?" she asked.

"Yes," Arrow told her. "And they're as amazing and strong as you are."

He loved the blush that pinkened her cheeks.

"I can't wait to meet them," Morgan said quietly. "It's been a long time since I've had the company of a woman."

"Is there anything specific you want while we're out?" Ball asked.

Morgan immediately shook her head. "No. It's been so long since I've worn anything other than this"—she indicated the T-shirt and tattered jeans she was wearing—"that anything would be heaven. But . . . Nina is obsessed with Elsa, from the movie *Frozen*. We talked about her a few times, how nice it would be if we could make a snowstorm appear in the stifling room we were kept in." She smiled. "If you can find anything related to that movie, it might go a long way toward making her trust you a little more."

"Consider it done," Black said. "I hate seeing that look of terror in any kid's eyes, especially when all we want to do is help."

And with that, the two men gave them chin lifts and disappeared out the door of the suite, leaving Morgan and Arrow alone, except for a sleeping Nina.

Chapter Eight

Morgan woke up a couple of hours later, momentarily confused and scared out of her skull. She was actually cold, which was unusual, and that was the first clue she wasn't a prisoner anymore.

She opened her eyes—

And immediately threw herself to the left, away from the man who was standing over her.

"Shit, Morgan. I'm sorry! It's me. Arrow. You're okay. *Fuck.*"

Arrow. Morgan blinked and slowly sat up on the bed. Nina was no longer next to her, and she and Arrow were alone in the room.

"Are you awake? I'm so sorry, beautiful. I thought you heard Nina wake up and climb off the bed. She's in the other room with Ball and Black . . . which is a huge step forward for her. They found a video of the movie *Frozen*, as well as a few toys. She's currently in little girl heaven, watching the movie and playing with the figurines."

Morgan appreciated Arrow talking to give her time to get her bearings back. "I didn't hear her leave," she said, stunned. "I can't believe it. When we were in that house, if she even so much as moved an inch next to me, I was immediately awake. I couldn't take the chance one of the men would decide they wanted her rather than me."

Arrow slowly sat on the edge of the mattress, giving her plenty of room. "I think a part of you knows that you're both safe here. Black and Ball would no sooner hurt her, or you, than they would any child who was under their care."

"I know. It's just . . ." Morgan's voice trailed off.

"Rex works with a therapist who specializes in crimes against women. I think it would do you a lot of good to talk to her."

Morgan wanted to immediately protest. To tell Arrow that she was fine and didn't need to talk to anyone about what had happened to her. But she knew she was kidding herself. She'd been through hell. And if she ever wanted to have a normal life, she needed to purge the hate and fear in her heart. For her captors, for whoever was behind her kidnapping, and even for herself. She wanted to be proud that she'd survived. But at the moment, all she could feel was disgust.

She hated that she'd done what she had. Hated that she'd stopped fighting her captors. It was easier, and less painful, to give in and let them take what they wanted rather than fighting back.

If talking with someone could convince her she'd done what she had to in order to survive, and would allow her to someday enjoy sex again, and hopefully allow her to have a relationship with a man, she'd do it.

Peering up at Arrow through her lashes, Morgan suspected he was a large part of why she wanted to feel normal again. Everything about him appealed to her. His height. His muscles. The scruff of a beard on his cheeks. The fact that he'd freely admitted to being claustrophobic. The way he held her tight when she needed it and kept his distance at times too. He was amazingly perceptive when it came to her, and the way he so easily and freely put her needs first was a heady feeling. No one had given a shit about her in so long.

Fear that she was feeling these things for him simply because he'd been the one to rescue her was the only thing keeping Morgan from throwing herself into his arms. She wanted to, though; oh, how she wanted to. She hadn't felt safe in forever, not like she did when he held her.

"Okay," she told him after way too many minutes had passed. "I'm not completely comfortable with talking about what happened to me, but I don't want this to beat me down. I don't want to be a homeless, crazy woman in ten years, still struggling to deal with my kidnapping."

"What *do* you want?" he asked seriously.

"I want to have a family. A little girl I can teach to stick up for herself and be empathetic to anyone who might be different from her. I want a son I can teach to be selfless and protective."

"And a husband?" Arrow asked.

"That too," Morgan whispered, not looking away from his intense gaze. "I want someone I can trust to help out with the kids and the household chores. I want to marry my best friend, who will make me laugh even when things are going wrong. I want to slow dance in my kitchen at midnight, simply because we can. I want to *live*, Arrow. Someone tried to take that opportunity away from me, and I refuse to let him succeed."

Arrow didn't say anything for a long moment, but she could see the longing and pride reflected in his eyes as he stared at her. "You'll have your family," he said. "I can't imagine anyone or anything getting in the way of what you want."

"Thanks," she whispered, feeling drunk as she lost herself in the admiration in his gaze. It had been a long time since she'd felt anything but disgust in the company of a man. She wasn't nearly ready for any kind of relationship, but she couldn't deny she liked what she saw when she looked at Arrow.

Clearing his throat, he said, "I came in here to see if you wanted to try to get those mats out of your hair. The guys found conditioner." He held up a white bottle.

Morgan brought a hand up to her head self-consciously. She knew how bad her hair was, had seen it firsthand in the mirror. She hadn't wanted to take a pair of scissors to it, but was afraid it was going to be inevitable.

"Sure. But I don't know if it'll do much good," she told him honestly.

Arrow stood and held out a hand to her. "We can try."

She liked that. *We.*

She lifted her hand to his and let him help her stand. As they walked toward the bathroom hand in hand, Arrow said, "Oh, and the guys got you and Nina some clothes while they were out. I can't guarantee they're the most fashionable things ever, but I, for one, would like to see those clothes you're in burned."

Morgan stopped in her tracks, and Arrow turned to see what the issue was.

"They got me clothes?"

"Yeah. Jeans. A pair of sweats. A sleep set. Panties and a sports bra. And a few shirts so you can decide what you like best. They got Nina most of the same . . . including a sleep shirt with Elsa from *Frozen* on it." He grinned like a little kid.

Morgan felt tears spring to her eyes, and she closed them tightly, trying to gain control over her emotions.

"It's okay," Arrow soothed. "I know it seems like a lot."

"No," Morgan countered without opening her eyes. "It's everything. I haven't had anyone do anything nice for me in months. Nothing that didn't have strings attached, that is."

She felt his fingers brush over her cheek in a barely there caress before he tugged on her hand, urging her to walk toward the bathroom once more. "Get used to it, beautiful," he said. "I'm finding that doing nice things for you could be my new mission in life."

Morgan chuckled. Somehow, the thought of Arrow doing things for her didn't make her uneasy, as it sometimes had in the past when men had gone out of their way to try to impress her. Maybe it was her time in captivity that made her appreciate the little things more.

Arrow grabbed the ice bucket on the way into the bathroom. Morgan stood there feeling awkward as Arrow set the conditioner on the edge of the bathtub, then put his hands on his hips, surveying the room. He turned to her and gestured toward the tub. "Go on and have a seat in there. I'll sit on the edge and work on your hair."

"Um . . . I'm not sure . . ." Morgan wasn't exactly sure how to tell him there was no way she was going to be naked with him in there, the previous night's bathtub incident notwithstanding.

Amazingly, Arrow blushed. "I didn't mean you should strip. I figured after we got through this, you can throw away that shirt and those jeans. You can keep them on while I work on your hair, and hopefully when I'm done, you'll be good to take a shower, and I'll go and get the things the guys bought for you today."

"Yeah, that should work," Morgan said in relief.

Arrow took a step toward her, and Morgan forced herself not to step back.

"I'd never purposely do anything to make you feel uncomfortable, Morgan. I know this is hard for you. And honestly, it's hard for me too. I'm not usually a gentle man. I swear too much, and I say and do shit that isn't respectable in polite society. I don't care much about fashion. But I'll do everything I can to make the transition back to your old life as easy as possible."

"I'm not sure I want to go back to my old life," Morgan blurted.

Instead of looking shocked or concerned, Arrow simply nodded. "I'm not surprised. You're a completely different person than you were a year ago. And that's not a bad thing. You went through shit that very few people experience, and you emerged from the other side a different Morgan Byrd."

"I already feel guilty," she admitted.

"Don't," Arrow fired back immediately. "You are who you are. If your old friends can't deal, then you get new ones who can. You don't have to prove yourself to anyone, and you don't have to answer to anyone except yourself."

"Thank you," Morgan whispered.

"You're welcome. Now, come on." He held out a hand. "Let's do this."

Morgan allowed Arrow to help her step over the lip of the tub, and she sat cross-legged with her back to him. She felt him settle behind her, his legs flanking her shoulders.

"You're going to get wet," she warned.

"Yup," he agreed.

He reached over and turned on the water, waiting until it got hot before filling up the ice bucket he'd put within reach. "Close your eyes and tip your head back," he said.

Morgan did as he said, and sighed in contentment as the warm water cascaded over her head. It also ran down her forehead into her face and onto the shirt she was wearing, but she didn't care. Within moments, her hair was soaked, and she heard Arrow uncap the bottle of conditioner. The cream felt cold against her now-warm scalp, but she was amazed at how patient and gentle Arrow was as he worked it into her hair.

"You're good at this," she observed after several minutes.

"I've had some practice."

Morgan stiffened. Oh shit. She hadn't even asked if he was married or if he had kids or anything. Was she attracted to a married man? Had she misread the signals he was sending? And if so, why was he acting as if he liked her? Liked her as more than just a chick he was rescuing?

Before she could freak herself out more, he said conversationally, "My sister is seven years younger than me. She was the ultimate tomboy. She was constantly rolling around in the dirt and muck. My dad died when I was young, and Mom worked a lot to make ends meet, so it was up to me to get Kandi to bed most nights, and that meant helping her with her bath and getting all the dirt out of her hair."

Morgan relaxed a fraction. Then she turned her head so she could look at him as she asked, "Your sister's name is Kandi?"

Arrow grinned. "Yup. I have no idea what my mom was thinking. She got teased mercilessly in school because of it. Now turn around, I'm still working."

Doing as ordered, Morgan couldn't help the chuckle that escaped. "Kids are brutal, but with a name like Kandi Kane, I guess I'm not surprised."

"Don't feel too sorry for her," Arrow said. "I taught her how to defend herself."

"I bet you did." And just like that, Morgan felt melancholy once more.

"What is it?" Arrow asked, perceptive as usual.

"I always wished I had a sibling," she told him.

"Kandi's a pain in my ass," Arrow told her. "You can have her."

Morgan chuckled again. She could hear the affection in his voice when he talked about his sister. "Does she live in Colorado Springs?"

"No. Thank God. I'd go crazy worrying about her all the time. She lives in Michigan with my mom. She's been dating the same guy for years, and I keep threatening to go up there and kick his ass if he doesn't hurry up and propose."

"Do you like him?"

"Yeah. He's a great guy. He keeps an eye on my mom since I can't be there. I send her money, but that doesn't help when she needs to put up the screens in the summer or get her grass mowed. I hate not being there for her."

"I bet she's proud of you," Morgan said.

"She is. I joined the Marines right out of high school. I know she didn't want me to, but she never let on. Always supported me in whatever I wanted to do. I got my degree when I was enlisted, and she cheered me on every step of the way."

"My parents love me, but not like that," Morgan said.

"What do you mean?"

She closed her eyes as Arrow's fingers caressed her scalp while he did his best to remove the stubborn mats in her hair. "It's just that I've been a bone of contention between them my entire life. They're always trying to one-up the other. My dad's got lots of money, and he never hesitated to use it to make my mom feel bad that she couldn't get me the things he did. Holidays were the worst. I mean, I loved getting toys and clothes and stuff, but I knew he bought them just to irritate my mom. And Mom never missed a chance to complain about Dad. She'd bitch about whatever woman he was dating and call her a slut, tell me to my face that Dad didn't really love me, that he was giving me stuff to take digs at *her*. It was . . . tough."

"Fuck, beautiful. I'm sorry. That sucks."

She shrugged. "Yeah. But eventually they stopped acting like three-year-olds, and it got better. My dad started giving me cash for birthdays and holidays, and I wouldn't have to try to hide extravagant presents from my mom. And she learned to keep her feelings about him to herself."

"I'm glad it got better. I can't stand to hear about kids being in the middle of squabbles between adults."

"Like Nina," Morgan observed.

"Exactly."

"I can't believe her dad just up and kidnapped her."

"Happens all the time. I'm just glad we were able to get on the case quickly and come get her."

"Me too," Morgan whispered.

She felt Arrow lean close, and was surprised to feel his lips on her cheek. He didn't say anything, merely continued to work on her hair, but Morgan knew she was blushing.

"Can I ask you something?" she blurted, determined to get this out of the way.

"Of course. Anything."

"Are you married? Or seeing someone?"

She wanted to say more. That she was beginning to like him, and if he told her he wasn't available or didn't want anything to do with her after this, it would be better to back away from him now rather than later.

"Look at me," Arrow ordered.

She didn't want to, but she steeled her spine and twisted so she could look him in the eyes.

"I'm not married or seeing anyone. I haven't been on a real date in years, and it's been about as long since I've been with a woman. I've never felt about someone the way I'm feeling about you, Morgan. And no, I can't tell you what that is, because I haven't figured it out myself. But I *do* know I want to see you when we get back to the States . . . and not to simply make sure you're doing okay. I mean, yes, that, but it's more . . . Shit, I'm messing this up," he said in agitation. His shoulders sagged, and he looked away from her.

"You're not," Morgan insisted, feeling ten pounds lighter at his admission. "I'm not sure I'm the best bet. I alternate between being scared out of my skull and being pissed at the world for this having happened to me. But . . . when I'm with you, things seem not as scary. I trust you more than I've trusted anyone in my life, and I don't think it's because you were the one to rescue me. I mean, I trust Black and Ball, but not the same as I do you. Does that make any sense?"

"Yeah, beautiful, it does." Arrow shoved his goopy fingers in her hair and supported her neck as she looked up at him. "We've got a bumpy road ahead of us," he warned. "Between your mental health, and trying to solve the mystery of who did this to you . . . my job, and the fact that we'll be living in two different cities . . . it's a lot."

Morgan swallowed and nodded, not sure what to say. Was he trying to let her down gently? Warning her that it wasn't going to work out between them, and not to get her hopes up? She just wasn't sure. It didn't help that it had been a full year since she'd had to deal with any kind of relationship issues.

"But all that notwithstanding," Arrow went on, "I want to try. Because I see something in you that I haven't seen in any other woman I've met. Yes, I feel protective of you. Yes, I realize that part of what I'm feeling is because of our situation. But, honestly, I think it's more than that. I want you to continue to trust me. To know I've got your back. No matter what you want to do. Harvest honey from bees or knit stocking caps in your house . . . I'll be there, supporting you and cheering you on. Whether that's as a friend or more remains to be seen. But I hope you'll be there for me too."

"I'm scared that I can't live up to your expectations," she admitted softly.

"Fuck that. You've already surpassed them, beautiful. The only thing you have to do is be yourself. We'll figure everything else out."

She nodded, then licked her lips and asked, "Do you think this is moving too fast? I mean, we've only known each other two days. Maybe it's the situation. Things might be different when we get home."

"It's possible," Arrow admitted. "But I don't think so. In case you're thinking this is some sort of protector complex I've got or that I feel responsible for you because I rescued you, think again. I can't even count the number of women I've rescued. And I haven't felt even a fraction for them what I'm feeling for you. Okay?"

"Okay."

He leaned down and kissed her forehead before saying, "I know we need to slow down. That it'll be a while before either of us is comfortable with any kind of serious intimacy. Sleeping next to each other is one thing, but *sleeping* with each other is something completely different. I'll give you all the time you need, but know that in the end, that's the kind of relationship I'm hoping for with you."

"You can't know that."

"I do. And I'm not saying that things won't change between us. We might get home and decide that we're better off friends than lovers. Or that we just don't suit. Or you might take one look at my neat-as-a-pin home and decide you don't want anything to do with me. Or Kandi might tell you one too many horror stories about my childhood, and you'll run screaming." He grinned to let her know he was teasing. "But the bottom line is that I want to try."

"I do too," she agreed. "But I think I'm the one with way more baggage than you. What if we never find out who did this to me? I'll have to spend the rest of my life looking over my shoulder, wondering if they're just waiting to pounce. And my folks aren't exactly poster children for mother and father of the year."

"We're going to figure out who took you," Arrow countered. "And if we can't, so be it. I'll be there to look over your shoulder with you. And I can handle your parents."

They stared at each other for a moment before she asked, "So . . . are we going steady now?"

He chuckled. "I haven't heard that term since middle school. I'll dig out my high school class ring and letter jacket and give them to you so everyone knows you're taken."

"Thank you," Morgan whispered. "Somehow talking to you always seems to make me less freaked out. You make me feel almost normal."

"That's because you *are* normal," Arrow fired back. "We'll make our own normal—together."

"I'd like that," she told him.

"Good. Now, turn around and let me continue working. I've almost got this one section done. It wasn't as bad as I thought."

It took another forty-five minutes, and by the time he was done, Morgan was shivering in the bottom of the tub, but he'd done it. Her hair was free of snarls and mats and fell freely down her back.

"Shower, beautiful. I'll go get your clothes. You're gonna feel like a brand-new person by the time you're done in here."

With that, he ran his hand over the top of her head and left the bathroom.

"I already do," Morgan said softly after the door clicked shut behind Arrow.

She stripped off her shirt and jeans and stood in the warm spray of the shower for at least ten minutes before soaping up, rinsing, and shutting off the water. A pile of new clothes sat on the edge of the sink, and she stared at them for a long moment before drying off and putting them on.

She wiped the mirror and stared at herself. She looked much like she remembered. A little thinner, perhaps, but otherwise, no one would be able to tell what she'd been through simply by looking at her. That seemed like both a blessing and a curse, because she knew she was fundamentally changed by her year in Santo Domingo.

"One day at a time," she whispered to herself, before opening the door to join the others.

Chapter Nine

Leaving Santo Domingo had been surprisingly easy. The private plane Rex had arranged for them was waiting at the airport. Morgan held Nina's right hand in her left and Arrow's left hand in her right as they boarded the plane.

Nina was still guarded around the men, but the *Frozen* toys, clothes, and movie had gone a long way toward loosening her up. The little girl still flinched around people she didn't know, but holding on to Morgan seemed to help.

Arrow had told her that Black and Ball hadn't found anything useful when they'd snuck back to the house where they'd found her and Nina. The two men said the house had been ransacked and pretty much destroyed from the inside out. All in all, it had been a frustrating dead end.

They landed at the small Colorado Springs airport after several hours in the air. Arrow had kept a close eye on Morgan, wanting to make sure she was all right with everything that had happened.

The second they landed, Black's phone rang. He answered it, and the look on his face told Arrow that whoever was on the other end of the line was telling him something he wasn't happy about.

He clicked off the phone and without beating around the bush said, "That was Rex. Morgan, he called and informed your father of your situation . . . and he's here."

"Rex?" Morgan asked, tilting her head in confusion.

"No. Your dad."

Arrow put his hand on the small of Morgan's back as they stood in the aisle of the plane, waiting to get off. He could feel her trembling, but when she spoke, her voice was strong and steady.

"Seriously?"

"Yes."

"And my mom? Please tell me she isn't here too. What a disaster that would be . . . to have both of them in the same place at the same time."

Black chuckled. "No, as far as I know, she's not here right now. Although Rex called and informed her of your well-being too."

Morgan nodded and turned to Arrow. "My dad is here," she whispered.

"You okay with that?"

She slowly nodded. "Yeah."

"You don't sound sure," he noted.

"It's just . . ." Her voice faded away. "I can't explain how I'm feeling."

"Excited to see him. Trepidation because it's been so long. Nervousness about what he's going to say?" Arrow asked.

Her lips twitched. "Yeah. That."

"You're allowed to feel all that and more. Don't think there's a correct or incorrect way to act and feel. You've been through a lot in the last year. You've changed. He probably has too."

"Will you guys . . . will you guys stay nearby? Seeing anyone I knew from before makes me feel nervous. I mean, it's my *dad*. He's not going to pull out a knife and shank me in the middle of a public airport, but . . ." Once more, her words trailed off.

"Of course we will," Ball said.

At the same time, Black exclaimed, "Damn straight we will be!"

Arrow leaned down and kissed her temple. "I'll be right here by your side, beautiful."

"Thanks," she said, and Arrow felt good when she leaned against him subtly. "I don't think my dad was the one behind my kidnapping, but I can't shake the feeling that it has to be someone I knew well."

"Shhh," Arrow soothed. "Don't think about it right now. Relax and enjoy being home. Me and my team will have your back. Nothing's going to happen to you. Okay?"

"Okay," she agreed.

"One more thing," Black said, and the look on his face made Arrow brace. "The press is here. I guess your father called them after he heard that you were found and on your way home."

One of Morgan's hands went to her hair. "Oh shit."

"You look fine," Arrow told her. "Relax."

"I don't . . . I can't—"

"You can," Arrow said. "You can do any-fucking-thing. Just ignore them. Rex is probably putting together a press conference right now where all their questions will be answered. All you have to do is be yourself."

"What if I don't know who I am anymore?" Morgan asked.

"One minute at a time, beautiful," Arrow said. "One minute at a time."

She nodded, and he watched her take a deep breath.

"Can we go now? I want to see Mommy," Nina said, squeezing around Arrow and latching on to Morgan's hand.

"Almost," Ball said. "Your mom is inside, and she can't wait to see you."

The smile that crossed the little girl's face was a thing of beauty. *This* was why Arrow and the others did what they did. The reunions allowed them to get through the low and dark points in their missions. Seeing the joy and relief on loved ones' faces was more precious than he could explain.

After another minute or two, they were stepping off the plane onto the tarmac. They got on a small shuttle bus, and then they were inside the terminal. The second the door opened, a female voice shrieked, and Nina tore her hand from Morgan's and ran toward the woman.

Arrow watched with a smile as Nina was scooped up and almost smothered in the bosom of a large woman who was sobbing uncontrollably.

Then they heard a man say, "Morgan?"

She froze in place, and Arrow wanted nothing more than to take her in his arms and protect her from the emotional angst she was so obviously feeling right now.

But like the strong woman he'd gotten to know, she straightened her spine and walked toward the man who'd said her name.

He was a little shorter than average for a guy, and even though Arrow knew he was only fifty-one, he looked much older. His face was creased with worry lines, and his hair was almost completely white. He'd seen pictures of the man from years earlier, when he had mahogany-brown hair. The stress of his daughter being missing hadn't done his looks any good.

But it was the relief and love in his eyes that made Arrow relax a bit.

He'd looked into the eyes of many a killer, and he'd bet almost anything that Morgan's dad was innocent. Of course, he'd also had a long time to adjust to the role of grieving parent, and he could be an excellent actor. It was for those reasons Arrow would keep his eye on the man.

"Dad," Morgan said as she approached him.

They embraced, and Arrow saw a tear fall down Mr. Byrd's face as he held his daughter.

"I never gave up," he said softly. "I prayed every night that you were out there somewhere and you'd be found."

"Thank you," Morgan told him.

"You don't have to thank me," he gently chided. "I'm your father. I'd move heaven and earth for you."

"I hear you pretty much did just that," Morgan joked as she pulled back.

Mr. Byrd ran a hand over her hair and kept his eyes locked onto her face. "Are you okay? I haven't heard all the details about what happened to you. All I know is that you were found down in Santo Domingo. How'd you get there? Did they hurt you?"

When Morgan cringed, Arrow stepped in. He returned his hand to the small of her back and caressed her briefly with his thumb. "There will be time for questions later," he told Carl Byrd. "How about we get out of here? The reporters are waiting outside the door, and the last thing Morgan needs is to have to deal with them right now."

"Of course," Morgan's dad said. "I'm so happy to see you," he told his daughter. "Leave the press to me. I've gotten pretty good at dealing with them over the last year. We're meeting back up at the Broadmoor, right? I've reserved a suite, so there's plenty of room for us to have our talk, and you'll have a room to yourself."

Arrow watched Morgan swallow hard, then turn pleading eyes up to him. It was crazy how easily he could read her after such a short period of time, but he knew without her saying a word that the last thing she wanted was to spend the night in a hotel room with her father—let alone talk about her ordeal with him.

"Actually, Mr. Byrd, for the time being, she needs to stay with me. There are some details about her rescue that need to be discussed further."

"Surely that can happen tomorrow? She's been through a lot, and she needs her family right now," Carl stated somewhat angrily.

"*She's* standing right here and can make decisions for herself," Morgan said firmly. "Dad, I love you, and I'm more grateful than you know that you didn't give up on me. But things have happened extremely quickly, and there are details that I need to discuss with Arrow and his team tonight. I'll see you tomorrow, and we'll figure out what to tell the press, okay?"

And just like that, the bluster faded from Carl's eyes. "Okay, baby. Whatever you need."

"Thank you, Dad," she said, and hugged him tightly.

Carl cleared his throat as he pulled back. "We need a diversion. I'll go out there," he said, indicating the doors that led to the public part of the airport, "and handle the press. Would you . . . maybe call me later?"

"Of course, Dad."

"I love you, baby. I hoped I'd see you again, but I wasn't sure I'd ever get the chance."

"I'm here, and I'm going to be okay," Morgan told him.

Nodding and pressing his lips together, Carl tugged on the suit coat he was wearing and marched toward the double doors to face the relentless media. Nina and her mom had been escorted away while Morgan had been talking to her father. Arrow knew Rex would follow up with the mom to make sure Nina was doing all right. He also most likely had already arranged for Nina to meet with the best child psychologist in the city.

"Ready to go?" Arrow asked Morgan.

"Yes."

"You didn't ask where we were going," he observed.

Morgan shrugged. "It doesn't matter. I trust you."

That. There. It was reason four hundred and twenty-seven why Arrow was falling head over heels for Morgan Byrd. She had no idea how much her words meant.

He curled his fingers around hers and squeezed. Then they followed Black and Ball in the opposite direction from where her father had gone.

~

Morgan was exhausted. She hadn't really slept on the plane, and the emotional reunion with her father had only drained her energy further. She didn't care where Arrow was taking her, as long as he'd be there.

When her dad had suggested that she stay with him in his suite at the iconic Broadmoor hotel, she'd internally panicked. She wasn't ready to be separated from Arrow. She wasn't ready to talk about what had happened to her, certainly not with her *dad*. His honest reaction to seeing her made her believe it hadn't been him who'd had her kidnapped, but she had a feeling whoever it was, they knew her well. Which made her leery of being around anyone she used to be close to.

Luckily, Arrow had come to her aid again. She didn't know if they really needed to talk about her rescue or the time she'd been in captivity, but at this point, she didn't care.

They'd made it out of the airport without being spotted, thanks to her dad, who had distracted the members of the media who'd gathered, and with the team, she was now inside a long black limousine.

"So where *are* we going?" she asked once they were settled and on the move.

Black and Ball had jumped into the limo with them. For someone who had been terrorized and abused by men for the last year, Morgan felt surprisingly at ease with the Mountain Mercenaries.

"Gray's house," Black said.

"Shit." Arrow sighed.

Morgan looked at him with concern. "What? Is that bad?"

"No, not at all," he soothed. "But I'm guessing Allye and Chloe will be there as well."

"And Ro and Meat too," Ball added.

"This isn't a good idea," Arrow mumbled.

"Why?" Morgan asked, clasping her hands together tightly in her lap.

Arrow noticed—of course he did—and put his hand over hers, squeezing lightly. "I'm just not sure on your first night back in the States that you need to worry about meeting everyone. That's all."

"Apparently, Allye is hoping for Morgan to stay the night," Black went on to explain.

"What the fuck?" Arrow asked. "She needs to relax and acclimate. Not have to worry about being a houseguest and being polite and shit."

"Again, *she* is sitting right here," Morgan said a little testily. "For the last year, I've had to deal with people talking about me when I was right in front of them. They made decisions about my life without getting my input or caring what I thought. Granted, I couldn't understand them, but I can understand *you*. I'd appreciate it if you guys would stop."

"You're right, sorry," Black said immediately.

"Sorry," Ball apologized.

She looked at Arrow expectantly. He stared at her for a long moment before nodding.

"Right, so . . . I'm okay with meeting everyone. I don't really want to be treated like a piece of fragile glass. I'll admit I've been curious about your friends since talking with them on the phone. And being around people . . . your friends . . . makes me feel safer at this point. I'm assuming Allye lives with Gray at the house we're going to? And Chloe is with one of your teammates, right?"

"You assume correctly," Arrow told her. "I'm sorry we didn't discuss with your dad where you'd be spending your first night back. In fact, I'm sorry we didn't discuss it with *you*. Honestly, we're so used to making decisions in cases like this, I didn't even think about it. So . . . here's the deal. We're going to Gray's house. He lives with Allye. The house is huge; it has a million bedrooms and enough security that Gray knows if a squirrel farts on his property. I know Allye would love to have you stay the night. She was in a situation similar to yours, but not exactly—"

"She was held captive?" Morgan interrupted.

"She was kidnapped by an obsessed man who wanted her to be his sex slave. Gray helped her escape, but she was taken again. We went in and found her almost immediately, though."

"I'm not sure it matters whether or not someone is held for one day or three hundred and sixty-five," Morgan said. "The feeling of helplessness is the same."

"Damn, you're wise," Black said with a small smile.

Morgan shrugged. "Pragmatic. I've had to learn to be that way."

Arrow picked up her hand and kissed the palm before putting it back in her lap. "You'll get to meet the rest of the team, and Allye and Chloe—she's with Ro; he's the British bloke. She recently lost her brother, who was the only family she had left. I'm sure she and Ro will invite you to stay with them, as well. Or I can take you to a hotel, if that's your preference. Or you can come back to my place with me. It's just an apartment, and not nearly as nice or fancy as Gray's house, but you'd be safe there."

"Do I have to decide right this second?" Morgan asked.

"No. And once you do decide, you can change your mind at any time," Arrow told her.

"Thank you."

"We need to talk about tomorrow and the press conference," Black said.

"Not to mention she really needs to get checked out by a doctor," Ball added.

Arrow held up his hand to stop his friends from saying anything more. "Right now, we'll celebrate the fact that Morgan is free. She's back home and safe with people who care about her. Everything else can wait until tomorrow."

Black nodded and relaxed in his seat.

Morgan could tell the other man was frustrated, but she gave him points for letting it go. And Arrow was right. She was overwhelmed, and the last thing she wanted to do was think, let alone talk, about dealing with the press tomorrow or seeing a doctor. She had no idea what to tell the media. They'd want to know what happened to her and where she'd been for the last year. They'd ask questions about who she thought had kidnapped her and other things she had no answers to. Just thinking about it made her head hurt.

"Don't," Arrow said softly.

She looked over at him. He'd shaved before they'd left Santo Domingo, but the scruff had grown back a bit, giving him a badass vibe. He and the others were still wearing the black cargo pants they'd had on in the Caribbean, but they'd taken off the vests and emptied most of their pockets.

"Don't what?" she asked.

"Don't think about tomorrow right now. One minute at a time, remember?"

She smiled. "Yeah."

He returned her grin, and Morgan did her best to relax. She'd trusted these men with her life, and they hadn't let her down. It had been a long time since she'd hung out with people for fun . . . since she was snatched, in fact, but this seemed different. More important. She wanted Allye and Chloe to like her for who she was. Not because she was another woman the Mountain Mercenaries had saved.

They drove for a while, and Ball explained that Gray lived north of Colorado Springs in a remote neighborhood where most of the houses faced Pikes Peak. Eventually, she saw fewer and fewer buildings and more and more trees. They drove down a street with tall pine trees on either side, and the limo turned onto a long driveway that Morgan wouldn't even have known was there if she'd been driving.

Then she was staring out the window at a huge house. The men in the limo with her hadn't been exaggerating the size of the place, after all. There was a garage off to the side of the main house, but all Morgan's attention was glued to the people standing on the front porch.

The limo stopped, and Black and Ball immediately jumped out, leaving Morgan and Arrow.

"They won't bite," Arrow teased.

Morgan turned to him. "I know. It's just . . . what if they don't like me?"

"Beautiful, they're going to love you. Come on." And with that, he scooted over to the door and held out his hand. Morgan took a deep breath and placed her hand in his. The second his fingers closed around hers, she settled. That was all it took.

They climbed out and headed for the group. Arrow kept a firm grip on her hand, as if he knew she was a second from bolting back to the limo, and stopped after they had climbed a couple of steps and were standing in front of everyone.

"This is Morgan Byrd," Arrow announced. "Morgan, meet the best group of friends a man could have."

"Hi," Morgan said softly. "It's good to meet you."

"No, it's good to meet *you*," Allye said, before stepping forward and hugging Morgan warmly.

Morgan stiffened for a moment, not sure how she felt about being hugged by a stranger, but Allye must've sensed her reticence, as she immediately let go and stepped back.

"I'm Chloe," the woman with the straight black hair said, holding out a hand. "We're so glad you're all right. We don't get to meet the women our guys help that often, so it's an honor to be your welcome party."

"I'm Gray," a man who stood over a foot taller than her said, and held out his hand.

Morgan shook it, keeping her left hand firmly tucked in Arrow's grasp.

"And I'm Ro."

The man with the British accent wasn't much shorter than Gray, but his blue eyes twinkled, giving him a less scary vibe.

"Don't forget me!" the last man said. "I'm Meat. Well, my name is actually Hunter, but these lugs call me Meat. I'm working on tracking down your belongings. It should be fairly simple, and—"

"Meat," Arrow warned.

The other man looked sheepish but kept grinning. "Sorry. Welcome home, Morgan."

"Thanks."

"Can we please get off the porch now?" Ro asked.

Chloe leaned toward Morgan and stage-whispered, "He's a little paranoid. But I can't blame him since the Mafia basically blew up part of his house to get to me."

"The Mafia?" Morgan asked, her eyes wide.

"Inside," Ro insisted.

Chloe winked at Morgan, and despite her words, she relaxed a bit. If the woman had been kidnapped by the Mafia and had such an amazing attitude about it, she admired the heck out of her already. Hoping to be as much like Chloe as she could about her own situation, Morgan followed the group inside.

∾

A few hours later, Arrow kept his eyes on Morgan as she smiled and joked with Allye and Chloe. They were in the kitchen putting away dishes and seemed to be having the time of their lives, giggling and laughing as if they'd known each other for years rather than just a few hours.

He hadn't been sure about bringing Morgan over here on her first night back, but it seemed she'd been right. She was definitely more relaxed than he'd seen her before. She'd hit it off immediately with the other two women, not that he'd doubted she would. They were very likable, and because they had so much in common, it was no wonder they took to one another.

But Arrow could also see the stress of the day catching up with Morgan by the lines in her forehead. She had a headache, but refused to admit it.

"She seems to be doing amazing," Gray noted quietly.

"I think she's buried a lot of what happened to her," Arrow said. "Time will tell how she does when it all hits her."

"She's going to be okay," Ro said. "She's strong."

"That doesn't mean she isn't going to need help," Arrow retorted.

"I didn't say it did. You're right, she *is* going to need help. It's going to take a while for her to fully trust again. She'll need to talk to someone about what happened to her, but she's going to make it. I can tell," Ro said.

"I've done some research on the people in her life," Meat said. "We need to talk about them."

"Not tonight," Arrow said.

"Of course not," the other man said. "But it needs to happen sooner rather than later. Maybe after the press conference tomorrow."

"Are we going to talk about that?" Black asked.

"I'll talk to her in the morning," Arrow volunteered. "She's about at the end of her rope tonight."

"Yeah, I can see that," Ball replied. Then added, "You like her."

"What?"

"You like her," he repeated.

"Of course I do. She's amazing," Arrow said.

"Don't be afraid to go after her," Gray said. "I made the mistake of thinking nothing could happen between me and Allye because she was an op. *Then* I made the mistake of thinking I knew what was best for her without even talking to her about it."

"Yeah, Morgan's already set me straight on that front," Arrow mused.

"I knew I liked her for some reason," Gray teased.

"Until we figure out who wanted her gone, she can't go back to Atlanta," Meat said.

"What are her options?" Ro asked.

"She could stay with her mom in New Mexico, stay with her dad in a hotel here, although he'll need to go back to Georgia soon, as he's got his business there, or she could stay here in Colorado Springs," Meat said.

"Speaking of her mom, do we know when *she's* going to show?" Gray asked.

"Rex told me he called Ellie Jernigan yesterday, and she said she'd be here in Colorado Springs tomorrow. She had to work today, but got the next few days off," Black said.

"When and where?" Arrow asked. He wanted to make sure Morgan knew. The last thing he wanted to do was blindside her. He knew she was anxious to see her mom, as they seemed to be close, but she'd had an emotional few days and needed the heads-up.

"Not sure. I'll call and find out. Maybe she can come to The Pit and meet us there tomorrow after the news conference?" Black suggested. "I know she doesn't get along with her ex, so it's probably better if we kept them apart in front of the media."

Arrow figured that for the sake of their daughter, Carl and Ellie could probably be civil, but he wasn't going to push it. Maybe they could ask Dave, The Pit's bartender, to close the place briefly, in case things with Morgan's parents got out of hand. "That sounds good."

"I like her, man," Gray said softly.

Arrow grinned at his friend. "I'm glad, but honestly, I wouldn't give a shit if you didn't."

Gray chuckled. "I didn't think you would, but seriously . . . I see myself in the way you look at her."

"How's that?"

"Like you'd sooner cut off your own arm than do anything that would hurt her."

"That's about right," Arrow muttered.

"You gotta go slow with her," Ro warned.

Arrow glared at his other friend. "I know that, asshole."

"No, I mean it. She's doing amazingly well. I can tell she's strong, but there's something behind her eyes that worries me. Remember that albino woman we rescued from Nightingale's sick human zoo?"

"Yeah?" Arrow asked, frowning. He remembered all too well how sadistic Gage Nightingale had been. He'd tortured the women he'd kidnapped and forced them to cater to his every whim. The woman Ro was talking about had been born without pigment in her skin and hair, and Nightingale had "collected" her, and done his best to break her. "Last I heard, she was living at home with her parents in South Carolina and doing well."

"She killed herself," Ro said bluntly. "Rex heard from her mother while you guys were down in the Caribbean. Even her mom thought she was doing okay, but they read her journals after they'd found her. On the outside, she looked like she was coping just fine, but she was utterly broken inside."

"Morgan's not like that," Arrow insisted, his eyes going to the kitchen to reassure himself that his words were true.

"I think if anyone can help her get through what happened, it's you," Ro said softly. "Give her space when she needs it, let her talk when she wants, but don't let her shut you out."

Arrow's shoulders slumped. "How am I supposed to do that? I've only known her a few days. She's most likely going to Albuquerque to live with her mom. My life is here."

"Where there's a will, there's a way," Gray said. "Allye's life was in San Francisco, but now she's here. We have no idea where this case is going to go in the next couple weeks and months. If you really want to give whatever is going on between you two a shot, you need to make sure she knows that you're not giving up on her. Call. Text. Take weekend trips to see her. New Mexico isn't that far."

Arrow straightened. "You're right," he said, more to himself than his friend.

"I know," Gray said arrogantly. "I'm always right."

"Ass," Arrow said as he shook his head and rolled his eyes.

"Be careful, though," Black added. "She's got some demons behind those pretty green eyes of hers."

"I know. I see them," Arrow said. And he did. He remembered the first time he'd seen her, defending Nina with a knife she'd somehow pilfered from her kidnappers. She'd looked determined . . . and desperate.

He was going to take it slow with Morgan. Slow but insistent. He planned to make her his in every way, but he'd give her whatever time she needed to be ready for the more intimate parts of a relationship.

Arrow realized he wasn't freaked out by the direction of his thoughts. He'd seen how quickly both Gray and Ro had fallen for their women. Instead of seeing their relationships as a hindrance to what they did, he knew it made them better mercenaries. They were even more careful when on a mission . . . because they had someone to go home to.

And Arrow wanted that.

Wanted Morgan.

Gray stood up and went into the kitchen. He wrapped an arm around Allye. "You ready to call it a night, sweetheart?"

Arrow had joined the others in the kitchen, and he stood near Morgan. Not touching her, but close enough that she definitely knew he was there.

"Yeah. Morgan looks wiped out. I think she's ready to go home too," Allye said gently.

Arrow's eyes whipped to Morgan's. "Home?"

She nodded. "If that's okay with you."

"Just to clarify, you want to go to my apartment with me?"

"Yeah. Allye said I could stay here with her and Gray, and Chloe also invited me to stay with them, but . . . if it's okay, I wouldn't mind going with you."

"It's definitely okay with me," he reassured her, reaching out and taking her hand in his. He turned to Allye and Gray. "Thanks for having us over tonight."

"Yes. It's been a long time since I've felt so . . . relaxed." Morgan hesitated before the last word, but no one called her on it.

Allye leaned forward and hugged her, and Chloe followed suit. "We'll see you tomorrow," Chloe said.

"Yeah?" Arrow asked.

"Yup. After the press conference and after you guys have your meeting, we're comin' to The Pit to play pool. Morgan said she's pretty good, so we challenged her to a game or two or three."

"You play pool?" Arrow asked Morgan, raising one eyebrow in surprise.

She blushed and shrugged. "I used to. I'm not sure if I'm still any good, though."

"I have no doubt you'll kick some ass, beautiful," Arrow said.

She grinned and turned her attention to the opening of the kitchen when the other guys wandered up to join the conversation. Arrow wouldn't have noticed Morgan stiffening if he wasn't standing right next to her, holding her hand. She didn't let any discomfort show on her face, but she was definitely not happy with being penned in by several large men.

He shifted until he was between his friends and Morgan and gestured for her to scoot along the counter. She did so without a word until they were standing on the outside of the space, rather than inside it.

Arrow knew the guys understood what he'd done immediately. Allye and Chloe weren't quite as dialed in, but then again, they hadn't seen what months of captivity and that kind of abuse could do to a woman like the team had.

"We're gonna get going," Arrow told the group. "Gray, thanks for tonight. If you could, tell Rex I'll call him in the morning to get the details about the press conference."

"Sure thing," Gray said. "We'll all see you tomorrow."

"You're all coming?" Morgan asked.

"Of course," Black responded. "We wouldn't miss it. Besides, if you need to escape, we'll run interference." He winked after he said it, indicating he was kidding, but Arrow knew he was dead serious. They'd all have Morgan's back, no questions asked.

"Come on, beautiful, you're sagging on your feet," Arrow told Morgan, then waved and tugged her toward the door.

"How are we going to . . . oh!" she said as they stepped outside. The limo they'd arrived in was still sitting in the driveway. "Has he been here all along?" Morgan asked in surprise.

"Who? The driver? Of course," Arrow said.

"But that's . . . so rude!" she exclaimed. "We should've invited him in!"

Arrow chuckled. "He's used to waiting on us, beautiful. Besides, he's getting paid to sit around. He's not exactly upset about it."

The driver hopped out of the car as soon as he saw them exit the house and hurried around to open the back door. When they were settled, he shut the door and headed back around the car.

"It's still rude," Morgan hissed.

Arrow grinned, wrapped his arm around Morgan's shoulders, and pulled her into him. He'd done it without thought, and immediately loosened his hold, not wanting her to be afraid of him, but she didn't struggle. Instead, she relaxed into him, putting a hand on his chest.

They stayed like that for a beat as the driver started up the car and headed down Gray's driveway. They had about twenty or thirty minutes before they arrived at his apartment. He leaned over and clicked her seat belt on, then did the same with his. Then he gathered her into his side once more.

"Close your eyes, beautiful. You've got time to take a quick nap before we get home."

She nodded, and within seconds he heard her slight snore.

Morgan resting against him, knowing she was safe, was a heady feeling. He silently swore to get to the bottom of who could dare want to torture her as badly as they had.

Chapter Ten

"If you're not ready for this, we can go," Arrow whispered to Morgan the next morning. They were in an office connected to the briefing room at the Colorado Springs Police Department, where the press conference about her recovery was about to happen. They'd talked about how the day would go, including stopping by a private clinic so she could get a complete physical with a doctor that the team frequently used to examine women and kids they'd rescued, then talking with the team at The Pit.

"I'm okay," she insisted for the tenth time.

But he knew she wasn't really. She was holding his hand in a death grip, and she'd eaten very little that morning, saying her stomach was queasy.

Her father stood on the other side of the office, and he was smiling and talking with anyone and everyone, not noticing how reticent his daughter seemed.

"Did I tell you about the time I had to give a briefing to a bunch of Marine bigwigs?"

She looked up at him then. "No?"

"I was scared to death. I wasn't prepared, and I had also gone out the night before and gotten shit-faced. I had the headache from hell, and I just knew I was going to embarrass myself and my unit."

"What happened?" Morgan asked.

Arrow was glad her attention was on him now and not on what was about to happen. They'd spoken with Rex that morning and gotten their story straight. No one wanted the Mountain Mercenaries bandied about on national television, but they had to say something to explain why and how Morgan had been found. Nina's mom was being interviewed at the moment, and soon it would be Morgan and her father's turn in the spotlight.

Arrow couldn't blame the general public for being interested and curious about both Nina and Morgan. Abductions were big news, but finding kidnapped people alive and well was *huge* news.

"I got up in front of the room and gave my thirty-minute presentation in fifteen minutes," he told her. "I was talking so fast because of my nervousness and because I was afraid I was going to barf in the middle of the presentation, and as a result, I breezed through my notes and slides way too quickly. When I was done, I didn't even ask if there were any questions. I just took my stuff and went and sat down."

"Did you get in trouble?" Morgan asked.

Arrow shook his head. "I actually had some of the top brass come up and congratulate me on the effective way I didn't open the floor to questions and thus 'muddy the waters,'" he explained. "One guy told me it was ballsy and gave the impression I was in charge, and that I knew what I was saying was one hundred percent correct. I think that's what you should do out there."

"What do you mean?"

"They want to hear from you, and I know a lot of America does too. They've been hearing about you for a year, thanks to your dad. They know all about your life. They feel like they know you. They'll be relieved that you're all right. So go out there, thank everyone for their well wishes and prayers. Tell them that you're thankful for being found. Then explain things are tough for you right now—don't explain how—and that you'd appreciate some space while you try to acclimate back to your life here in the States. Then smile, nod at the cameras, and leave the platform. Ignore the questions and come straight back here to me. I'll get you out of here."

"But I'm supposed to stay and answer questions," Morgan said, though Arrow could clearly see the relief in her eyes.

"You don't owe anyone *anything*, beautiful. Let the cops handle the questions. And your dad. He's been dealing with the press for a year now. Trust him to keep doing it."

Morgan bit her lip.

"What is it?" Arrow asked.

"What if he's the one who orchestrated this?" she whispered.

Arrow dropped her hand and cupped her face in his palms. "Don't think about that right now."

She reached up and grabbed his wrists. "How can I not?"

"Your only job is to go out there, say your thing, and come back to me. Can you do that? We'll talk about who might be behind it later this afternoon. Even if it *was* your dad, he's not going to do anything in front of all those cameras. He loves the limelight as much as you dislike it. Just keep in the back of your mind a younger me, trembling because I was so fucking scared to talk to those head honchos in the Marines while I was hungover. And do what I did. Fake it until you make it, beautiful."

She gave him a small smile then. "I'm good at faking it."

Arrow couldn't help it. The words came out of his mouth before he thought about what he was saying. "You won't be faking anything with me, beautiful. I'll have you so desperate, you're begging for it."

When her eyes widened in surprise, he swore.

"Shit, sorry. Forget I said that. Dammit, I'm an idiot. I—"

"Well, *now* I'm not thinking about the damn press conference anymore," she said softly with a small grin, interrupting his self-recriminations.

Arrow was relieved he hadn't freaked her out. "This isn't the time or place, but . . . I like you, Morgan. A lot. I want to see where this crazy connection we seem to have can go. I know your life is up in the air, but I hope you're ready for me to be in it somehow. Any way you'll let me."

"I . . . I'd like that, but I feel so off balance right now. I have no idea what's going to happen in the near future."

"Whatever happens, I'll be there to help you. We're going steady now, remember?" he asked with a grin. "I think being there to help your girl is a requirement in the going-steady handbook."

Morgan grinned.

Arrow heard the reporters raising their voices to fire questions at Nina's mother. The little girl hadn't made an appearance in front of the cameras—she was in another room with her aunt—but from what Arrow could tell from the sidelines, her mom had done an amazing job dealing with the press. It was almost Morgan's turn.

He pulled her into his embrace and sighed in contentment when her body fit perfectly against his. Her arms wrapped around his back and clutched him to her. She smelled fresh and clean, nothing like a few days ago when they'd lain together under debris, hiding from their pursuers.

"It's time," he told her reluctantly. "You've got this. Remember what I said. Short and sweet and walk away without looking back."

Morgan took a deep breath. "Right. I can do that."

"You can do anything," Arrow said, then stepped back as she turned around and headed for the door that entered into the conference room. She stepped up on the small stage with her dad at her side.

The second she was far enough away, Meat stepped up next to Arrow and said, "I did some research on her boyfriend. He seems to be in the clear, but I'm not so sure about his brother. That Karen person doesn't exactly have the best taste in men either."

Arrow nodded, but he was only half listening. His attention was glued to Morgan. She sat in a chair behind a small table. Flashes were going off nonstop, and he hated that she had to go through this. He hadn't exaggerated when he'd found her and told her everyone knew who she was. And because of that, everyone needed some sort of closure about what she'd been through because, thanks to her dad, in some ways, they'd been through it with her.

He'd seen it time and time again. With Elizabeth Smart, Jaycee Dugard, Shawn Hornbeck, and even Danielle Cramer. The general public was horrified by what the missing children had been through but fascinated by their stories of survival.

Arrow knew that Morgan would be no different. She wasn't a child, but with her diminutive stature and haunted eyes, she'd be seen in the same sort of light. Not to mention her connection to Nina Scofield.

"Did you hear me?" Meat asked.

"I heard you," Arrow said, not taking his eyes from Morgan. "But at this moment, I can't do jack shit about it. I can't talk about it because I need to be here in case Morgan needs me. I can't fly to Georgia and get Lane or Lance Buswell in a room to beat the shit out of them until they tell me what they know. I can't make Karen tell me about her asshole ex-boyfriends or whoever you found in her life that might've been a threat to Morgan. All I can do is trust you and the others to figure this shit out while I'm concentrating on making sure Morgan doesn't break down into a million pieces."

"Uh . . . right. Got it," Meat said. "You're still going by the clinic right after this, then bringing her to The Pit?"

Arrow nodded. "She's not happy about seeing the doctor, but knows it needs to be done. Her mom is meeting us at The Pit afterward. They need to see each other. Every little girl needs her mother to make things better."

"True. Okay, Black and Gray are on their way there now. They'll get with Dave and make sure the back room is closed until we're done. Allye and Chloe will meet us there later in the afternoon, and the rest of us can handle any problems with the press being overzealous."

Arrow took his eyes off Morgan long enough to look at Meat. "Thanks, man. I appreciate it."

"Fuck off," Meat responded. "You'd do the same for me. Besides, we're a team. There's no *I* in team."

Arrow rolled his eyes. "Please tell me you're not getting a poster with that bullshit saying on it."

Meat chuckled. "I wasn't. But now I am. Gonna put it up in our corner at The Pit. Maybe I'll get it embroidered on a pillow and give it to you as a wedding present."

"First, there's no way Dave would allow that shit to be put up in his bar," Arrow said, referring to the gruff bartender. "Second, if you get us anything that's embroidered, I'll kick your ass."

"No protest about the wedding thing?" Meat asked.

Arrow smiled and turned back to look at Morgan. "Nope."

Meat clapped Arrow on the back and said, "Happy for you, man."

"Don't be happy yet," Arrow warned. "There's a long road ahead of us both."

"Good thing you're stubborn, then, isn't it?" Meat asked. His face turned serious. "If something happens, get Morgan out of here. We'll deal with everything else."

Arrow nodded. He'd planned on it. But he was aware his teammates knew that was the plan. They'd had a similar plan when Chloe had faced the press after what had happened to her.

The next twenty minutes were the longest in Arrow's life. He hated seeing how uncomfortable Morgan was with the way her dad was talking as if he'd single-handedly swooped down to the Dominican Republic and rescued her himself. He was a bit of a braggart, and pompous, but Arrow supposed that came with being a CFO, and the excitement of having his daughter back.

The press asked a few questions, but it was obvious they were holding back to ask Morgan the real juicy things they wanted to know. Then it was Morgan's turn to speak. She stood up slowly and walked to the microphone on the podium.

Flashes from cameras went off constantly, and she blinked in the harsh lights. After she cleared her throat, she said just what Arrow had suggested.

"Thank you very much for your concern, and for every tip that was called in after I disappeared. Knowing no one gave up on finding me means the world to me. I'm still acclimating to being back in the States, and I hope everyone will give me some time to come to terms with everything that has happened over the last year, and recently. For those of you who have missing loved ones, the best thing you can do is *never* stop believing they'll come home. Thank you."

Then she nodded at the cameras and turned to walk toward Arrow.

The reporters lost their composure when they realized she wasn't going to take questions and began shouting at her as she walked away. Some tried to get in front of her, to block her from leaving.

Arrow was on the move immediately. He shoved one woman with a small tape recorder out of his way as he strode toward Morgan. She looked up with big green eyes filled with tears. Without a word, he tucked her under his arm and made his way to the exit.

He felt her arm come around his waist, and she buried her head in his chest as they walked. She couldn't see a thing that way, and Arrow felt his heart swell with the trust she was giving him. She might not be ready for more than friendship right now, but she would be. He knew it.

Within seconds, Ball, Ro, and Meat had pushed back the reporters enough to allow Arrow to escape out the side door with Morgan. He quickly made his way through the hallways of the police station, nodding at the officers he passed. No one tried to talk to them or block his passage. He pushed open the back door and made his way toward his beat-up pickup truck, parked there for exactly this reason.

He'd hoped that things would stay civilized and they wouldn't need to make a quick exit, but experience had made him always have a backup plan, just in case. He helped Morgan climb inside before reaching over and putting on her seat belt for her. She seemed a little shell-shocked, and Arrow wanted to take the time to comfort her then and there, but didn't dare. He needed to get her away from the station before someone saw them and tried to follow. The press was useful in a lot of things the Mountain Mercenaries did, but this was not one of those times.

Arrow ran around the front of the truck and hopped into the driver's seat. He started the engine and put on his seat belt at the same time. He pulled out of the parking lot as calmly as possible, not wanting to bring undue attention to them. The limo they'd arrived in was still sitting in front of the police station, acting as a decoy. Meat had driven Arrow's truck to the station and parked it in the back.

Once they were safely away from the station, Arrow still didn't say a word. He simply reached over and grabbed Morgan's hand. She intertwined their fingers together and held on tightly. Knowing she needed some time to process the press conference before he took her to the clinic, Arrow drove them to Memorial Park. It was a large green space not too far from the police station, with a large lake.

The day was beautiful, and he knew the park would be crowded and no one would take a second glance at them. He pulled into a parking spot and shut off the engine. He continued to hold Morgan's hand and didn't say a word, letting her process the morning in her own way.

"That didn't exactly go as planned," she said after a long while.

Arrow chuckled. "Things usually don't, but I actually think it went as well as it could've. There was no way those vultures were going to let their chance to ask you questions go."

"I would've preferred that things went how they did with you and your Marine speech you gave," she said.

"Actually, I didn't tell you the entire story," Arrow admitted.

Morgan looked up at him for the first time since she'd gotten into his truck. He hated the pain behind her eyes, but rejoiced in the curiosity he saw there as well. "Seriously?"

"Yup. The top brass didn't give a shit about my short presentation because they'd already sat through three others that day, and they were bored out of their skulls. It was just a learning opportunity for Marines like me. So they didn't care and were thrilled mine was so short. But my commanding officer *definitely* cared. After we left and got back to his office, he chewed me a new asshole and told me I was a disgrace and that my briefing was the worst he'd seen in his twenty years on the job."

Morgan's eyes widened. "What happened?"

"I was lucky I wasn't demoted a rank. He just made my life a living hell for the rest of the time I served under him . . . and made sure I never forgot what an ass he thought I'd made of myself."

"Well, I'm glad you didn't tell me *that* part of the story," Morgan said with a shake of her head and a little chuckle. Then she turned to him. "Thank you."

"For?"

"For being with me. For getting me out of there. For . . . everything, really."

Arrow loosened his hand from hers and brought it up so he was cupping the back of her neck tenderly. He leaned over until he was resting his forehead against hers. It felt as if they were the only two people in the world at that moment. "Mark my words, beautiful. I'll always be there for you. No matter if I've got three bullet holes in me or have had my leg blown off. I'll do everything in my power to be there when you need me."

"I think that's a bit extreme," she said with a small smile, but Arrow noticed that she'd gripped the side of his T-shirt with one hand and held on tightly. "Zombie Arrow might scare me more than whatever situation I'm in."

He grinned but said, "My point is . . . don't count me out. You and me, we're a lot alike."

"I doubt that," she huffed.

"We are. We fight for what we want. You fought to stay sane and alive until someone could find you or you could make your escape. And I'll fight for *you*. I was a Marine, Morgan. We don't let anything stop us when the shit hits the fan."

"Do you think the shit's going to hit the fan?" she asked quietly.

"I have no idea. But rule number one is to plan for the worst and hope for the best."

"That's kinda depressing."

It was Arrow's turn to chuckle. "I think you of all people can appreciate that saying."

"True," she agreed. Then she said quietly, "I'm scared, Arrow."

"Of what?"

"Everything. What if my mom doesn't want me to live with her? I'm afraid of being kidnapped again. I'm scared that what I'm feeling for you right now is just gratitude that you saved me and that when I leave, you'll come to your senses and realize how much of a mess I am and thank your lucky stars that I'm out of your life."

"You are never going to be out of my life," Arrow vowed. "You've already burrowed yourself in here." He picked up her hand and placed it on his chest over his heart. "If your mom doesn't want you living with her, which I highly doubt, you can stay here with me. I can't do anything about your being afraid of being snatched again, except reassure you that me and my team are doing everything we can to figure out who was behind it and make sure they never, ever get the chance to get near you again."

Morgan took a deep breath, then nodded again.

Arrow lifted his forehead from hers, brought his fingers to her chin, and tilted her face up. "May I kiss you?"

He didn't lean forward. Didn't do anything to pressure her. Simply waited.

She dipped her chin down a fraction of an inch.

Arrow's lips quirked up, and he closed the distance between them. He brushed his lips against hers once. Then twice. Then he pulled back and said, "Thank you."

She blinked. "That's it?"

"What? Not good enough?"

Morgan's brows furrowed, and she shook her head.

"Why don't you kiss *me*, then?" Arrow challenged.

He saw the spark of determination in her eyes a second before she said, "I will." Then her lips were on his—and she was *kissing* him.

Arrow had never been so turned on in his entire life.

Morgan kissed him as if her life depended on it, as if she was desperate for him. He followed her lead and let her take control. When her tongue came out and traced his lips, he couldn't stop the small groan that escaped. He opened for her and tightened his hold on her neck when her tongue swept inside his mouth.

She tasted like the mint he'd seen her pop into her mouth right before the press conference started. He wanted her under him, over him, wanted to be inside her. But he reined in his libido and tried to enjoy the moment for what it was: two people taking the first step toward the rest of their lives.

She finally pulled back and licked her lips as she stared at him with pink cheeks. Seeing her tongue swipe over her lips made him want to kiss her all over again. Arrow satisfied himself by bringing a hand to her face and tracing her wet lips with his thumb. "That was amazing," he told her.

"I haven't kissed someone in a year and a half. Not like that," she blurted.

"Yeah?"

"When I was . . . you know . . . there was no kissing. That's not what they wanted. And before that, with Lane, we gave each other pecks on the lips, but we hadn't *really* kissed each other in months."

Arrow said, "It's been a while for me too, beautiful."

She shot him a skeptical look.

"Seriously, the last time I went on a date was . . ." Arrow paused, trying to remember. "I have no clue. I think nineteen sixty-four." He smiled to let her know he was teasing.

Morgan rolled her eyes. "I'm not an idiot, Arrow. I've got eyes in my head. You're gorgeous. There's no way you haven't had women throwing themselves at you."

Arrow got serious. "Just because they might be interested doesn't mean I did anything about it. I've been way too busy with the team and our missions and even my electrician gig on the side to worry about women."

She looked so hopeful, Arrow continued speaking. "With that said, if I *had* been interested in someone, I would've made the time for them. I'm not so married to my job that I'd give up the chance to find some-one to spend the rest of my life with. I want that. It might not be cool to admit, but it's true. I see how happy Gray is with Allye and Ro is with Chloe. I want that for myself. But no one has grabbed my attention. Not like you did."

She snorted. "Right. I grabbed your attention all right. With my beautiful hairdo and smelly clothes and body."

"Don't do that," Arrow warned. "Don't denigrate yourself. You want to know what I saw the first time I laid eyes on you?"

"No."

He went on as if she hadn't answered his rhetorical question. "I saw a woman who was scared out of her skull, but wasn't afraid to stick up for a small child who needed her. I saw a woman who had been through hell, but somehow the goodness in her still shone from her every pore. I consider myself a strong man. I've been through some bad shit in my life, and I've seen things that I wish I could unsee. But nothing prepared me for the punch in the gut I got when I saw you in that room. Even before I knew who you were, and what your story was, I knew you were special. That you would change my life."

"Arrow," Morgan whispered.

But he kept talking, wanting her to understand how he felt. "I can't predict the future, but I'm going to do what I can to nurture whatever it is we have going on. I enjoy being with you. I like the way you don't back down. How you say what's on your mind, and how you somehow, with all you've been through, have managed to trust me and my team. That's a rare thing, and I want to encourage that. I told you before, and I'll say it again—I like you, Morgan. I want to be in your life. I'm happy to take things as slow as you need them to go. I don't want you to feel any pressure whatsoever when you're with me to do anything you don't want to do."

"But we can keep doing the kissing thing, right?" she asked with a small smile.

Arrow returned it. "Oh yeah, we can keep doing the kissing thing." And with that, he pulled her toward him gently and kissed her again. He took his time, taking the lead. Sipping and nipping at her bottom lip before twining his tongue with hers.

She was with him every step of the way. Digging her nails into his arm as they made out, making little pleased noises in the back of her throat that went straight to Arrow's dick. Everything about her made him hard as a rock. He couldn't wait for the day he had her spread out on his sheets, naked as the day she was born, moaning just for him. Begging him to make love to her.

But he *would* wait, as long as it took, to have that. He knew a good thing when he saw it, and he wasn't going to give anyone else a chance to horn in on what he considered his.

He caressed her cheek as he pulled back and did his best to memorize the content, satisfied look on her face. He'd seen her experience a variety of emotions in their short acquaintance, but this was how he always wanted to see her. Relaxed and happy.

"You ready to get the visit to the doctor over with?"

She wrinkled her nose, but nodded. "I know I need to get checked out, but I hate it."

"I know. This doctor is really good, though. She'll answer any questions you might have, and from what the other women have said, she makes the entire process as painless as possible. You know you won't get any results from the STD testing today, though, right?"

Morgan nodded. "I know. I'll just be glad to get it over with."

"I think you'll find The Pit an interesting place," he said, changing the subject. He wanted nothing more than to bring her back to his apartment after her appointment and let her decompress, but he knew the team needed to talk about her situation . . . and her mom was going to meet them there as well.

"What's up with this Pit place?" she asked. "It sounds like a dump."

"From the outside, it *looks* like a dump," he told her honestly, reluctantly dropping his hand from her neck and starting the engine once more. As he pulled out of the park and headed for the clinic, he said, "But inside, it's extremely clean, and Dave doesn't put up with any shenanigans from the patrons."

"Dave? And really . . . shenanigans?" she asked. "Who says that?"

"I just did—really. And Dave is the bartender, who we all think secretly lives under the bar. We're not sure he ever goes home."

"Does he own it?"

Arrow thought about her question for a beat before saying, "You know what? I don't know. I hadn't really ever thought about it. But it makes sense. He's there all the time, and if people destroy shit or do something he doesn't approve of, he takes it extremely personally."

"So what makes it so special . . . besides Dave the bartender?" Morgan asked. "It's just a bar, right? With a few pool tables?"

"Yes. And no." Arrow shrugged. "I'm not sure. Maybe it's because it's where me and the rest of the guys all met for the first time. Rex had us meet there for an 'interview,' and I think I told you before that he never showed up, so we all played pool and got to know each other.

We were so pissed when Rex never bothered to come interview us, and we thought it had all been a joke, bringing us to the Springs on a wild-goose chase."

"It's really interesting how the Mountain Mercenaries came to be," she said.

"Yup."

"Okay. So I'll withhold judgment until I see this paragon of a bar," she teased.

"Appreciate it," Arrow said, smiling over at her.

"I don't know how you do it," Morgan mused.

"What?"

"Make me feel completely normal when half an hour ago I felt like complete shit."

"That's my job, beautiful," Arrow told her.

"Since when?"

"Since I walked in on you protecting Nina with a piece-of-shit knife." Arrow could feel Morgan looking at him, but he kept his attention on the road, giving her time to process his words.

Finally, she said, "You're serious about us, aren't you?"

"Good thing you're finally cluing in," he teased. Then he said seriously, "Yeah, Morgan. I'm dead serious. Anything you need. Whenever you need it."

"We don't even know each other."

"Which is why I'm giving us time to *get* to know each other."

"I'm most likely going to New Mexico to live with my mom," she protested. "Maybe even today."

"Albuquerque isn't Jupiter, beautiful. It's not that far away, all things considered. And there are these things called phones that everyone has nowadays. And the internet. Where there's a will, there's a way."

"You're going to a lot of trouble, Arrow."

"No, I'm not. It's called being in a relationship. It's what people do."

"Just because we said things in the heat of the moment when we were down in Santo Domingo doesn't mean we have to follow through with 'going steady' now that we're back in the States."

"It wasn't heat of the moment for me," Arrow said, a little frustrated now. "I want to continue to get to know you, to date you. But this isn't a one-sided decision. If you've decided that you don't want anything to do with me, I'll be honest—I'll do my best to change your mind. But if you don't, then that'll be that. I don't want to be with someone who isn't as committed as I am to the relationship. I just . . . There's something about you that I'm drawn to. No, fuck that. You're like a glass of water, and I'm a man dying of thirst."

After his admission, neither of them said anything until they pulled into the parking lot of the clinic.

"Okay," she said as he turned off the engine.

"Okay?"

"Yes. We'll get to know each other. Talk on the phone. Text. Visit. See if there's anything to this relationship thing."

Arrow smiled. "Cool."

"Yeah. Although I still think you're insane. I'm not a good bet, Arrow. The things that happened . . . I . . . I don't know when, or if, I'll be ready to be intimate with anyone again."

"Baby steps, beautiful."

"But that's not fair to you."

Arrow shut off the engine and turned to her, making sure to not crowd her as he said, "Fuck fair. Life's not fair. My dick isn't going to fall off if we don't make love. We can get creative if you aren't comfortable with penetration. And I can always masturbate. There's more to a relationship than sex."

She was blushing, but Arrow hoped she was truly hearing what he was saying.

"You really do like me, huh?"

He couldn't help it. He chuckled. "Yeah, Morgan. I really do like you. Now, come on. Let's get this over with so you can get over to The Pit."

An hour and a half later, they were parking in front of The Pit. Morgan hadn't said much about her visit with the doctor, and he didn't press. Having to be tested for sexually transmitted diseases wasn't exactly fun, and he'd already told her that he'd be there for her no matter what. He didn't want to continue to harp on it.

Glad that she'd gotten that done and off her plate, Arrow turned off the engine.

Neither said anything, but the silence wasn't uncomfortable. Finally, Arrow said, "I'm sure Dave knows we're here and is wondering why we're sitting in the parking lot instead of coming inside."

"What, does he have cameras set up out here or something?" Morgan asked.

"Yup."

"He does?" she asked in surprise. "I was kidding."

"There are cameras all over this place. Does that bother you?"

"No. Should it?"

"Nope. But I wanted to warn you anyway. Don't be leaping on me to suck face if you don't want it on video." She chuckled, as he'd intended. "Stay there. I'll come around," he ordered as he climbed out of the truck.

He took her hand as she jumped down from his truck. He frowned as he realized for the first time how tall his truck was. He'd never even thought about it, but seeing how hard it was for Morgan to get in and out made it more than obvious. He'd need to get some steps for her, or running boards. Better yet, maybe he'd finally upgrade his truck for a newer model that would be more comfortable for her. His mom and sister had been bugging him for years to get a new one, but he'd blown them off.

He threaded his fingers with Morgan's, and they headed for the front door of The Pit. "Ready?" he asked as he grabbed the handle.

"Lead on, my mighty Marine."

Arrow knew she was teasing, but he liked when she called him hers. He opened the door and gestured for her to enter ahead of him.

The second they walked into the dark space, a female voice cried out, "Oh my God! My baby!"

Chapter Eleven

Morgan stiffened at the hysterical cry, but quickly relaxed. It had been a while, but she'd recognize her mom's voice anywhere.

She dropped Arrow's hand and ran toward her mom. The older woman was standing stock-still in the middle of the bar, frozen as if in shock. She obviously knew Morgan had been found alive, had probably even watched the news conference, as the TV in the bar was on, but hearing someone say your daughter was all right and seeing it for yourself were two completely different things, Morgan knew.

She threw her arms around her mom, and the two hugged and cried together in the middle of the bar, not even caring who was watching. She buried her head in her mom's hair and inhaled, smelling the familiar scent of coconut. Her mom had used the same shampoo for years, and smelling it again after all she'd been through was almost too much.

"My baby," Ellie Jernigan said again, rocking her daughter back and forth. "I never thought I'd see you again. Everyone told me to stay positive, but I'm not an idiot. I know when someone disappears, it's usually only a matter of time before their body is found in the woods, half-gnawed by wild dogs."

Morgan chuckled against her mom. She'd always been overly dramatic. Pulling back, Morgan smiled, held out an arm, and said, "I'm okay. See? No gnawed bones."

"The others said you were at the clinic getting checked out. Are you okay? I know you had that implant, so you shouldn't be pregnant, but you never know about anything else."

Morgan blushed and stared at her mom in embarrassment. She couldn't believe she'd brought that up, blatantly acknowledging what Morgan must have suffered. Morgan wasn't an idiot—she knew there was a chance she could have some sort of disease, but the last thing she wanted to do was talk about it in front of everyone. "I'm not pregnant," she settled on saying quietly, biting her lip in mortification.

"How about you two come over here and sit?" a man with a southern accent said, and Morgan felt him take a gentle hold of her elbow and steer her toward a couple of chairs.

Glad for the interruption, so she didn't have to go into detail about her visit to the doctor with her mom, Morgan allowed herself to be led toward the chairs.

"Morgan, this is Dave," Arrow said from her other side.

Turning toward the man who'd interrupted her and her mother, she looked up at him. He was not only a foot taller than her—he was massive. He had muscles on top of muscles. Arrow and his friends were well built, but not like this man. He was also older than them too. If she had to guess, she'd say he was closer to her mom's age than her own. Maybe in his mid- to late forties. He had short hair with a bit of gray in it, as well as a beard, also liberally sprinkled with gray.

He was extremely tan, but it was the large scar snaking down the side of his neck, disappearing into the collar of his T-shirt, that she couldn't take her eyes from. It looked like whatever had happened had almost decapitated him or, at the very least, severely slit his neck open.

Her hand was lifting toward the scar before she thought about what she was doing. Luckily, she caught herself before she'd actually touched the man. Flushing in embarrassment again, she froze with her hand in midair and stared up into his brown eyes.

"You must be Morgan," he said, his deep voice sounding like Morgan Freeman's . . . except with a southern twang to it. He gripped her hand in his, shaking it before letting go.

"I am."

"Welcome to The Pit," he said, as if she hadn't just made a complete fool out of herself in front of him by almost touching his scar. "I'm Dave. Can I get you something to drink? A soda? Water? Something stronger?"

"I haven't had alcohol in months," she said softly. "Probably not the best idea."

"That sounds wonderful," her mom said from next to her. "I could definitely use a mimosa."

Morgan swallowed hard and turned to stare at her mom once more. She eyed her up and down and realized that she looked good. She'd always taken care of herself, but it seemed in the year Morgan had been gone, and since the move away from Atlanta, Ellie Jernigan had gotten more comfortable in her own skin.

She'd always been taller than Morgan, but the two-inch heels she was currently wearing put her half a foot taller. She had on a fitted blouse that hugged her ample chest, and her knee-length skirt was tight. "Have you lost weight, Mom?" Morgan blurted. "You look amazing."

Ellie blushed and ran a hand down her thigh self-consciously. "When you went missing, I didn't eat that much. I was too worried about you. I knew I needed to get out of Atlanta. Everywhere I turned there were reminders that you were gone. One of the women in the office told me she had a friend who lived in Albuquerque and said there were lots of openings for hygienists. So one day, when I was particularly depressed, I made the decision. I quit and moved. I've met so many wonderful friends there, Morgan. I also joined a workout club and have been on the keto diet. I think it's been paying off."

Morgan felt Arrow's hand on the small of her back. They hadn't yet sat in the chairs Dave had indicated.

On one hand, Morgan wanted to be mad at her mom for moving on with her life. She'd gotten new friends and had been busy making herself look better . . . all while Morgan was being abused. But it would be petty to be upset. There was literally nothing she could've done, and it was better that she'd moved on rather than sinking into a pit of despair. "You look great, Mom."

"Thanks, baby." She lifted a hand to Morgan's blonde locks, fingering them. "Look at your poor hair. I wish your father would've given you time to do something with it before putting you on national TV."

"You should've seen it before Arrow got his hands on it," Morgan quipped, trying to ease the tension. She hated when her mom disparaged her dad. She'd gotten used to it, but it had been over a year since she'd heard the snark. She smiled up at Arrow, who stood at her back, and said, "I'm lucky he didn't need to cut it all off."

Ellie looked horrified. "Cut it off? Oh, that would've been downright awful. You've always loved your hair."

Short hair wouldn't have been *awful*. Not compared to what she'd been through. It would've been the least of her worries. She'd lived through hell, and her mom was worried about her hair?

"I think your daughter is beautiful no matter what she's wearing or what her hair looks like," Arrow said, leaning into her a bit.

Morgan was thankful for his support at that moment. His speaking up kept her from saying something she'd probably regret later.

Ellie's gaze focused on Arrow. "So you were the one who found my daughter? Did you kill the people who had her?"

"I was one of the three men, yes. And no. Our only objective was to get Nina home safely. We alerted the authorities about where we'd found both your daughter and the little girl, and they were going to go after Nina's biological father. We're still waiting to hear if they were able to catch any of the other men who were involved."

"Hmmm."

Morgan was embarrassed that her mom was being so rude. She should be kneeling at his feet and thanking him for finding Morgan and bringing her home. Come to think of it, even her dad hadn't said much in the way of thanks to Arrow and the rest of his team. He'd been too worried about what news stations would be at the conference and whether the story would go national or stay regional.

She turned and saw Meat, Ro, and Ball enter the bar. She knew they'd stayed behind at the press conference, giving her and Arrow time to make their escape. She smiled shyly at them and saw Arrow give them a chin lift in greeting.

"Who are they?" Ellie asked.

"Those are the other men on the team that rescued me," Morgan told her. "Ball was actually in Santo Domingo, but the others were back here, helping out with information."

Instead of asking to meet them, her mom turned away, as if they weren't important, and faced her daughter. "Morgan, you're coming back to Albuquerque with me, right? You're not going to go back to Atlanta, are you? I'm not sure that's the best idea. Whoever took you the first time could be waiting for you to go home. He could do it again. Not to mention the fact that your father is there, and I know he'll want to parade you in front of all the cameras for his own benefit."

It was a backhanded way of asking her to live with her, but Morgan couldn't exactly argue. She was leery of going back to Atlanta as it was, and the last thing she wanted was to have to give interviews to all the people her dad had met and worked with over the last year.

Though she was quickly remembering why she'd been so happy to move out of her mother's house in Atlanta too. Morgan loved her mom, but she could be extremely petty at times.

Looking from her mom to Arrow and back, Morgan said, "I . . . if that's all right with you, Mom. Yes."

"Of *course* it is!" Ellie exclaimed and reached for her, enfolding Morgan in her embrace once more. "You're my daughter, and I'm so happy to have you back from the dead. I wouldn't dream of you going anywhere else!"

Morgan hugged her mom back, hiding her face and trying to regain her composure. Now that her living arrangements were settled, for some reason she wanted to reconsider. Maybe she hadn't thought this out well enough. Maybe she could get an apartment here in Colorado Springs or something.

Then Ellie pulled back and said, "Oh, and I called Lane and let him know that you were found, and he's very anxious to talk to you."

Morgan could only stare at her mom. Ellie had always loved Lane. She'd thought they were perfect together. But Morgan definitely wasn't ready to talk to him. They'd been on the verge of breaking up when she'd disappeared, but she hadn't really told her mom about that, so she wouldn't know.

"Mrs. Jernigan?" Arrow asked.

"It's Ms.," Ellie corrected. "Yes?"

"We're going to need to steal Morgan from you for a bit. We need to go over some more things about her kidnapping."

"Are you sure that's necessary right now? She's still vulnerable after everything that happened. I don't want her having to relive anything that will distress her. Maybe you should wait a month or so."

"It's very important that we talk to her while everything is fresh," Arrow said with an apologetic look at Morgan. "I promise we'll go easy on her. Her well-being is of utmost importance to me and my friends."

"Then I don't see why I can't go with you." Ellie pouted. "I'm her mom. We share everything."

That wasn't exactly true, but Morgan didn't contradict her. She knew from experience that the woman would just dig in deeper and get more stubborn if she didn't distract her. "Mom, I could use your help in getting me some clothes and stuff. Maybe you can order some things online for me to be delivered to your place while I'm talking with Arrow and his friends? I'm sure we won't take too long."

"Shopping?" Ellie said, perking up. "I'd be happy to! I should've already thought about that. Do you think someone has a computer I can borrow? I could use my phone, but it would be easier on a laptop."

"I'm sure that can be arranged," Arrow said, looking over at Dave, who'd been observing the conversation closely without saying a word, and lifting his eyebrows comically.

The bartender took the hint and nodded. "I've got one in the back office you can use, Ellie."

"Thank you," Morgan's mom said, batting her eyelashes. When Dave held out his arm to her, she smiled even wider and hooked her arm around his. "And such a gentleman. I like it."

"Mom?" Morgan asked before Ellie walked away.

"Yes?"

"Do you think you can make your world-famous five-layer lasagna when we get home? It's been forever since I've had a home-cooked meal."

"Oh, baby . . . of course. And I'll make those marshmallow cookies you like so much, as well."

"Thanks."

"I'm so glad you're all right. I might not be the greatest mom in the world, but I love you and only want what's best for you."

"Thanks, Mom. I love you too."

When Ellie and Dave were out of earshot, Arrow leaned down and asked, "Are you all right?"

"I'm fine. I guess I should've warned you about my mom. She's a little . . . over the top sometimes."

Arrow chuckled. "I guess that's as good a word as any to describe her."

"She means well. She's just a bit outspoken and doesn't always think about what she's saying before it comes out of her mouth."

"She didn't know about you and Lane, did she?"

"About us breaking up? No. I don't know why I didn't tell her we weren't working out. Maybe I didn't want to disappoint her or something. But I hadn't gotten around to telling her that we were going to break up soon." She looked up at Arrow. "I guess I should've called him, huh?"

"Come on," Arrow said, taking her hand in his. "We can have this conversation with the guys. They'll be interested to hear that he wants to talk to you."

"I hate this," Morgan said as she dutifully followed Arrow through the door in the back of the room to a large area that held pool tables. He turned to the right and led her over to a table at the side of the room. Black, Ball, Ro, Meat, and Gray were already seated and looking through some papers.

"I know, and I hate that you have to go through this shit, as well. But it's necessary. You do know that, right? I mean, we wouldn't need to have this conversation if we knew who took you, and why."

"I know, Arrow," Morgan reassured him, putting her free hand on his arm. "I'm not saying I don't *want* to do this, just that I don't like it."

"It'll be too late for you and your mom to leave this afternoon when we're done here," Arrow said. "Any chance I can interest you in dinner at my apartment? I'm not the best cook in the world, but I'm not the worst either. I can grill us up a mean steak with some grilled asparagus and rolls on the side. It's as close to home cooking as I get. Do you want to invite your mom over? Or your dad?"

Morgan stared up at him and felt like she wanted to cry. He could've asked her to go out to dinner with him and his friends. He could've invited Allye and Chloe and the others over to eat, as well. She liked even more that he was willing to make her happy by inviting her parents to eat with them.

"I'd love a steak," she said softly. "And . . . maybe since it's my last night here . . . we can keep it just the two of us? I'll have plenty of

143

time with Mom since I'm going down to New Mexico. And Dad will just want to talk about what happened—when he and Mom aren't arguing—and I have a feeling I'll be all talked out by the time tonight comes."

She watched as Arrow's gaze dropped to her lips and then her chest before coming back up to her eyes. She felt like squirming under the intense look he gave her, but resisted the urge. She liked this man. Maybe there was something to love at first sight, after all. She didn't know that she loved him, but she sure did like everything she knew about him so far.

"Whatever you want, I'll do my best to make sure you have it," Arrow told her.

"Okay. I'll talk to my mom after we're done and let her know the plan," Morgan said.

"Sounds good. If you need a break when we're talking, just tap on my knee twice."

The gooey feeling inside her grew at his words. "I'll be fine."

"I know you will. But still, the offer is there. Don't think you have to power through this if it's too much."

"I won't."

"Good. You ready?"

"To talk about the people in my life who I thought were friends and try to figure out who might hate me enough to have me kidnapped and held captive in a foreign country? No. But I *am* ready to get on with my life."

"I don't know whether to hug you or give you a high five," Arrow admitted.

"Come on, you two," Meat called out. "We got shit to do and rats to ferret out."

"Charming," Arrow muttered as he walked Morgan over to the table.

He waited until she was seated before pulling out the chair next to hers.

Morgan wasn't sure if she was supposed to just start talking or how this was going to work, but she needn't have worried. Meat jumped right in, as she was realizing was his way, and said, "So, Morgan Byrd, tell us about every single person you knew back in Atlanta."

Chapter Twelve

Arrow could tell Morgan was exhausted. They'd been talking to her for two hours—or rather, she'd been talking to *them* for two hours.

Meat had told her not to filter her words at all. If she had weird feelings about someone, she needed to tell them. He'd taken the lead on the questioning, and he'd been pushing Morgan hard.

When they were still in Santo Domingo, they'd heard about her inner circle, Lane and Lance Buswell, Karen Garver, Thomas Huntington, and Sarah Ellsworth, but Meat had insisted on getting the names of as many of her friends, acquaintances, customers, and suppliers as possible. He'd even gone so far as to press her for the names of her parents' friends. Since her dad was a CFO, any rivals he had couldn't be overlooked.

Morgan hadn't balked. She'd answered every question they'd thrown at her and had told them as much as she knew about each person.

As a result, they now had a list of about a hundred people, and at this point, *everyone* was a suspect. He knew Morgan was still holding out hope that her kidnapping was random, but it didn't feel like it to Arrow. And he knew the rest of the team was on the same page.

If she'd been abducted by a stranger, they wouldn't have gone to such lengths to keep her down in the Caribbean. They would've done what they wanted with her, then killed her. But drugging her, transporting her to the small country, then paying a group of thugs to keep her there, and unseen, was way above and beyond a random kidnapping.

No, whoever was behind this knew Morgan personally. They had one hell of a grudge against her as well, which baffled Arrow. Granted, he hadn't known her long, but he couldn't imagine she'd ever do something that would make someone want to torture her like they had.

So they'd start going down the list of people she knew, starting with her friends and ex-boyfriend and his brother, and go from there. The better someone knew her, the more likely it was that they were the one behind her kidnapping.

"It looks like Lane is dating someone new, has been for almost a year," Meat said. Then, looking up at Morgan, he belatedly added, "Sorry."

She waved off his words. "I told you guys that we weren't really dating that last night we went out. It's fine."

"Right, so he started dating a woman named Rebecca Low. She's got a hell of a list of ex-boyfriends of her own . . . including a few felons."

"What'd they get booked for?" Black asked.

"Armed robbery, assault, and domestic abuse."

"Shit. I'm guessing Lane was a huge step up from that?" Ball asked Morgan.

She nodded. "He didn't even like to speed."

"Yup. Lane Buswell is a Boy Scout for sure," Meat said, staring at the computer screen in front of him. "But maybe Miss Rebecca wanted Morgan out of the picture so she could have Lane for herself. She certainly knew people who could do the dirty deed."

"Lance isn't much better, is he?" Ro asked. "He's got his own record."

"True. Mostly petty stuff, though, like public intoxication and disturbing the peace . . . oh, but he had a DUI that was pending when Morgan disappeared."

"Sarah came in contact with all sorts of people as a bartender," Gray threw in. "She could've paid someone to follow Morgan out of the club that night and nab her."

"Oh, this is interesting," Meat said as he clicked away on his computer.

"What?" Gray asked.

"Karen Garver's *brother* is in a motorcycle gang in Miami. If she had a beef with Morgan about something or thought she was being charged too much, she could've flipped and had her brother step in."

Arrow had been concentrating so hard on the list of names in front of him, and on the theories the others were throwing out, that he hadn't been paying attention to Morgan. It wasn't until he felt a tentative tapping on his knee that he looked over at her.

She was pressing her lips together in agitation and didn't have much color in her cheeks at all.

Fuck.

Throwing out every piece of information they had and brainstorming was how the team worked best. They didn't tend to hold back when they were doing it either. Morgan had been so helpful, and had been so even-keeled when talking about her friends and acquaintances, he'd almost forgotten she wasn't one of them. This wasn't merely a case she was discussing—it was her life.

"It's getting late, guys," Arrow said firmly. "Allye and Chloe should be here soon, and I know Morgan probably needs a break before that happens."

She nodded enthusiastically from next to him.

Gray immediately realized their error and said, "Sorry, Morgan. You've done an amazing job. Seriously. I know this was tough."

"Yeah," she agreed. "I never thought I'd have to think about the mailman as someone who hated me so much he'd have me kidnapped and tortured for a year. Guess I should cut back on my catalog ordering, huh?"

Arrow had opened his mouth to soothe her when they heard a commotion from the front room.

"I do not *believe* this!" Ellie Jernigan shouted.

"Calm down, Ellie," a deep voice responded.

Morgan stood up so quickly her chair fell over behind her, the sound loud in the large room when it landed. "Oh shit," she exclaimed.

"Who is it?" Black asked, coming around the table, looking alert and ready to defend Morgan from anyone who might burst into the back room and try to hurt her.

The others had followed suit, and they'd surrounded Morgan, putting themselves between her and whoever had entered the bar. It made Arrow feel good . . . but he had a feeling the person who needed protecting wasn't Morgan. "It's Carl Byrd," he informed his teammates.

"Her dad?" Gray asked.

"The one and only," Morgan mumbled and headed for the door. "I hope you guys are ready for this. If there were ever two people in this world who hated each other, and shouldn't be in the same room together, it's them."

Feeling protective of Morgan, and kicking himself for not watching her more carefully when they were discussing who might want her gone, Arrow walked slightly in front of her as they approached the doorway.

Carl Byrd was standing just inside the bar, and Ellie Jernigan was in his face, yelling at him.

"You can just turn your ass around and walk out of here," she said, wagging her finger in his face. "Morgan doesn't want to see you. Haven't you realized how hard today was for her? That you parading her in front of those vultures was the wrong thing to do? How could you be so insensitive?"

"Those 'vultures' were the ones who kept Morgan's case in the spotlight," Carl said calmly. "Without me working my ass off to make sure no one forgot about our daughter, she would still be in that hovel in the Caribbean."

"That's a joke!" Ellie said. "She wasn't found because of anything *you* did. It was an accident! If that other man hadn't taken his little girl down there, she'd still be in their clutches. So don't give me that bullshit that it was all *your* doing that she's home safe and sound."

"I didn't see *you* doing anything to find her," Carl said, his composure slipping. "You hightailed it out of Atlanta so fast after she disappeared, I wondered if you were trying to hide something."

The crack of Ellie's palm hitting Carl's cheek echoed in the mostly empty room. "How *dare* you," she screeched. "*You're* the one who did everything in your power to exploit her being kidnapped! Stocks for your precious company went through the roof after you went on TV, crying about *your* poor daughter and how much you missed her. Maybe you should've spent more time with her when she was little and less time screwing your secretary!"

"That's enough!" Dave boomed, stalking over to the couple.

Arrow blinked and pulled Morgan off to the side of the open door, making room for the others to wade into the fray. He'd never seen Dave look so enraged. He was the most even-keeled man Arrow had ever met. He didn't get upset when people got drunk and disorderly in his bar. He didn't blink when someone tried to pick a fight with him. He didn't seem to give even the smallest shit when he was stiffed on a tip.

But at the moment, he looked like he was going to murder one, or both, of Morgan's parents.

Gray and Ro flanked the man, while Ball went to Carl's side and Black went to Ellie's.

"How dare you *both*," Dave hissed at the couple. "Your daughter coming home is a fucking *miracle*, and you're standing here bickering at each other like five-year-olds. I don't care what your history is, you should at least be civil to each other at a time like this."

"You're right," Ellie said, dropping the bitter edge to her voice, her shoulders sagging. "Having Morgan back *is* a miracle, and I'm more than happy she's here. I've just been so stressed and worried. Nothing is more important than having my baby home."

"Except maybe missing out on your own five minutes of fame since you weren't invited to the press conference," Morgan's dad said under his breath, but loud enough for everyone to hear.

"Enough!" Dave said once more. "For God's sake! *You* two are what's wrong with the world today. Out. Get. Out."

"But I wanted to talk to Morgan," Carl argued.

"You had your chance," Ellie said. "She's going home with me to Albuquerque tonight. I'll make sure she's not left alone for one second. I'll make sure she's *safe*."

Carl looked over to Morgan then. "Seriously? You need to come home to Atlanta, honey. I'll put you up in an apartment in my building. There's a doorman and everything. You'll be safe there."

"Maybe I shouldn't go with either one of you," Morgan said evenly. "I'm sick of the two of you acting like babies. You got divorced decades ago. You need to start acting like adults and stop pulling at me like two dogs with a bone."

Dave nodded at Black and Ball and walked to the door of the bar. He opened it as the other two men grabbed hold of Morgan's parents' arms.

"Hey, let go of me!" Carl protested.

Ellie turned to her daughter as she was being led to the door. "I'm so sorry, baby. I'll do better, I promise! I just . . . I've missed you so much, and I need to know you're all right. Please reconsider coming with me. I won't say anything about your father. I swear."

"Morgan will be in touch," Dave told Ellie. "She's staying the night here in Colorado Springs, and you two can be on your way tomorrow. I suggest you both chill out and think about Morgan for once in your lives. If she decides to stay here, know that she'll have all the protection she needs. If she decides to go with you to New Mexico, Ms. Jernigan— and that's a big if—you had better be prepared to be there for her one hundred percent. I recommend you spend your evenings thinking about what your daughter has been through and how you can best help *her*, rather than what's most convenient for you."

And with that, Black and Ball gave both adults a gentle shove out the door, and Dave closed it in their faces. He turned around and walked straight to Morgan.

She was standing next to Arrow with her eyes wide and an embarrassed look on her face.

Dave came up to her and pulled her into his embrace without a word. Arrow didn't see any fear of the older man, or anything that showed she didn't want Dave's hug. She closed her eyes and rested her cheek on his chest.

"I'm sorry about that, hon," Dave said.

Morgan shrugged in his embrace. "It's okay. It's not the first time I've seen them fight, and it won't be the last."

"They should be there for you," Dave protested, not ready to give it up.

Morgan pulled back a bit and looked up at the older man. "They've been like that my entire life. The more time that went by since they divorced, the worse they got. It's like they both refuse to give up the anger they have toward each other. I don't get it, but I've learned to deal with it. Besides, they're not always like that. My mom is generally pretty clingy. Once my dad leaves, she'll go back to her normal loving self."

"Still." Dave sighed. "I'm sorry. And you *are* a miracle. I know you must've gone through hell, but you're here. You can deal with anything that happened because you're alive. Remember that." Then he turned to Arrow. "You guys done?"

"Yeah, we're done for now."

"Good. Morgan needs a drink," Dave announced. Then he transferred Morgan into Arrow's arms and spun and headed for his bar.

"He's a little intense," Morgan noted quietly when he'd taken several steps away.

"Actually, no, he's not," Arrow countered. "He's usually very easygoing."

"I don't know how to feel about that," she admitted.

"Special," Arrow said. "You should feel special. Now . . . are you okay? I'm sorry about that back there." He gestured to the back room with his head. "I should've realized that talking about your friends that way wasn't cool."

She immediately shook her head. "No, it's okay. I just . . . I was just overwhelmed for a second. It's not like I haven't already thought all the things you guys were saying. I've had a year to think about my kidnapping and wonder 'Why me?' But I never would've guessed someone was paying those men to keep me there."

"Um . . . do you guys know there's a couple in the parking lot yelling at each other?" Allye asked as she entered the pool hall with Chloe.

"Yeah, we know," Gray told her as he went up to her and wrapped his arm around her shoulders.

"Are you going to do anything about it?" Chloe asked.

Ro bent and kissed his girlfriend deeply before pulling back and saying, "We already have. Why do you think they're out there in the parking lot and not in here?"

"Hi," Morgan said, self-consciously trying to pull away from Arrow. He refused to let her go.

"Hey," Allye said.

"Ready to kick some pool ass?" Chloe asked.

"Yeah, I think I am," Morgan told her.

"Here," Dave said, handing bottles of water to both Chloe and Allye. He carried a bright-blue drink over to Morgan. "And this is for you."

"What is it? Do I want to know?"

"It's called AMF. It has vodka, rum, tequila, gin, blue curaçao liqueur, sweet-and-sour mix, and is topped off with 7UP."

Morgan stared at him in disbelief. "Dave, I haven't had any alcohol in a year."

"All the more reason."

"Um . . . okay," she stammered. Dave nodded in satisfaction and turned on his heel and went back to the bar without another word.

Morgan looked up at Arrow. "I'm kinda scared to drink this," she admitted.

Arrow smiled at her. "Don't be. Dave is the best bartender I've ever met in my life. He's also one of the most protective when it comes to the ladies. If he thinks you need that, you do."

"What does AMF stand for?" Morgan asked as she took a sip of the blue drink.

"Adios, motherfucker," Dave yelled from across the room.

Morgan choked on the sip she'd just taken and stared at him for a beat, then asked Arrow, "Did he really hear me from all the way over there?"

"Did I fail to mention that Dave has the hearing of a bat?" Arrow asked with another smile.

"Uh . . . yeah." Then she raised her voice and asked Dave, "Are you bidding *me* adios, my parents, or telling me that I'm not going to remember anything after I drink this thing?"

"Yes," the other man yelled back, and he turned his attention to wiping down the already clean bar top with a small grin.

"He's never made *me* a drink," Allye whispered when she got close.

Chloe also sauntered up and uncapped her water. "Me either. All we ever get is water. In a bottle, of course."

Both women laughed and Morgan's brow furrowed in question.

"He refuses to serve women water in glasses because he's afraid they can be drugged too easily," Arrow told her.

"Seriously?"

"Well, yeah. The likelihood of anyone daring to do that shit in here is extremely low, but Dave isn't taking any chances."

"Are you guys done with her?" Allye asked. "Can we steal her and play some pool?"

"We didn't show up too early, did we?" Chloe added.

"No. Your timing was actually perfect," Arrow told her, then turned to Morgan. "You want to stay . . . or have an early dinner?" A part of him wanted her to say she wanted to go home with him right this moment, but he also wanted her to loosen up and have some girl time. Allye and Chloe were amazing women, and if anyone could make Morgan feel better, it would be them.

"I'd like to stay and play some pool . . . if that's okay."

"Of course it is," Arrow told her immediately. "Take your time. Me and the guys will continue with our conversation we were having earlier."

She looked relieved with his answer. "Okay."

"Okay." Then, without feeling an ounce of uneasiness or awkwardness, Arrow leaned down and kissed Morgan's lips briefly. "Have fun."

Then he strode away. But not before he heard Allye say, "Giiiiirl. Did I see right and Archer Kane just kissed you?"

Morgan grinned as she walked arm in arm with Allye, Chloe close on their heels, and said, "Yup."

"High five!" Ally exclaimed as all three girls chuckled and disappeared into the back room.

Arrow felt the other five men on the Mountain Mercenary team walk up to him, but his attention was on the doorway Morgan had disappeared through.

"That's a big list of names we need to investigate," Black commented.

"Yeah," Arrow agreed.

"There seem to be a lot of felons in the woodwork that could be connected to her," Meat added.

"Yup," Arrow said.

"It's going to take a while to investigate them all," Ball threw out.

"Uh-huh."

"Maybe she had *herself* kidnapped and was having herself a yearlong vacation," Ro said dryly.

"Maybe," Arrow mumbled.

Gray smacked Arrow on the back of the head. He flinched and turned to glare at his friend. "What the fuck was that for?"

"Just trying to get you to pay attention," his friend said. "Come on. She's fine with Allye and Chloe. Dave will keep his eye on them. We have shit we need to discuss if we're going to narrow down this list of suspects, and we need your head in the game."

"You could've just said so," Arrow complained as he rubbed his head.

"For what it's worth . . . we like her," Meat said. "She's kept her head, and had some amazing insights into who might not like her and why. She gave us a real head start on working on these names."

"She's amazing, all right," Arrow agreed. He followed his friends into the back room, not able to keep himself from looking for Morgan. She was laughing at something one of the other women had said, and he inhaled sharply. He'd already thought she was beautiful, but seeing her right then, relaxed and happy, made him realize he hadn't even begun to see all the different sides to her.

He wished she could stay here in Colorado Springs, but he'd be damned if he let a few hundred miles keep him from what he wanted—namely, Morgan.

Chapter Thirteen

Morgan lay on Arrow's couch hours later, too full to move, too comfortable to even think about getting up and going to bed. Arrow sat on the other end of the sofa, her feet in his lap, giving her the best foot massage she'd ever had.

He was watching television as he worked on her feet, seemingly not paying any attention to her. But Morgan knew he was as tuned in to her as she was to him. When she shifted, he immediately asked if she was comfortable and if she needed another pillow. When she closed her eyes for a second, enjoying the feel of his hands on her sock-clad feet, he asked if she was tired and wanted to go to bed.

His apartment *was* as neat as a pin. He'd warned her he was a bit of a neat freak, but she hadn't been prepared for how immaculate the place was. Morgan supposed it was a result of being a Marine, but taken to the extreme. The glasses in his cupboards were lined up precisely, the pantry arranged as if a professional organizer came in after he went to the grocery store, and there weren't many extra personal touches in the room to gather dust.

There were only two pictures on his bookshelves: one of him and two women she assumed were his mom and sister, and one of Arrow standing with the other five men from Mountain Mercenaries. They were all grubby and dirty, but each and every one had a huge smile on his face.

As clean and orderly as the place was, Morgan immediately felt comfortable there. She wasn't a neat freak, not even close, but after the last year of living in squalor, being in Arrow's clean space felt freeing somehow. Calming.

"Did you enjoy dinner?" Arrow asked in a low voice.

"Immensely," Morgan answered. "I have no idea how you got all those spices to stick to the meat, but it was amazing."

"Not overdone?"

"No way. It was perfect."

"I'm glad."

"Arrow?"

"Yeah, beautiful?"

"Thank you."

"For what?"

"For today. For staying by my side. For looking out for me. I was nervous about the press conference, but you reassured and distracted me when I needed it most. I know you guys needed as much information as possible about my friends and acquaintances, but when it became too much, you let me take a break. Thank you for letting me play pool with Allye and Chloe. I like them a lot, and they help make me feel normal. And that's a big deal, because I haven't felt normal for a very long time. Thank you for not freaking out when my parents did their thing. And finally, thank you for tonight. I needed a quiet dinner, away from the oppressive stares of the general public. I'm . . . I'm going to miss you."

Without a word, Arrow shifted until he'd pulled her upright, turned her in his embrace, and reclined, with her back to his front. His arms were looped loosely around her waist, and she could feel his breath against the side of her face and hair as she lay against him.

"You can stay here, you know," he told her after a while.

Morgan sighed. "I know. And I appreciate it more than *you'll* ever know. You didn't see my mom at her best today. She's normally not like that. Most of the time she's almost suffocatingly sweet. She hovers over me. I think . . . I think I need that right now. You've got your job and all, and . . . I just need some Mom time."

"I can understand that," Arrow said, tightening his arms around her. "But remember that you're always welcome here. If things don't work out in Albuquerque, all you have to do is call, and I'll come and get you."

"I appreciate that."

"And you should know, I'm going to miss you too," he told her. "You've only been here two days, and you've made your mark on my place, and now I'm not going to be able to do anything without seeing you here."

"You mean I'm a slob, and I dirtied up your kitchen, left my shoes in the middle of the floor, and made you go grab a blanket so I could snuggle up on the couch," she joked.

"No. Just by your presence, you've made this apartment more of a home than it's been since I moved in. You've filled it with your energy and goodness."

"Arrow," Morgan protested. She knew he was being melodramatic, but she loved the sentiment all the same.

"I'm serious. And if you come back here, you should know that you won't be an imposition. Not a bother. As you can see, I haven't quite left the Marines behind when it comes to being tidy. That was drilled into us from day one of boot camp. But the thought of you being here, of sharing my space, doesn't freak me out in the least. I could get used to seeing a crumpled blanket on the couch and shoes on the floor if I knew they belonged to you."

"How did this happen?" Morgan asked.

"What?"

"This. Us. Less than a week ago, I was barely living, thinking I was going to die in that damn hovel. But now . . . we're . . . well, I don't know what we're doing."

"Fate," Arrow said with conviction. "Things happen in the world that we can't explain. Kids who are way too young to know how, discover they can play the piano as if they'd been doing it their entire lives. Pets that ran off years ago reappear and are reunited with their families. People who thought they were alone in the world suddenly find out they have a huge family they knew nothing about."

Morgan looked back at Arrow and saw the serious look on his face. He wasn't just blowing smoke up her ass. He truly believed what he was saying.

"I know," he said with a huff of breath. "You think I'm crazy. But I've seen enough things in this world that can't be rationalized with a simple explanation. People who have survived a direct hit on their house with an RPG and walked out without a scratch. Soldiers who should've died from their injuries but didn't. Lovers who were reunited after being apart for fifty years. I don't question it anymore. And sometimes two people just click. Maybe they knew each other in a past life, and their souls are drawn together in this life. I don't know, but from the first time I saw you, I knew you'd change *my* life. How, I've yet to figure it out, but I know with everything that's in me that it's true."

Morgan swallowed hard. His words were unexpected. She hadn't thought much about reincarnation or souls, but what he said resonated with her. "I'd like to believe that . . . but I'm not sure I can."

"That's okay," he told her. "I believe it enough for both of us. All you have to know is that if you need me, I'm here. I admire you, Morgan. And more than that, I believe in you. I don't know what's in store for the rest of your life, but if you want me in it, I'm here. Now . . . lie back and close your eyes. Morning will come quickly."

"I'm nervous about figuring out what I want to do with my life. Do I try to start up my bee business again? Do I look for an apartment? Will people recognize me and want to talk about my ordeal? Everything just seems so up in the air."

"One day at a time, beautiful," Arrow said. "I don't have any answers for you, but when you feel overwhelmed, you call me. Shoot me a text, and I'll be there for you."

"Thanks," she whispered.

She felt Arrow kiss her temple softly. He didn't pull his lips away from her skin for the longest time.

Just as she was drifting off to sleep, she heard Arrow whisper, "I'm already counting down the hours until I can see you again, beautiful."

~

The next morning, Arrow backed away from Ellie Jernigan's Subaru Forester and kept his eyes on Morgan's. He'd woken up on his couch with her still in his arms. He was stiff from the awkward sleeping position, but he wouldn't have changed it for anything in the world. Morgan had woken up not too much later and had been surprised that she'd slept through the night without having any nightmares.

He hated that she was having them, but wasn't surprised. She'd been to hell and back, and it would take a while for her to recover. He'd texted Rex while she was showering and asked for some recommendations of people Morgan could talk to in Albuquerque. The faster she began talking about her experience, the faster she'd be able to deal with it and recover.

Ro had showed up an hour ago and dropped off a new phone for Morgan as well. He hadn't stayed long, just enough to say hello and goodbye to her before heading out again. She'd tried to refuse the phone, but Ro had finally said, "It's yours. Deal with it," before heading back to his car and leaving her no choice but to accept it.

She had rolled her eyes but kept the top-of-the-line phone. Arrow had put in his own number, as well as Rex's and those of the other guys on the team. Allye's and Chloe's were added as well.

She didn't have a lot to pack up, as she hadn't gotten around to buying many clothes yet . . . and then it was time for her to go. Her mom called Arrow—he'd contacted her to tell her where he lived and what time Morgan would be ready—and now she was leaving.

Arrow kept his eyes on Morgan's face for as long as possible, before the SUV backed out of the parking space and was gone.

How long he stood there watching as the car disappeared, Arrow didn't know, but eventually he pulled out his phone and typed a quick text.

Arrow: You haven't even been gone five minutes, and it feels like forever.

Her response was immediate.

Morgan: I feel the same way. Tell me again why I'm leaving?

Arrow tapped away on the keys as he walked back into his apartment building. He gave Robert, the doorman, a chin lift and continued toward the elevators to take him back up to the third floor. He usually took the stairs, but he wanted to concentrate on what he was typing.

Arrow: Because you're strong. Because your mom needs some time with you to understand that you're truly home and safe. Because you're a good daughter. Because you need to know that you can stand on your own two feet without me hovering next to you. Because you know that if things don't work out, you'll always have a place to go: back here to me.

He unlocked his door and headed into his apartment. He had to get ready to go back to The Pit and discuss Morgan's case some more. Meat had been doing some investigating on his computer and wanted to discuss what he'd found. Arrow wanted to stare at his phone until Morgan responded, but he forced himself to put it down and go shower.

Ten minutes later, he was back in the kitchen and saw he had a text waiting for him.

Morgan: Just when I don't think you can get any better . . . you prove me wrong.

Arrow smiled and tucked his phone into his pocket. He wanted to write her back. Wanted to call her and hear her voice. But the best thing he could do for her right now was give her space. Let her be who she was meant to be. In the meantime, he'd figure out who the hell was behind her kidnapping and make sure she never, ever had to worry about that happening again.

Chapter Fourteen

Morgan smiled as she texted Arrow. They'd been texting almost nonstop since she'd left his apartment a week earlier.

Morgan: Is it weird that the mattress in my mom's guest room is too soft?

Arrow: No. You could get some boards to put under it to give it more support.

Morgan: I'm not sure that would help. I slept on the hard ground so long that I think it ruined me.

Arrow: You slept on the bed in the hotel and on my couch in my arms and were just fine. It'll just take time to acclimate.

Morgan: I did, didn't I? :)

Arrow: Yup.

Morgan: What are you doing today?

Arrow: Grocery store, meeting with Meat, then working out.

Morgan: Are you sure you have enough time? I mean, it'll take you hours to organize your pantry after shopping.

Arrow: Are you making fun of me?

Morgan: Maybe. :)

Arrow: What about you? What's on your agenda for the day?

Morgan: Well, I wanted to stay in today because I have a headache and my stomach hurts, but I have something I need to do.

Arrow: I'm sorry you don't feel good. Where are you going?

Morgan: The women's clinic downtown.

Arrow: Why? Are you okay? Are you sicker than you're letting on? Do you need me to arrange for you to see a doctor?

Arrow: Why didn't you tell me you needed a doctor? Dammit, beautiful . . .

Morgan: I'm fine.

Morgan: Seriously. Stop panicking.

Arrow: I can't. Not when you tell me you're going to the doctor and your mom isn't there to go with you. Do you need me to come down?

Morgan: If I said yes, you'd come?

Arrow: In a heartbeat. I'd see if I could get Rex to let me borrow the plane. I could be there in around two hours.

Morgan: Wow. As much as I'm tempted, this is something I need to do on my own.

Arrow: Call me.

Morgan: No. I can't talk to you about this.

Arrow: Seriously, call me, Morgan.

Morgan: No.

Arrow: I'm annoyed with you. You should know.

Morgan: Why does that make me smile?

Arrow: Because you know it means I give a shit. Now tell me what's up, or I will show up and track your ass down.

Morgan: I know I was tested when I first got back and everything came back negative, and I'm sure the doctor I saw was good, but I can't shake the feeling that maybe she missed something. I don't know what, but because I've been feeling so rotten lately, I thought maybe I should go to the women's clinic here and get retested . . . just to make me feel better and to make sure I'm clean.

Morgan: Arrow? Are you there?

Arrow: I'm here. Although I'm contemplating flying back down to Santo Domingo and hunting down the assholes who had you and killing them slowly.

Arrow: I can't type fast enough to get all this out, but since you won't call me . . .

Arrow: I think it's a good idea to go.

Arrow: I hate that I'm not there to go with you.

Arrow: I'm no doctor, but I don't think your symptoms really coincide with an STD. But no matter what the doc says today, or any doc says in the future, it's not going to make me want you any less.

Arrow: I've said it once and I'll say it again. If you decide you want to give whatever's between us a go, I'm the lucky one. I'm fully aware that I'm not the best catch.

Arrow: I'm OCD when it comes to neatness.

Arrow: I have a job that takes me out of town way too much.

Arrow: If I'm not on a mission, I'm usually tinkering with electronics.

Arrow: I'm slightly claustrophobic and overprotective with those I love.

Arrow: Will you call me later?

Morgan swallowed hard before responding.

Morgan: How do you always know what to say to make me feel better?

Arrow: Because. Now, will you call me later?

Morgan: Bossy. Yes. I'll call.

Arrow: Good. Have you talked to your dad lately?

Morgan: Nice change of subject. And yes, he called yesterday.

Arrow: And?

Morgan: He keeps trying to get me to agree to the one-on-one interviews.

Arrow: You should only do what you want to do, beautiful.

Morgan: Thanks. I told him I'd think about it. Arrow?

Arrow: Yeah?

Morgan: I miss you.

Arrow: Not as much as I miss you.

Morgan: It's only been a week.

Arrow: And?

Morgan: My mom suggested that it's just because you saved me. That it's some sort of savior syndrome. That I'm latching on to you because you swooped in and rescued me.

Arrow: What does your psychiatrist say?

Morgan: That it's possible.

Arrow: We'll talk about that tonight too.

Morgan: Bossy.

Arrow: :)

Morgan: Okay, I have to go. My appointment is in an hour, and I have to call for a ride.

Arrow: Be careful.

Morgan: I will.

Arrow: Text me when you get home so I know you're all right.

Morgan: Okay. Have fun at the store.

Arrow: It's shopping. There's no fun to be had.

Morgan: You've never been shopping with me. :)

Arrow: It's one of a million things I'm looking forward to doing with you, beautiful. Have a good day and try not to worry. Remember, you're a kick-ass, strong woman who has the rest of her life ahead of her.

Morgan: I'll talk to you later.

Arrow: Yes, you will.

Morgan stared at her phone for a long moment before putting it aside. She really did need to leave if she was going to make it to her appointment on time, but she couldn't resist a few more minutes thinking about Arrow . . . and how much she'd already grown to like him.

He'd been a lifeline the last week. Her mom was excited to have her home, but her overprotectiveness, always a bit much, was now almost oppressive. She'd taken the first couple of days off work, and then she'd arranged to work half days for the foreseeable future. Morgan felt terrible, already wanting space from her mom, but she could only take so much.

Ellie constantly asked how she was doing and if she wanted to talk about what happened. She kept telling Morgan that it wasn't healthy to keep everything inside, that she needed to talk. And Morgan *was* talking . . . to a therapist. She didn't have the energy to rehash everything with her mom because she definitely wasn't comfortable telling her about some of the awful things she'd endured. She was working to put the past year behind her and get on with her life, but that was difficult to do when her mom was constantly asking if she was all right and if she needed anything.

Morgan didn't have any friends in Albuquerque she could talk to or hang out with, and she missed Arrow even more than she wanted to admit. Their text conversations and the nights she'd called him had been the highlights of her week. She wanted to ask if she could come back up to Colorado Springs, but felt that wasn't fair to her mom.

Ellie was a grown woman with her own life. Living with her adult daughter, who was dealing with some pretty serious issues, had turned out to be a little harder than either of them had imagined. Morgan wasn't an idiot; she knew her issues wouldn't magically disappear if she was closer to Arrow, but she honestly felt he was better equipped to deal with them because of his experience with kidnapping victims.

Sighing, she forced herself to get up. She pulled up an app on her phone and ordered a ride downtown. She was dreading the appointment, but until she reconfirmed that none of the men had given her a sexually transmitted disease, she wouldn't be able to relax.

~

Arrow paced his apartment and ran his hand over his closely shorn hair for the tenth time. He was trying to be patient and wait for Morgan to call him, but he kept finding his phone in his hand. He could tell she wasn't happy staying with her mom. It sounded like the woman meant well, but it was obvious she was smothering her daughter.

He'd planned on asking Morgan to come back up to Colorado Springs even before he'd met with Meat and the rest of the team, but after the phone call Rex received today, he had even more reason to see if Morgan would consider it.

The second his phone rang, Arrow clicked on the button to answer without letting it ring a second time.

"Morgan?"

"Hey, Arrow."

"How'd the doctor visit go? What'd they say?"

"Wow, just jumping right to it, huh? No asking how I am, or telling me to say hi to my mom for you?"

"Morgan . . . ," Arrow threatened. "Just tell me."

"They went over the results I got from the clinic there, and they said there wasn't anything that alarmed them with my blood work. But they went ahead and retested me for herpes, HIV, hepatitis, chlamydia, gonorrhea, and syphilis again. The fastest they can have most of the results is tomorrow afternoon sometime, but they said that I wasn't exhibiting any physical symptoms, so they're pretty sure I'm in the clear. The doctor suggested the stomachache and headaches were most likely a result of the stress I've been under. He said if they don't get better to come back and he'd do more tests."

"Thank fuck," Arrow breathed. "I'm sorry you're still feeling sick, but I wouldn't care if the doctor had said you had *all* that shit. It wouldn't change the way I feel about you. But I'm glad for your sake that everything looks like it will turn out all right."

"Me too," Morgan whispered.

"Now that that's pretty much out of the way . . . how's your mom?" Arrow asked.

"Good, I guess. We were watching TV tonight and a commercial came on for Oreo cookies. I made a comment that I hadn't had them in forever, and the next thing I knew, she had her keys in her hand and was on the way out the door to get some for me."

"She hasn't calmed down on the smothering then, huh?" Arrow asked.

"No. Not in the least. I swear I can't go to the bathroom without her asking me where I'm going and if I'm all right and if I need anything. I should be happy that she cares so much, but it's annoying. And then I feel guilty that I'm annoyed."

Arrow hated that she had such conflicted feelings toward her mom. He wasn't sure what he thought about Ellie, himself. She hadn't exactly put her best foot forward when they'd first met, but he was trying to give her a second chance. Changing the subject, he said, "Right. So I have something to tell you and a question to ask."

"Oh shit."

"It's nothing bad . . . well, not really."

"Okay."

"Trust me, Morgan. I'd never do or say anything that would cause you distress if I could help it," Arrow told her.

"I know. It's just . . . today was hard. And I miss having friends to talk to. And my mom is confusing me. You know I talked to my dad yesterday, and I'm stressed about that too. It's just been a weird day."

"I'm sorry I'm not there to help you end it on a better note," Arrow said.

"Me too. Although in a way you *are* here with me and helping the day get better," she said.

"You're sweet."

"No, I'm not. I'm a badass survivor who isn't going to let shit get me down anymore," she retorted.

"Fuck yeah, you are," Arrow agreed. "And there's nothing that turns me on more than a strong woman who knows who she is and what she wants."

"I'm not sure about those last two things, but I'm trying to be stronger . . . at least outwardly."

"Trust me, you are, beautiful. Inside and out."

"You always know exactly what to say."

"I try. How are you feeling at the moment? You said your stomach hurt this morning. Do you still have a headache?"

"Yeah. My stomach feels a little better. I made some soup earlier, and I'm trying to drink a lot of OJ. Mom's been buying it by the gallon for me. It's been forever since I've had it. I'd forgotten how much I love it, even if it's almost too sweet for me. I've been watering it down, and that makes it more palatable."

"I'm sorry you're sick, beautiful," Arrow said.

"It's okay. I guess it's the stress of adjusting to normal life. And that's sad because it's not like I'm really getting out much, but I've had to interact with more people recently than I had to in the past twelve months combined. Now . . . what did you have to tell me, and what's the question?"

"Nina's mom talked to Rex today. She's having a hard time."

"A hard time? How? What's wrong?" Morgan asked.

"She's not sleeping well at night and is having nightmares."

"That sounds familiar," Morgan muttered.

Arrow hated that for her, but kept going. "She wakes up at night screaming your name. She's convinced that the bad men—her words—have found you and have taken you away again. She thinks it's her fault, and no matter how many times her mom tells her that you're safe, that the bad men don't have you, she refuses to believe it."

"Oh shit," Morgan said. "I need to see her. If I leave tonight I can be there by morning. I'll have to rent a car, but—"

"Morgan," Arrow interrupted. "Take a breath."

He heard her inhale then say, "Sorry. I just . . . I hate to even think of her that way. She was so scared when she was thrown into that room with me. Every time one of the men came to the door, they'd threaten to take her if I didn't do what they wanted. They learned pretty fast that I'd be extra compliant if they threatened Nina. I didn't think she really understood what was going on, but I guess I should have. She's smarter than I gave her credit for."

"My question was going to be if you'd consider coming back up here for a while and maybe going to therapy with Nina. I think if she sees you on a regular basis, and you guys talk about what happened together, that she might relax and she could heal faster," Arrow said. "But I can tell I don't even need to ask."

"No, you don't." Her voice dropped to a whisper, as though she was scared if she spoke too loudly, her mom would hear her from wherever she was. "I'm not happy here. I love my mom, but I miss you. And I'd like to get to know Allye and Chloe better."

"I can come down and pick you up tomorrow," Arrow said, his entire body sagging with relief. He hadn't thought she'd refuse, but hearing her say the words was enough to make his stress levels even out.

"Awesome," Morgan breathed.

"I'd love it if you stayed with me, but I also talked to Allye and Gray, and they said you were more than welcome to crash at their house. I'm sure Ro and Chloe would be happy if you stayed at their place too. All I'm saying is that you have options, beautiful."

"Do you want me to stay with Allye or Chloe?" she asked, the uncertainty easy to hear in her voice.

"Fuck no," Arrow said. "That night I held you in my arms on the couch was one of the best sleeps I've had in months, simply because I was near you. I want you here, but I don't want you to feel any pressure about anything. You know how I feel about you, about how I want our relationship to be . . . I haven't hidden that from you. But the last thing I want is for you to agree to do something you're not comfortable with. When I say there's no pressure about this, I mean it. If you decide to stay with Allye, I'm okay with that, but I'm guessing Gray will get sick of seeing my ugly mug. Same goes for Ro if you decide to stay at his place."

He relaxed a bit when he heard her chuckle. "If you get tired of having me there, you'll tell me, right?" she asked.

"Morgan, the day I get sick of you being in my space is the day Rex will need to commit me for having lost my mind."

"If you're sure, I'd love to stay with you at your apartment, Arrow," Morgan said.

"Awesome. I'll see if Chloe can go to the store while I'm on my way tomorrow and stock up on orange juice for you."

Morgan chuckled again. "Sounds like a plan."

"Is your mom going to be okay with you leaving so soon after you got there?" Arrow asked.

"I'll try to make sure I talk to her every day to make her feel better about it. She won't be thrilled, but I'm twenty-seven. I need to get past what happened to me and live my own life. I can't stay with her forever, as much as she might want me to. I'm sure it'll be fine."

"If it's not, you call me," Arrow ordered.

"I will. But my mom will get over any disappointment and worry," Morgan insisted. "What time should I expect you tomorrow?"

"Before ten. I'm going to head out of here around four, four thirty. I'd leave right now, but I didn't get enough sleep last night and don't want to risk passing out behind the wheel of my truck."

"Please drive safe, Arrow. I couldn't handle it if something happened to you because of me."

"Nothing that happens to me is your fault, beautiful. Now, go drink some more OJ—it's good for you. Get some sleep, pack your things. I'll be there before you know it."

"Thank you."

"No, thank *you*," Arrow told her. "Not a lot of people would be willing to drop everything for a kid they don't even really know."

"I might not know her all that well, but spending a week together under the crappy conditions we did seems to have forged an unbreakable bond."

"As did spending a day hiding under a bunch of cardboard boxes," Arrow said dryly. "I'll see you soon, beautiful."

"Bye, Arrow."

"Bye."

Arrow had to consciously refrain from telling Morgan that he loved her before he hung up. Shaking his head at himself for how sappy he felt, he forced himself to dial Rex's number and let him know that Morgan had agreed to come back to Colorado Springs to help Nina. After that was done, he called Chloe and asked if she would stop at the store for him tomorrow, and he gave her a list of things he wanted her to buy so Morgan would hopefully feel more at home in his apartment.

Just when he'd gotten settled into bed, his phone rang. It was Meat.

"Hey. What's up?"

"Just calling to give you a heads-up that Ball and Black are headed to Atlanta tomorrow."

"Why?"

"To have a little chat with Lance and Lane Buswell."

"What did you find out about them?" Arrow asked, sitting up in bed.

"Nothing that you didn't already know, but we all agreed that it would be better to talk to them in person to see their reactions to certain questions and revelations about what Morgan went through. They're planning on talking to Sarah and Karen as well. A trip to the nightclub she disappeared from is also on their agenda. Basically they just want to get the lay of the land in person and see if anything sticks out."

"Keep me informed?" Arrow asked.

"Of course."

"I'm headed down to Albuquerque tomorrow to pick Morgan up and bring her back here."

"It's about time," Meat said.

"She's only been down there a week," Arrow protested.

"Exactly. It's about time," Meat repeated. "Later."

Arrow shook his head in exasperation at his friend. Meat was certainly the most unique of their bunch. He made incredible furniture and definitely knew his way around computers, but he was also the most outspoken at times. If Arrow had to guess, he'd say the man had some sort of attention deficit disorder. Something that made it hard for him to sit still, and ensured his hands had to be busy at all times. Something that led to him blurting out whatever crossed his mind, whether it was entirely appropriate or not.

But Arrow and the rest of the team had been around him enough to find it endearing instead of annoying. Meat was just . . . Meat.

Arrow lay back and forced himself to close his eyes. He had to get some sleep if he was going to be able to drive for ten hours round-trip the next day. The last thing he would ever do was put Morgan in danger.

It was hard, as he wanted nothing more than to fantasize about having her in his space once again, but eventually he fell into a light sleep.

Chapter Fifteen

"Hi, Nina. How are you today?" Morgan asked as she hugged the little girl tightly.

In the last week since she'd been back in Colorado Springs, she'd seen Nina every day at therapy. The sessions had been tough, but necessary. She'd had sessions with Nina, by herself, with Nina and her mom, as well as a couple with Arrow.

She hadn't liked feeling vulnerable in front of Arrow. She wanted to be the strong woman he thought he saw when he looked at her, but the therapist had shown her that she could be struggling with what happened to her and still be strong at the same time.

"Hi, Morgan!" Nina chirped. "I'm good. How're you?"

"Good. I fell asleep at eight o'clock last night and didn't wake up once until I had to pee at six in the morning! What about you?"

Nina beamed. "Me too! Well, I got up when it was still dark and checked to make sure Mommy was still there, but then I went right back to sleep."

"Good for you!" Morgan praised. She hated that the little girl was still waking up to make sure she wasn't alone, but that was much better than waking up with night terrors or crying hysterically. Today was their last session together—at least, she was hoping it was. If Nina needed to talk something through later, Morgan would always be available.

"Hi, Arrow," Nina said with a small smile as she stepped away from Morgan.

"Hey, girl. I like your hair."

Nina beamed. "Thanks! I had Mommy braid it like Merida's."

"The girl from the movie *Brave*. You know, the archer," Morgan whispered behind her hand as she pretended to scratch her face.

"Ah, the archer," Arrow said as he wrapped a hand around Morgan's waist. "Morgan and I watched that movie the other night. She's something else, huh?"

Nina nodded agreeably and started describing her favorite part of the movie.

"Thanks for the save," Arrow said softly as the little girl went on and on. He leaned in and nuzzled Morgan's hair.

"You're welcome," Morgan told him as she gave him her weight. The more time she spent with Arrow, the more she fell for him. He wasn't perfect by any stretch. He had a tendency to forget clean clothes in the dryer, and he followed behind her to double check some of the things she'd already done, like locking the door. He also straightened things in the cupboard that she'd just put away. But all the wonderful things he did for her more than made up for the small quirks. If those were the worst things he did, she could definitely live with them.

"How's your stomach today?" he asked when Nina had wound down and run off to tell her mom something.

"Good. I must've had a twenty-four-hour bug or something," Morgan told him.

"It was a lot longer than twenty-four hours, beautiful," Arrow reminded her.

"I know. Whatever. I feel much better now. Must be all that OJ you forced me to drink," she teased.

"Forced?" Arrow asked and dug his fingers into her sides, tickling her.

Morgan choked back the screech that threatened to break free and tried to squirm away from his fingers. "Stop!" she ordered.

He did, immediately, but gripped her hips tightly as he held her to him. Morgan hooked her fingers together at the small of his back and leaned against him. She'd always hated being shorter than everyone else, but with Arrow, she loved it. Loved how she fit against him perfectly. Loved how he seemed to surround her with his strength.

"Do you have an individual meeting today? Or just the joint one with Nina?" Arrow asked.

"Just the one with Nina and her mom."

"I know I ask too much, but are you really doing better here?" he asked. "And don't lie just because it's what you think I want to hear. I've loved having you with me for the last week. I love falling asleep with you on the couch. But if you have any doubts, or if you need your space, I'm not going to be upset if you tell me that you want to get your own apartment or go back to Albuquerque."

"Do *you* want me to go?" Morgan asked instead of answering his question.

"Abso-fucking-lutely not," Arrow said with conviction.

"What if I said I was tired of sleeping on the couch?" Morgan asked.

"I've been camping out on the couch because you said you aren't sleeping well by yourself. But if you're ready to stay in the guest room, I can make that happen. All I need is for you to tell me."

"I don't want to sleep in the guest room," Morgan said, trying to sound as certain as she felt inside. "And I've gotten used to sleeping with you . . ."

She watched as Arrow's eyes closed. When they opened, she saw a mix of emotions. "Tonight, we can sleep in my bed and see how it goes."

Morgan smiled. "Good."

"I'd like you to consider something else," Arrow said.

"What?"

"Not calling your mom tonight." He held up a hand when she opened her mouth to protest. "I know, I know. She's worried about you and isn't taking it well that you moved back up here. But she's stressing you out. All I'm suggesting is that you maybe back off a little on how much you talk to her, not that you push her out of your life altogether or anything."

Morgan knew he was right. Her mom *was* stressing her out. She'd flipped when Morgan had told her she'd be going back up to Colorado Springs. Even when Morgan had promised she'd call her every day and let her know how she was doing, Ellie still pressed her to stay. Morgan understood. She was Ellie's baby and had been missing for a year. So it was understandable that her mom was leery over her moving out. But the nightly whining and begging for her to come back to Albuquerque had started to take its toll.

"Okay," she told Arrow. "My dad still wants me to talk to Diane Sawyer. He's going to call tonight to talk to me about the interview again."

"Have you thought any more about it?" Arrow asked.

Morgan nodded. "Yeah. I think I'm going to do it. I watched her interview with Jaycee Dugard, and she was very respectful and didn't ask any invasive questions. My dad has a point, I do need to give some interviews so the press will back off, but I guess I'm just scared."

"You know whatever you decide, I'll support, right?" Arrow asked.

Morgan nodded immediately. "Yeah. And I appreciate it. It's just that I'm so sick of being between my parents. My dad thinks one thing, and by default, my mom will take the other side. And when Mom wants to do something for me, Dad decides it's not healthy and tries to throw money at me to get me to do what *he* wants. It's exhausting."

"Speaking of parents . . . I need to get you up to Michigan to meet my mom and sister."

"Um . . . what?" Morgan croaked.

"What, what?" Arrow parroted.

"I can't meet your mom and sister!"

"Why not?"

"Because," Morgan blurted.

"That's not an answer."

"I just . . . they're your family. Your only family."

"And I love them very much and want them to meet the woman I want to spend the rest of my life with," Arrow retorted. "What's wrong with that?"

Morgan could only stare at him in shock.

Arrow shook her slightly. "Morgan, me wanting to be with you shouldn't be a surprise. Hell, I practically told you that the same day we met. I'm not going to change my mind. Besides, I've met *your* family, why shouldn't you meet mine?"

Morgan smacked his arm. "I swear you're going to give me a heart attack one of these days," she complained.

"What'd I do?"

"Meeting a guy's parents is a big deal, Arrow. You can't spring that on me out of the blue." She didn't know why she was complaining, really. She knew how Arrow felt about her. Knew he was the most patient man she'd ever met, and she wanted the right to call him hers more than she'd ever wanted anything. Okay, not more than she'd wanted to escape her captors, but almost.

She was still confused about what it was he saw in her, but through his every action and every word, he was convincing her that he was serious. He liked her. *Really* liked her. Even though she was still dealing with the psychological aspects of having been kidnapped. He told her over and over again to cut herself some slack, that it would probably take years to get over what had happened—if she completely got over it at all. She didn't want to think about still having flashbacks and nightmares years from now, but when Arrow had told her that he'd be there for her no matter what, it made her feel better.

He leaned down and kissed her forehead. "They're waiting for you," he said, and nodded to the now open door that led to the offices where the doctors had their sessions. "I'm proud of you, beautiful," he told her. "I'll be back in an hour to pick you up. I'm going to stop by a friend's house and take a look at a few of his outlets that aren't working properly. Call if you need me before then."

He took a step back and reluctantly dropped his hand from her waist.

"Thanks, Arrow."

"Anytime, beautiful. Anytime." Then he was gone.

~

"Hey, Morgan," Allye said as she came through the door to Morgan's doctor's reception area. Two hours had passed since Morgan had said goodbye to Arrow, and when he hadn't been there when she was finished, she'd been worried. But then she remembered belatedly that she'd turned off her phone for the session, as were the rules.

She'd missed a text from him saying that he wouldn't be able to pick her up, and that Allye would be there as soon as she could after her dance class.

"Hi," Morgan said. "Do you know where Arrow is?"

Allye frowned. "He didn't tell you?"

"Tell me what? Is he all right?"

The other woman waved her hand. "Yeah, he's fine. But someone slashed his tires. All four of them. He had to call a tow truck to take the car to Ro's."

"Slashed his tires? Seriously? That sucks!" Morgan exclaimed.

"He definitely wasn't pleased," Allye said. "Especially since his were the only ones damaged in the parking lot at his friend's condo complex. You ready to go?"

Morgan nodded, thinking about Arrow's tires as she followed Allye out to her car.

"Arrow told me to just bring you to Ro's place. Ro's a mechanic, if you didn't know, and he's putting new tires on Arrow's truck now. I hope that's okay."

"Of course," Morgan told her. "Did he say who he thought did it?"

Allye scrunched up her nose. "No, not to me. Gray and the other guys still think I need to be protected against every little thing. I told Gray that hearing about kidnappings and burglaries isn't going to throw me into a funk because of what happened to me, but he still treats me extra carefully when it comes to talking about his job or other bad shit that happens in the world."

"Can I ask you a question?"

"Of course. You can ask anything," Allye said.

"From what Arrow has said, you and Gray got together pretty quickly . . . how did you know he was the one?"

"I was resistant at first. I mean, I figured there was no way a man like Gray would really want to be with me. First, I was a mission for him. Second . . . well . . . I just figured he'd be happier with someone more like him. Someone who loved adrenaline rushes and wanted to be out lifting weights, exercising, and generally kicking ass."

Morgan chuckled. "You mean that's not you?"

Allye returned the laugh. "I mean, I love to dance, and I guess that's exercise, but I swear if I wasn't a dancer I'd be about fifty pounds heavier because I love sitting at home, watching TV, and chatting with my friends."

"So how did you know?"

"Honestly? I think it was when I couldn't imagine myself *not* being with Gray that I was convinced. After I was rescued—the second time—I could've stayed in San Francisco and gotten on with my life there. But even being with Gray for the short time I was, I came to crave seeing him in the morning and every evening. I loved talking with him about his day, and I loved simply watching him at his desk working on someone else's taxes. It's silly, but I had never felt as comfortable around someone as I did Gray."

"That's exactly how I feel," Morgan said. "But it's crazy . . . isn't it?"

"No. Listen, men like the Mountain Mercenaries live their life at full blast. They like what they like, they hate what they hate, and they love who they love. Period. They'll defend their friends and family to the death, and if necessary, they'd do the same for anyone they were sent to rescue and/or protect."

"That's what I'm afraid of. That when he realizes that I don't need protecting anymore, he'll come to his senses and wonder what the hell he's doing with me," Morgan said.

"I can't tell you not to feel that way because, honestly, I still feel a little bit of that. But what I've come to realize is that Gray didn't feel that way about the hundreds of people he rescued before me. He didn't ask *them* to move in with him. He didn't kiss *them* as if he couldn't get enough, and he certainly didn't make love to them. I can't tell you why he was attracted to me or what made him decide he wanted to spend the rest of his life with me, over every other woman he'd ever met. But, in the end, it doesn't matter. It *is* me he picked. It *is* me he wants to sleep with every night. I make his eyes light up when he sees me, and I make his pupils dilate when he sees me naked.

"And I don't ask myself why anymore. I accept it for what it is, and I'll fight tooth and nail to keep it. To keep *him*. I deserve him. I deserve to have a man who treats me like the most precious thing in his life. If he wants to protect me by not letting me watch the news and by doing his best not to talk about the missions he goes on with his friends, I'm okay with that because it means he loves me. And that love is the most precious thing in my life. Does that make sense?"

Morgan nodded and tried to blink away the tears in her eyes. For the first time since she'd met Arrow, she stopped thinking about why he seemed to like her as much as he did, and tried to think about it the other way. Why *shouldn't* he like her? She was a good person. She'd not only managed to survive what had happened to her, but she hadn't been broken by it—at least not beyond repair. She deserved a man like Arrow. She'd earned him, in a sense.

Allye was right. It wasn't as if Arrow was living in a bubble. She'd seen more than one woman shoot him flirtatious glances. She'd been sitting right next to him when a waitress slipped him her phone number. But he hadn't been interested in them. He'd continued to treat *her* as if she was the most important person in his life.

She was as worthy of love as the next person, and why shouldn't she grab hold and give a relationship with Arrow her best shot?

She couldn't stop the smile that curled her lips.

"I take it by that smile you've made a decision about something?" Allye asked.

"Yeah. I've been telling myself what *you* used to, that I'm too messed up. That what happened to me made me somehow less worthy. But I think I should be thinking about the entire situation differently. I need a man who can help me pick myself up and dust myself off, not someone I need to try to suck up to, or feel like I have to always look my best for. Hell, Arrow spent an hour trying to get mats out of my hair, and not once did he curl his nose at my looks. Why *shouldn't* I get a man like Arrow? I'd say that I deserve him more than the average woman does."

"Right on!" Allye cheered. "That's exactly right. We didn't ask for what happened to us. And we ended up with men who could appreciate us for who we are and what we went through. They don't hold us down or back—they prop us up and help us keep going when things get tough."

"I'm still concerned that it's too fast," Morgan admitted.

"Don't be. As I said, these men know what they want. And if Arrow has decided he wants you, that's it for him. *You're* it for him. Don't fight it. Just go with the flow. Trust me, it'll be the best thing that has ever happened to you."

"Okay."

"Okay," Allye agreed as she pulled down a long driveway with pine trees surrounding the property.

"This is so beautiful," Morgan breathed. "I would love to wake up to a view like this every morning."

"Don't say that in front of Arrow," Allye warned.

"Why?"

"Because if he's anything like Gray, he'll buy a piece of property and start plans to build a house before you can blink."

"Oh shit, you're right," Morgan said.

"I know I am," Allye said as she turned off the engine. "Other women would take advantage of their men wanting to give them every little thing they wanted, but not us."

"No," Morgan agreed. "Not us. Thanks, Allye. I . . . It helps to talk to someone who's been where I have."

"Anytime," she said. "I mean it. Our men are a lot alike. They can be hard to figure out at first. I'm here anytime you want to chat."

"I appreciate it."

Morgan startled when the door next to her opened, but she relaxed when she saw it was Arrow standing there. He held out a hand, and Morgan took it, allowing him to help her up and out of Allye's car.

"You okay?"

"Of course. Are *you* okay?" she asked back.

In answer, his head tilted, and he squinted his eyes as he looked her over. "Something's different," he declared.

"What?"

"About you. Something's different. I take it the talk with the therapist went well?" he asked.

Morgan looked over at Allye, who was busy kissing Gray, and smiled. "You could say that," she said mysteriously. "But seriously, what's up with your tires?"

Arrow shrugged. "Some asshole decided he was bored," he said. "Come on. Ro's almost done, then we can leave."

Morgan smiled at Allye as she passed her and Gray and gripped Arrow's hand tighter as he towed her to Ro's garage.

"Hey, Ro," she said as she entered, feeling more confident after her talk with Allye.

Arrow's truck was up on a lift, and Ro was standing by a tire when she called out her greeting. He looked over at her and raised one eyebrow. "Hey," he replied. "Looks like the session with Nina went well today."

Morgan nodded. "It did. I think she's finally getting over the hump. She's not one hundred percent over what happened, but I have a feeling she's not going to wake up screaming anymore . . . at least I hope."

"And you?" Ro asked, wiping his hands on a rag. "You're okay too?"

"I'm getting there," Morgan told him honestly. "I've got good days and bad days, but I'm thankful to be alive. I didn't ask for what happened to me, and I've got too much life left to live to wallow in misery for the rest of those years."

Arrow wrapped his arms around her from behind and held her to him. His lips brushed against her temple as he said, "I'm so proud of you."

Morgan shrugged. "I'm kinda proud of myself, actually."

"Good girl," Ro mumbled, and turned his attention back to the tire in front of him. "I'm almost done, Arrow," he said.

"Thanks."

Ro waved off the gratitude. "Did Meat have any luck finding surveillance footage to see who did this to your truck?"

Arrow shook his head. "No. There were cameras in the lot, but they were all pointed in the opposite direction from where I parked."

"I'm assuming you educated them on the correct way to use surveillance cameras and they've changed the positioning of them now?"

"Meat did," Arrow said. "After he chewed them a new asshole and told them they were opening themselves up to a hell of a lawsuit if someone got hurt in their parking lot when all their fucking cameras were focused on the entrance to the building instead of the cars."

"Bloody wankers," Ro said under his breath.

Morgan wanted to giggle, but refrained. She loved listening to Ro. His slight British accent was sexy, and the phrases he used now and then were so quintessentially British, she found herself almost sighing in pleasure when she heard them.

"Hey, no mooning over my friend," Arrow scolded.

Now Morgan *did* giggle and turn in his arms. "I'm thinking I need to find myself a nice Brit. Or maybe a Scot. There's just something about a Scottish accent that does it for me. I loved watching *Outlander* before I was taken."

"If you want a Scottish accent, I can do that," Arrow said, in a per-fect imitation of Jamie Fraser from *Outlander*. "Maybe you want me to throw you over my shoulder and take you back to my castle and have my wicked way with you?"

Morgan burst out laughing and threw her arms around Arrow's neck. "I didn't know you could talk like that!"

Arrow smiled back and said in his normal voice, "There's a lot of things you don't know about me, beautiful."

She sobered. "I know. But I want to learn every single one of them."

The look in his eyes felt like it scorched her where she stood. She realized for the first time just how much she'd been holding back with Arrow. Hadn't told him how much it meant, spending time with him. How much she liked him. She'd still been afraid if she admitted it out loud, somehow he'd change his mind about her.

But after her talk with Allye, she realized that everything the woman said was dead-on. Arrow wasn't the kind of man to mess with anyone's head. He wasn't with her because he wanted sex. She was about the worst bet he could get, as far as that was concerned. He was with her because he liked her, and she'd be an idiot if she let him slip through her fingers.

The timing was a bit awkward, as she wasn't sure she was completely ready for a boyfriend and all that having one entailed, but Arrow had promised to go slow with her . . . and she trusted him.

It was that bone-deep belief that he would never go any faster or further than she wanted, as well as her talk with Allye, that allowed her to let go of some of her fears when it came to Arrow.

"You ready to go home?" he asked.

"With you? Yes," Morgan told him, not shying away from looking into his eyes as she said it.

"You *are* different," he said quietly.

"Me and Allye had a good talk," Morgan admitted.

"Remind me to thank her later."

Morgan smiled at him.

"Hopefully this was a fluke," Ro said as he threw the keys to the truck to Arrow, who caught them one-handed. "But keep your eyes peeled just in case. It wouldn't be cool if someone was trying to get rid of you to get to Morgan."

The words were said offhandedly, as if the other man didn't really believe what he was saying, but they had an immediate impact on Morgan.

She stiffened and turned to stare at Ro with worried eyes.

"Ro . . . ," Arrow warned belatedly.

"Bloody hell," Ro said under his breath.

Morgan turned to Arrow. "Do you think that's what happened? Is whoever wanted me gone here, in the Springs? Are they watching me? Will they try to kill you to get to me?"

"Shhhh," Arrow soothed. "No, that's not what we think happened today."

"Then what? I mean, it's not normal to have all four tires slashed. One, maybe, if someone was just having fun. But all four? That means you were targeted. How did they know where you'd be? Are they following you? Oh my God, maybe I should leave!"

"Morgan," Arrow said sternly, grabbing her shoulders and forcing her to still. "Look at me."

She brought her eyes up to his and tried to slow down her breathing. The last thing she needed was to pass out in Ro's garage because she was hyperventilating.

"I'm fine. Nothing's going to happen to me. You're safe. Hear me?"

She nodded, even though she wasn't convinced.

"I don't think anyone is after me. We've been keeping tabs on your ex and others back in Atlanta. They're still there. No one has traveled up here to Colorado to try to get me."

"They could've hired someone," Morgan whispered.

"True. But as annoying as this was, they're only tires. It was probably punk kids. We're all going to be a bit more vigilant as a result, but no one thinks you're in any danger. This is what we do. We come up with possible scenarios and either prove or disprove them. It's how we work. Ro was merely throwing the possibility out there. Not stating it as a fact."

"No one can get to your apartment, though, can they?" Morgan asked, staring up at him. "I mean, it's safe, right?"

"Absolutely," Arrow said. "I've got a doorman, and we're on the third floor. There are cameras all over the building. In the lobby, stairwells, parking lot, elevator. You're safe with me."

Morgan knew she was freaking out, but she couldn't help it. It had been a long time since she'd felt safe, and it was as if someone had pulled the rug out from under her once more. She didn't want to be taken again, but she also didn't want Arrow or any of his friends hurt while protecting her either.

Something else occurred to her. "What about my mom and dad? Are they safe? Should we tell them to be on the lookout?"

Arrow palmed her face and brought his forehead down to hers. "I'll have Meat call them. But we have no reason to think anyone is in danger, beautiful. I swear to you that if we think that has changed, we'll take care of your parents. Get bodyguards for them or something. You're safe. We're safe. Your family is safe."

"Why is this happening?" she whispered.

"We don't know that *anything* is happening," Arrow said.

"But your tires were slashed," she protested.

"They were. But that does *not* mean that whoever kidnapped you is going to try again. Take a deep breath."

She did.

"And another. Good. Now look at me."

Morgan pulled back just enough so she could meet Arrow's gaze.

"Do you trust me?"

She nodded before she'd even thought about his question.

"Then trust that I'd never do anything that would put you or your loved ones in danger."

"Okay."

Arrow leaned down and kissed her before wrapping an arm around her waist. Ro had given them some space, but seeing they were ready to go, he came forward.

"I'm sorry, Morgan. I shouldn't have said anything."

"No," she said firmly. "You should've. I'm not a helpless five-year-old like Nina. I need to know what's going on. Don't keep things from me. I need information if I'm going to protect myself. How would you feel if you knew I was a target again and didn't tell me, and I went to the store one day by myself, thinking everything was fine, and I got taken again? You'd feel guilty, and I would be so pissed at all of you. So don't ever *not* tell me what's going on to try to protect me."

Interestingly enough, Ro was smiling by the time she finished speaking, which angered her.

"Don't laugh at me," she hissed.

The smile left his face immediately. "I'm not laughing at you, love," Ro said. "I'm chuffed that you're so fierce. I like it."

"Well . . . okay then," Morgan said, at a loss for words.

"Come on. Let's go home," Arrow said, tugging her forward.

"I didn't get to say bye to Allye or Chloe," Morgan said.

"I'll have her call you later," Ro said as Arrow helped her into the passenger side of his truck.

The second his door shut, Morgan said, "Don't get hurt because of me."

Without outwardly reacting, Arrow started his truck and backed up before putting the vehicle in drive and heading down Ro's driveway. "Here's the thing," Arrow said seriously. "I've spent almost my entire adult life fighting for other people. In the Marines, I was fighting for all Americans in general. I fought for the repressed and downtrodden. When I got out and joined the Mountain Mercenaries, I was fighting for women and kids who needed a champion."

He glanced over at her, and Morgan inhaled at the look in his eyes.

"But for the first time in my life, my fight is personal. I'm fighting for *you*. For *us*. At this point, I honestly don't care who was behind your kidnapping or why they did it. All I care about is making sure they don't get a chance to do it again. I've never felt as passionately about something in my life as I do about keeping you safe. So if someone wants to come after *me* instead of you? I say bring it, because they'll make a mistake. Assholes always do. And when they do, I'll be ready to stomp them into the ground.

"But you have to let me do my job, Morgan. I've been hurt before, and I'll probably be hurt again in the future, but until my heart stops beating in my chest, I'll keep fighting. I can deal with pain. What I can't deal with is seeing *you* in pain. So you're just going to have to come to terms with that, beautiful."

"I . . . I don't know what to say to that," Morgan admitted. "On one hand, I think it's sexist and a little naive for you to sit there and tell me it's okay for you to get hurt, but not me. And you're not Superman. If something happens to you, you can't just jump up and take on an attacker if you're bleeding to death or something. But on the other hand, what you said makes me want to weep. I've never had anyone who put me first like that. Ever."

"You do now," Arrow said, and put his hand on her knee.

Morgan didn't say anything else during the ride back to his house, but neither did he. She was scared, but somehow Arrow made everything seem less frightening.

By the time they arrived at his apartment complex, she'd calmed down. Yeah, having his tires slashed sucked, but it didn't mean that her kidnapper was waiting in the wings to snatch her. Maybe she'd overreacted.

Smiling at Arrow when he stopped the engine, she asked, "What's on the agenda for the rest of the day?"

"Grocery shopping, dinner, and relaxing in front of the TV," he replied.

"Sounds perfect. Although eventually I need to start thinking about what I want to do with the rest of my life," Morgan mused. "I can't mooch off you or my mom forever."

"Why not?"

"Because," Morgan said firmly. "That's not me. I need to work. I like working."

"Okay, okay," Arrow said, holding up his hands in capitulation. "But not tonight."

"Not tonight," she agreed.

As they walked to the door of the building, Morgan couldn't help but surreptitiously take a look around. She saw nothing out of the ordinary. Robert the doorman greeted them warmly as they entered and headed for the elevator.

Satisfied that she'd overreacted, Morgan let herself relax into Arrow. She was safe. Arrow was safe. Her family was safe. Things were just fine.

Chapter Sixteen

The next few days were uneventful, as far as new information about Morgan's kidnapping went. Arrow ripped Ro a new one when Morgan wasn't around. He hadn't wanted to worry her about anything, but Ro's casual comment about watching his back had blown that out of the water. She'd tried to convince him that she was fine and that she'd rather know about his suspicions than be kept in the dark, but he hated seeing her so jumpy.

It wasn't that he was going to keep information about her kidnapping from her, but he'd wanted to give her time to truly relax first.

Her parents weren't helping the situation at all. Her dad was hounding her to talk to the press. As much of an asset as he'd been when she'd disappeared, keeping her case in the public eye and not letting anyone forget about her, he was now a liability when it came to Morgan moving on with her life.

Carl was still making the rounds on the morning shows, talking about Morgan as if he was the one in charge of her recovery. He'd flat-out lied in several interviews, saying he was right by Morgan's side as she integrated back into society.

And her mother wasn't much better. While she was avoiding the press, Ellie was hounding Morgan to come back to Albuquerque. She was adamant her daughter was too fragile to be in a relationship right now, and that she needed to be with family so she could heal properly.

She texted day and night, constantly needing reassurance that Morgan was all right. It was driving Arrow crazy. He was glad Ellie seemed to genuinely love her daughter and was worried about her, but the emotional strain it was putting on Morgan was the final straw.

They'd argued about how much Morgan spoke with her mom, and in the end, Morgan had agreed to only talk to Ellie twice a week, and he'd agreed to not complain about the woman.

Morgan was researching what it would take to start up her bee-and-honey business in Colorado, and Arrow had begun the process of looking for a house and property so she could have the bees she loved so much. Her landlord back in Atlanta had rented her home to someone else when she hadn't returned after several months. Her dad had packed her things up and put them in storage.

Arrow hadn't told her that he'd started looking for a piece of land that would work for her business, deciding that things needed to settle first. Once she figured out what she needed to do to get her business back up and running again, he'd talk to her about living arrangements.

They'd been sleeping in his bed every night since his tires had been slashed. At first it had been awkward for both of them. For Arrow, because he'd never actually had a woman spend the entire night in his bed, and for Morgan because of her abduction.

But after that first night, things had seemed . . . right. Arrow wore a pair of cotton sleep pants to bed, and she wore a tank top and boy shorts. She was absolutely gorgeous, gaining weight slowly and in all the right places. Arrow went to bed and woke up with a hard-on every night and day. But he'd suffer through a million hard-ons before moving one step in a direction she wasn't yet ready to go in.

And she definitely wasn't ready to go there.

Arrow knew it as easily as he knew his name.

It was five thirty on the sixth morning after they'd begun sleeping in the same bed together, and Arrow woke with Morgan wrapped around him. She clung to him from the second she climbed into bed until she woke up. She held on to him as if he'd disappear if she didn't.

He loved having her close, but it was also torture. Her leg was hitched up over his lap, pressing against his cock. Her breaths were slow and even, and every time she exhaled, he felt her warm breath waft over his chest. His nipples were puckered into little points. If she moved her head a fraction of an inch, she could take one of those nipples into her mouth.

The thought was intoxicating, and he couldn't help but close his eyes and fantasize about her moving over him. Down his chest to his pants, pulling them down over his engorged dick and taking him into her mouth. She'd look up at him coyly as she slurped and sucked.

He came back to reality when he felt Morgan stiffen against him.

Opening his eyes, he looked into hers and saw she was staring at him with trepidation. She was stiff as a board against him, as if she was scared to move a muscle.

"Morning," he said easily.

"Good morning," she returned carefully.

Arrow wanted to punch someone in his frustration. She'd come a really long way in her recovery. He knew she wouldn't ever be the same as she was before she'd been kidnapped, but he hated seeing her scared of *him*.

"You're safe with me," he said softly. "I'd never do anything that caused you pain."

At his words, she relaxed against him once more. "I know," she mumbled, dropping her eyes. "I just . . . I woke up and felt your . . . *you* against my leg, and it threw me back there for a second."

"I figured that's what happened. It's fine."

"It's *not* fine," she said with heat. "I hate that I can't show you how much I like having you here with me. That I can't be normal with you."

"What's normal, anyway?" Arrow said lightly. "Normal is what we make it."

Susan Stoker

"I want to be able to wake up and not immediately freeze, thinking I'm back *there*, and wonder if today's the day they'll kill me after they take what they want. I want to be able to wake up with my boyfriend's mouth on my body and not think about what they took from me without permission so many times. I want to be able to get lost in your touch, not flinch because it reminds me of *them*."

"You will," Arrow said, keeping the fury from his tone by sheer force of will.

"When? By the time I don't think of them every second of every day, I'm afraid you'll have gotten sick of waiting for me. I'm afraid of losing you before I've even really had you."

Arrow couldn't stop himself from pulling her on top of him, making sure to pull her up so she was straddling his stomach instead of his lap. The last thing she needed was his cock pressing against her pussy.

"You will *never* lose me," he said firmly. "I am not going to get sick of waiting for you. There's no timetable on recovery from rape. You know that. As I told you when we were talking with your therapist, I'm in this for the long haul. I will never force you, beautiful. Whatever you choose to give me, whenever you choose to give it, is up to you. I'll spend every day making you feel safe again. Inside this apartment, in this bed, and even out in the real world. Your safe place will be right here, in my arms. Whatever happens out there has no effect on my feelings for you. I love you, Morgan. You're *it* for me."

Tears fell from her eyes as she stared down at him.

He used his thumbs to wipe them away from her cheeks before pulling her down so she was resting on his chest. He said nothing else, feeling helpless as she sobbed. All he could do was hold her and rub her back. He didn't tell her not to cry. He didn't tell her everything would be all right. He just held her tightly, trying to tell her without words that he was there for her, and he always would be.

Eventually her sobs tapered off and she sniffed against him.

"Better?" he asked softly.

She nodded.

"Good. Want to get up and shower, or lie here a bit longer?"

"Lie here," she said softly.

"Okay, beautiful. I'm going to get up, shower, and get breakfast started. You snooze. I'll wake you up when your omelet is done."

"You're too good for me."

Arrow snorted. "Hardly. I'm still waiting for you to come to your senses and realize that you could do so much better than me." Then he scooted out from under her and covered her with the blanket. He kissed her temple and headed for the bathroom.

He was in the shower with his back to the door when he heard something behind him.

Looking over his shoulder, Arrow could only stare in disbelief as a naked Morgan stepped into the small enclosure and shut the door behind her.

"What—"

He forgot what he was going to ask when she wrapped her arms around him from behind and her hands reached for his semihard cock. The second she touched him, all the blood in his body went to his dick, and he grew in her hands.

He grabbed her wrists and held her still as he turned his head and asked, "Morgan? What are you doing?"

"I would think it's obvious," she replied, but didn't struggle in his grip. "I just . . . I'm tired of feeling so helpless. I'm not ready for you to . . . you know. But I want to give this to you."

"Are you sure? I love your hands on me, but this is not something I expect from you until you're absolutely ready."

"I'm not at a place yet where I can say that I love you back," Morgan told him. "But I can tell you that I've never felt for anyone else what I do for you. Thinking about you hurting when I can do something to help makes me feel physically ill. I want to touch you, Arrow. I want to be the one to make you feel good."

"You make me feel good just by being with me," he reassured her. "If at any time you get overwhelmed with memories, I want you to stop. It'll hurt *me* if you're suffering just to give me pleasure."

"Arrow, believe me, this is *nothing* like what happened to me before. Not even close. I'm freely giving this to you. I want you to orgasm by what I'm voluntarily doing."

He chuckled and took his hands off her wrists, giving her the freedom to do what she wanted. "Beautiful, I feel as if I'm always on the verge of orgasming when you're around, and you don't even have to touch me to make me hard."

"Turn sideways and put your hands on the wall," she ordered.

Arrow wasn't a man to follow orders when it came to sex, but for her, he'd do whatever she wanted or needed. He was putty in her hands. He turned so the water hit his side, and he groaned when Morgan squatted next to him, a hand on his hip to steady herself.

He looked down and saw her breasts dripping with water. Her hair hung damp around her shoulders. Her gaze was locked on his dick. She licked her lips, and his cock jerked in response.

Groaning, Arrow tore his gaze from her, threw his head back, and stared at the ceiling.

He felt her hand move, going from his hip to his stomach as she traced the muscles there before sliding down and wrapping around his cock again.

"Oh shit," he breathed, locking his knees.

She began to stroke him up and down while her other hand came to rest on his thigh to keep her balance.

"This isn't going to take long," Arrow warned as he dropped his head to stare down at her. As much as he wanted to make this last, he knew there was no way he'd be able to keep his normal iron control over his libido.

He'd dreamed of this moment for weeks, not expecting anything like this so soon. She was a miracle. *His* miracle. She was braver than anyone he'd ever met.

"Let me know if I'm not doing this right," she murmured, biting her lip in concentration as she stroked him.

"You're touching me, so you're doing it right," Arrow managed to say. He watched as the head of his cock peeked out from her tight fist on every downstroke, then disappeared on the upstroke of her hand. He wanted to touch her, to hold her hair in his fist as she pleasured him, but he forced himself to keep both hands on the wall. "Faster, baby," he said desperately.

She immediately sped up her strokes, and moved her other hand to cup his balls. That was all it took.

"Oh fuck, I'm coming," he breathed. Seconds later, he was spurting come all over the wall and her hand. Groaning, he thrust his hips forward as she slowed, caressing him instead of jerking him off.

When he dared open his eyes once more, she was looking up at him and smiling in wonder, as if she'd just passed the hardest test she'd ever taken . . . and he supposed in some ways, it truly felt that way for her.

"Can I hold you?" he asked, wanting nothing more than to haul her into his arms and squeeze her tight, but he wasn't sure where her head was at and refused to do anything that would hurt her psyche.

"Please," she said softly.

Immediately he leaned down, helped her stand, and brought her into his embrace so fast, their bodies made a smacking noise as their skin slapped together.

If Arrow thought Morgan felt good against him when they were fully clothed, it was *nothing* compared to holding her skin to skin. Her nipples were hard against his chest, and while she still needed to gain some weight, the feel of her softness against his hardness was enough to make his dick twitch already.

"I'm not sure I'll ever be able to give you a blow job," Morgan said against his chest.

Arrow's dick immediately deflated at her words. Not because of the thought of never getting her mouth on him, but because of the meaning behind *why* she felt that way.

"I don't care."

"All guys care. They all want that," Morgan protested.

Arrow put his hand under her chin and lifted her head so she had to look at him while he spoke. "I don't," he said firmly. "Beautiful, I just shot my load after you touched me for, like, two-point-three seconds. I don't care *what* part of you is touching me, as long as you are. I am not 'all guys.' When we're together like this, it's just you and me here. No one else. What we do together is no one's business but ours. Having you here in my shower is like a dream come true. Intimacy between us is what we make it. Screw everyone else and screw what 'all guys' want."

Morgan nodded and tucked her chin once more. Arrow held her to him, turning so the warm water hit her back so she wouldn't be cold. They stood like that for quite a while until he asked, "Do you want me to wash your hair?"

He felt her take a deep breath, then she looked up. "No. I'm hungry. I need you to go and start my omelet."

Arrow couldn't help the silly smile from spreading across his face. "You got it, beautiful. Thank you for this morning. You'll never know how much it meant to me."

"Me too," she said shyly. "Thank you for not pressuring me for more."

"You don't have to thank me for that," he scolded. "I'll never pressure you for anything more than what you want to give me." Then Arrow slowly leaned down and kissed her lips lightly. She tugged him back down when he started to straighten and deepened the kiss.

By the time he got out of the shower, he was hard once again, but he didn't care. He had a feeling he was going to spend most of his time around her hard as a fucking rock . . . and he'd love every second of it.

Morgan got dressed slowly and tried not to blush thinking about what she'd done to Arrow. She hadn't planned it, but as she lay on his bed listening to him in the shower, she'd gotten mad. Mad at herself. Mad at her captors. Mad at the men who'd taken what she didn't want to give. So she'd decided to take the bull by the horn, so to speak, and the next thing she knew, she was naked with Arrow.

She'd been nervous at first, scared he'd take her coming to him the wrong way, but she should've known better. He hadn't pressured her. Hadn't even touched her while she was pleasuring him. It had been empowering. She'd felt the need to warn him that she didn't think she'd ever be comfortable taking him in her mouth, not after what the men in Santo Domingo had forced her to do, but she'd felt safe telling him because she knew he'd answer exactly as he had.

For the first time since she'd moved in with Arrow, she thought maybe she'd get to a point eventually where she could make love with him and not freak out.

Today wasn't that day, but she could see herself giving her trust to him. He wouldn't hurt her. Wouldn't rush her, and would do everything in his power to make her feel safe.

She hadn't missed how he'd pulled her on top of him when she'd cried, rather than rolling over and putting her beneath him. He was cautious and ever mindful of where her head might be when he was with her in an intimate situation. It made her love him all the more.

Wait . . . what?

Love?

Did she love him?

Morgan wanted to deny it, but she couldn't.

Even when she'd first started seeing Lane, she hadn't felt like she did with Arrow. She was giddy with excitement, yes, but it was more than that. It was the bone-deep realization that she trusted him with her darkest secrets . . . and that he'd protect them with everything he had.

He knew about her less-than-perfect family, and it hadn't chased him away.

He didn't care that she might never be the same person she used to be.

Smiling, Morgan quickly finished getting dressed and didn't bother to dry her hair before rushing to the kitchen to see Arrow. Her stomach growled when she smelled the delicious omelet he'd made for her.

"Morning, beautiful," he said as she came to him.

She snuggled under his arm and smiled shyly. "Hi."

He chuckled. "I never would've pegged you for the shy type," he said with a smirk.

Smacking his arm, Morgan shook her head. "Whatever. Give me that plate, mister, before I upend it on your head."

"You wouldn't dare waste a good omelet that way," he retorted, handing her the plate.

"True," she conceded. "Thank you for making it for me."

"No problem."

She took the plate, hauled herself up onto one of the barstools next to the island, and dug in. The eggs were cooked perfectly, like usual. He joined her, placing a large glass of orange juice in front of her, and tucked into his own fried eggs.

Just as they were finishing, Arrow's phone rang. He pulled it out and answered.

"Hello? Oh hi, Robert . . . What? No, I didn't . . . Absolutely not . . . keep her there for me. I'll be down in a second."

Morgan frowned. "What was that about?"

"I need to go downstairs for a second." He pushed away from the island and turned to head to the bedroom, where he kept his shoes.

"Wait. What's going on?"

Morgan saw him hesitate before turning back to her. "That was the doorman. He said a . . . woman was here, saying that I'd called for her. He wanted to know if he should let her up."

"A woman? Who?" Morgan asked.

"I don't know, but Robert thinks she's an escort."

Morgan blinked. "A *what*?"

"A prostitute."

"Are you serious? You wouldn't call for someone like that."

"Of course not," Arrow said with conviction. "I'm guessing someone is messing with me."

"One of your friends?" Morgan asked hopefully.

At that, he took the few steps back to her side. They were close to being eye to eye since she was still sitting on the high stool. "No, beautiful. They'd never do that, especially knowing you're here."

Morgan's stomach sank as the implications settled in. "Someone wanted to upset me, then."

"That's my guess," Arrow said evenly. "But whoever did it underestimated you. Underestimated how much we care about and trust each other . . . right?"

Morgan nodded immediately and brought her hands up to grip his hips. "I trust you, Arrow. I know you wouldn't do that. But . . . what are you going to do?"

"I'm going to go downstairs and talk to whoever this woman is. See who hired her and gave her my address. This is a good thing, Morgan."

"It is? How?"

"Because with everything they do, they leave more of a trail. Eventually we'll gather up all the breadcrumbs, and it'll lead us right to him."

"I hope so."

"I know so. Now, I need to grab my shoes and get downstairs. Will you be all right up here? Don't open the door to *anyone*, and don't answer your phone. I'll be back as soon as I can."

"Should I call Gray or someone?"

Arrow shook his head. "No. I want to talk to this woman first. Then I'll call Rex and Meat and get them on the case. Then I'll call the others."

"Okay."

Arrow stared at her for a beat longer, then smiled. "I love you. Thank you for not freaking out and for trusting me."

"Of course."

He kissed her quickly, teasing her with a swipe of his tongue over her bottom lip, then he was gone, headed for the bedroom to grab his shoes. He was back within seconds and stalking toward the door. "Remember, don't open this to anyone."

"I won't."

Then he was gone.

Morgan hopped off the stool and picked up their plates. She wasn't hungry anymore and knew if she tried to finish the delicious omelet, it might reappear in an unappetizing manner, so she dumped it in the trash and put the dishes into the sink. She refilled her glass with orange juice—it was weird how much more she loved the stuff now—and went into the living room to sit and wait for Arrow to return.

It took an hour before he finally reappeared. He didn't look pissed or upset in the least.

"What happened?" Morgan demanded.

He kicked off his shoes, came over to the couch, and sat next to her, pulling her against him. "Nothing."

"What do you mean, nothing?"

"I mean, nothing. The woman was pissed that she'd been set up on a wild-goose chase. Her services don't exactly come cheap, if you know what I mean. I ascertained that she was working of her own free will, that she wasn't forced to come meet with me. I informed her that what she was doing was illegal, then asked politely if I could inquire as to what she knew about the person who'd hired her."

Morgan couldn't help but giggle at his explanation. "What'd she say?"

"Nothing very useful. She works with a group of other women, and they have ads on several different sites on the web. They take turns replying and accepting the various jobs. This one came in late last night through a generic Gmail address. Apparently that isn't unusual, as most people who hire them don't want to be identified. The instructions stated that she was to show up this morning right at seven o'clock and to bypass the doorman if at all possible. She had my apartment number and my name and was even informed that the 'lady of the house' might be willing to partake in a threesome if the opportunity arose."

Morgan wrinkled her nose at the thought.

"Right? But Robert was on duty and didn't let her sneak by. He called me, and that was that."

"Can you track who hired her?"

"If they'd actually paid her ahead of time, maybe. But the woman was promised that *I* would pay for her services, plus a twenty percent tip. The email is probably a dead end, but I've already got Meat on it. At the very least he can get the IP address, which will give us the general location of the sender. We can go from there."

"Do they have any more leads from Lane or Lance?" Morgan asked.

"No. But both seem to be in the clear for now. Meat is having a harder time following the trail of the men Sarah associated with. Motorcycle gangs are notoriously good at keeping their mouths shut, and it's been a long time since you were taken from that parking garage."

"I know," Morgan said morosely. "I was just hoping. As much as I'd hate for any of my friends to be behind this, not knowing is worse."

Arrow didn't know what to say to make her feel any better, and it frustrated him. Eventually, he simply asked, "Are you okay?"

She scowled and shook her head. "No. I'm not all right. I'm pissed." Pushing to her feet, Morgan paced in front of Arrow. "It's not cool that someone's messing with you. And messing with you means that they're messing with *me*. And that sucks! I mean, didn't they do enough? Whoever did this is demented and sick. They don't care that they've hurt me, want to *keep* hurting me. How could someone think this is okay? What's next? Are they going to burn down the apartment? Maybe they'll put a bomb under your truck and blow us up. Maybe they'll lie in wait at the grocery store. Or better yet, they'll grab Allye or Chloe and threaten to do to them what they did to me. When will this end? What did I do that was so horrible to deserve this?"

"Nothing," Arrow said from right next to her. "You didn't do anything wrong."

"It's getting harder and harder to believe that," Morgan said, knowing she was seconds from losing it but not caring. "I'm the one who was tortured for a year. I'm the one who they're still trying to torment. It doesn't make any sense! I'm just a bee lady. I've never hurt anyone that I know about. But I had to do something to *someone* for them to be so pissed off at me. I just don't get it!"

"Morgan—"

"No. I'm done. This is crazy. Who do I need to talk to in order to get this to stop? The police? The FBI? This Rex guy? Who?"

"Morgan . . . ," Arrow tried again.

But she was on a roll. "Maybe I'll see if I can find someone in the mob. Or maybe I can find a motorcycle club who doesn't mind offing people. Who do you know that I can talk to? Oooh, I know, I'll find one of those Mexican drug lords and sic *them* on the case. They'll figure it out and—*umph!*"

Her words were cut off by Arrow putting his shoulder to her belly. He had her over his shoulder before she could finish her thought.

"What are you—Arrow! Put me down!"

"Nope," he said calmly, and headed for the front door.

Morgan struggled for a moment, then stilled when she felt his hand land on her ass with a smack. "Calm down, beautiful," he said.

In shock, she shut up . . . and then started grinning. By the time they'd reached the elevator, she was giggling. Maybe she *was* losing it. "Arrow, I'm not wearing any shoes," she protested.

"You don't need shoes," he told her as he put her on her feet in front of the elevator.

"I don't have my purse and haven't even styled my hair."

"Don't care. You are in need of some serious nature therapy."

"What's that?"

"You'll see," Arrow said. Then he sobered and said, "I'm going to fix this for you, beautiful. This is not your life, so don't get used to it."

"Don't get used to being able to speak my mind, freak out, and have my gorgeous boyfriend haul me over his shoulder to stop me from said freak-out and have him take me somewhere I know is going to be awesome and beautiful?"

"*Do* get used to that," he said with a small smile. "But not the freak-out part. This is going to end. You'll be safe to do what you want, where you want, with who you want."

"I know the second two things, but I'm still working on the first," Morgan told him shyly, and was rewarded by the blinding smile that crossed his face.

The elevator chimed as it opened, and Morgan said, "I really should go back and get my shoes."

"Nah," Arrow told her, and pulled her into the elevator. "I'll carry you."

"You're going to get sick of hauling me around."

"Never," Arrow vowed.

That felt good. "And I'm not back to my fighting weight." Morgan patted her belly. "But I'm working on it."

"Anything I can do to help?"

"I should call my mom and get her cookie recipe. She makes these amazing, gooey, sinful s'mores cookies that are to die for."

"You can ask her when you talk to her in three days," Arrow said firmly.

Morgan knew she still had a few days to go before she should call her mom again, and she'd been okay with limiting how much they spoke, but it was times like this when she really missed her mom.

"I'm sure she's sorry for pushing so hard," Morgan said in a conciliatory tone.

"You promised," Arrow reminded her.

Morgan huffed out a sigh. She *had* promised to give her mom some cooling-off time. She'd told her exactly why she was going to limit her calls, and even though Ellie hadn't been happy, she'd agreed to try to be less aggressive in pushing Morgan to move back to Albuquerque.

"Fine. But you're going to be sorry once you taste these cookies, because they're absolutely amazing."

"That much sugar isn't good for you," was Arrow's response.

Morgan rolled her eyes. "Whatever."

On their way out, Arrow stopped to say something to Robert, who smiled and nodded. Arrow picked Morgan up, bride style this time, with one arm under her knees and the other around her back, and carried her to his truck. He got her settled and climbed in next to her.

He didn't start the engine immediately, and just when she was going to ask him why, Robert came jogging out of the building carrying a pair of flip-flops for her.

Arrow tipped Robert and thanked him, handing the shoes to Morgan.

"I thought you said you were going to carry me everywhere," she teased.

Arrow merely shrugged. "I was, but then I thought that was a bit impractical. Besides, I can't protect you if I'm holding you."

Morgan's smile died.

"Shit, beautiful. I didn't mean to bring you down."

"No, it's okay. I mean, I hadn't thought about that either. I would never want to be a burden to you."

"You are *not* a burden," Arrow growled. "Don't ever say that again or even *think* it."

Morgan couldn't help it: she smiled. "Okay, okay. Sorry."

"What are you smiling about?" he said grumpily as he finally started the truck.

"Just that it feels good."

"What does?" Arrow asked as he pulled out of the parking lot.

"To be loved," Morgan told him softly. She knew she was blushing but couldn't help it.

In response, Arrow picked up her hand and kissed the palm before twining his fingers with hers and resting her hand on his thigh.

She had no idea where they were going or what they were doing, but ultimately, she didn't care. She was with Arrow, and that was all that mattered.

Chapter Seventeen

Arrow didn't really have a destination in mind. He just needed to get out of the apartment as much as Morgan. He was pissed at the prostitute, who hadn't seemed to care that she was being used to try to hurt Morgan. All she cared about was being paid for her time.

He was pissed at whoever seemed to be one step ahead of him and the Mountain Mercenaries as well. They needed to figure this out so Morgan could relax. She'd been through enough.

He wanted to take Morgan somewhere they could just be themselves together. The morning had started out so well, and now it was . . .

He wasn't sure what it was. But he was determined to get them both back to the feeling they'd had in the shower. A feeling of being connected. Loved.

He knew she loved him. Felt it deep in his bones. But saying it would take a while. He got that. In the meantime, he'd bend over backward to make sure she heard it from him often, and felt it even more.

All his life, his job had taken priority. First the Marines, then the Mountain Mercenaries. But no longer. Morgan came first from here on out. Period.

They spent the rest of the morning walking around Memorial Park and enjoying the antics of the dogs, kids, and couples who were there enjoying the beautiful Colorado weather. They had lunch at an Italian restaurant, and were on their way to Gray's house to visit with him and Allye when Arrow received a call.

"Hello?" Arrow answered, and the voice came through the speakers in the car.

"It's Gray. We have a situation."

"Morgan's here with me," Arrow warned his friend. Then he asked, "What is it?"

"Dave was attacked."

"Dave?" Arrow asked. That was the last person he'd expected to hear about.

"Yeah. He was coming in for his shift today and was jumped in the parking lot."

"Shit. Is he all right?"

"Yeah. More pissed than anything else. He's at the emergency room getting stitches."

"Tell me it was caught on tape," Arrow ordered.

"It was caught on tape," Gray dutifully replied.

"Thank fuck. Where are you?"

"At The Pit."

Arrow pulled into a grocery store parking lot and did a U-turn. "We're on our way."

"See you soon," Gray said, then clicked off the connection.

"Should we go to the hospital to check on Dave?" Morgan asked worriedly.

"No. He'd expect us to look for the fucker who jumped him. If Gray says he'll be fine, he'll be fine."

"Do you think this is related to me?"

"I don't know, beautiful. But it doesn't matter. We'll find whoever did it and get to the bottom of why."

The rest of the drive was done in silence. Arrow couldn't help thinking that this probably *was* related to Morgan, and whoever was harassing him. The Pit wasn't exactly in the best part of town, but it wasn't in the worst either. They'd never had any issues in the parking lot before, and especially not in the middle of the day. He knew he'd have to wait and see the tapes for himself before he made any conclusions, but he couldn't help but feel uneasy about the entire situation.

Glad he'd made sure Morgan had shoes, he led her into The Pit twenty minutes later. He headed straight for the back office, where he knew he'd find his teammates poring over the surveillance tapes.

Nodding at Noah Ganter, the other bartender who worked at The Pit, both alongside Dave and when he was off, Arrow didn't bother to stop and introduce Morgan. He went into the back hallway and through the office door, not stopping until he was in front of one of the comfortable armchairs Dave had brought in a few years ago.

"Sit, beautiful. And stop worrying," he ordered.

"I can't help it," she said.

Arrow kissed her on the forehead and turned to his friends. "Tell me he's on there."

"He's on there, all right," Meat said, not looking up from the screen he was peering at with an intensity that was kind of scary. "We've got him from several different angles. Looks like he didn't drive in, but was waiting for Dave."

"Are we sure he was waiting for *him*, or did Dave just happen to arrive at the wrong time?" Arrow asked.

Both Gray and Black turned to him at the same time.

"Got something you want to tell us?" Gray asked.

Arrow sighed and told his friends about the prostitute from that morning.

"So you're being targeted," Gray concluded. "Whoever this was could've been waiting for *you*."

"But I had no plans to come to The Pit today," Arrow argued. "I haven't been here in a few days."

"Whoever beat up Dave didn't know that," Black noted. "He might've been casing the place, and when Dave showed up, just decided to go after him because he knows you. Dave was busy grabbing a grocery bag. You know how he likes to get fresh fruit for his cocktails," Gray mused.

"Show me the tape," Arrow ordered. "Maybe I'll recognize him."

"I want to see it too," Morgan said, standing.

"No," Arrow responded immediately. At the scowl on her face, he gentled his tone. "Let me watch it first, beautiful. The last thing I want is for you to have to come face to face with any more violence."

"I want to help," she said in a pleading voice.

"I know you do. And if we need your help, I won't hesitate to ask you for it. Okay?" He stared at her, praying she understood that he was trying to protect her. That he didn't want her to have to see the violence that had happened to someone she knew.

"Okay," she agreed after a tense few seconds.

"Thank you," Arrow said, then turned back to the screen. He nodded at Meat to play it and squinted, trying to get a better view of the perpetrator.

The person was wearing some sort of coveralls. Brown. With a hat pulled low over his brow. He wasn't very tall or big—that much was obvious when he snuck up behind Dave, who was bent over picking up a bag from the back seat of his car. He used some sort of crowbar to stun Dave. Once the bigger man was on the ground, the punk hit him twice more. Once in the thigh and once in the ribs. Dave had done the smart thing and immediately covered his head with his arms, but that had left the rest of him vulnerable.

The punk turned and ran off as soon as Dave rolled to get up. At no time did the person turn to face the cameras, keeping his back to them at all times. He never looked up, as if he knew exactly where they were and how to keep his face from being caught on film.

Arrow looked at Meat in frustration. "That's it? We don't have anything else?"

"No. But we haven't talked to Dave yet."

213

"He was wearing gloves," Black noted.

"And we have his height," Gray added.

"Play it again," Arrow asked Meat.

The other man nodded and cued it up once more. Arrow watched the video again from start to finish. He could just see the man hiding in the trees as Dave pulled into the parking lot. Then the second his back was turned, the punk sprang into action, walking calmly but quickly.

Something about the perp niggled at the back of Arrow's brain, but he couldn't bring it into focus.

"What is it?" Gray asked, seeing Arrow's frustration.

"I don't know. I feel like I've seen the perp before. There's something about his movement that seems familiar."

"Maybe on another op?" Black asked.

"Maybe," Arrow agreed.

"It could be someone who has a beef with the Mountain Mercenaries," Gray threw out there.

"Yeah," Arrow said.

"But you don't think so," Meat concluded.

Arrow shook his head. "If it was, why wouldn't he have stayed to make sure Dave was really down for the count? I mean, yeah, he was hurt, but he was on his way up. If someone really had a problem with us, I can't help but think they would've shot him or brought a knife or something. A crowbar seems . . . opportunistic. And desperate."

"Could it be someone connected to Chloe's brother?" Gray asked. "I'd like to think we nipped that in the bud, but someone could still hold a grudge."

"Doubtful," Meat said. "There's no one left who is all that loyal to Leon Harris."

"We could've missed someone," Gray said.

"No. I don't think so. He would've made his move before now." Arrow turned to Meat. "Check on the Buswells. Make sure they're still in Atlanta. Lane is about the right height."

"You think Lane is here? That he attacked Dave?" Morgan asked from across the room.

Arrow made his way to her and squatted down in front of her chair. "I don't know anything right now," he soothed. "But we can't count anyone out. They've upped the game. Slashing tires and ordering a prostitute to visit my apartment is child's play. But assault is a whole 'nother story. We should be able to count Lane in or out pretty easily. He's either in Atlanta or he isn't."

"Lance is about the same height as his brother," Morgan volunteered. "Of course, everyone seems tall to me, but Thomas is taller than both of them."

"Carl is the right height," Meat muttered as he clicked on his laptop.

Arrow swore under his breath when Morgan froze.

"My dad? You think my *dad* hurt Dave? Why? Why would he do that?"

"He's been acting more desperate for you to talk to the press," Arrow said gently. "You said yourself the last time you talked to him that you didn't understand why it was so important to him that you go on television."

"But . . . he's my dad," she said.

Arrow hated to see the pain and confusion in her eyes.

"He could've orchestrated the whole thing to drum up attention, make people feel sorry for him, or to further his career," Gray said.

"And he *has* done extremely well in the last year . . . in part, thanks to his missing daughter," Black added.

Morgan shook her head. "He wouldn't do that to me," she protested.

"We have to admit, he has the connections," Arrow said as gently as he could. "Because of his job as CFO, he travels internationally a lot, and I think there's even a branch of the organization in Puerto Rico. That's not too far from the Dominican Republic."

"My *dad*?" Morgan said, her eyes filling with tears. "Not my dad."

"Here," Meat said, turning the computer toward Morgan. "I agree with Arrow that I don't think you should watch all of the video, but I've cued it up from the beginning so you can see if you recognize the person."

Morgan stood and crossed to the desk. Leaning over the laptop, she concentrated on the figure on the tape. Meat let it play until just before the mysterious man started hitting Dave.

"Can you play it again?" Morgan asked.

Meat didn't say a word, just clicked the time bar and played it again.

After it was finished, Morgan sighed and stood up straight. "I don't recognize him. There's just not a clear enough view of his face. I'm so sorry."

"You have nothing to be sorry about," Arrow told her, and wrapped his arm around her shoulders.

"I'm pretty sure it's not my dad, though," she added. "He moves with more . . . *purpose* or something. I don't know."

"No, that's a good observation," Meat said. "And I agree."

"We're going home," Arrow told both Morgan and the others. "If anything more comes up, you know where to find me."

"I'll stay on it," Meat told him, looking at Morgan with sympathy in his eyes.

"We're going to do whatever we can to figure this out," Gray told her.

"Try not to worry," Black threw in.

Arrow knew that last one was impossible, but he appreciated his friends doing what they could to reassure Morgan.

He led her past the bar. Noah asked if they wanted water for the road, which they both declined. Arrow made a mental note to text Gray as soon as he could and suggest they look into the other bartender as well. There was a possibility that the attack on Dave wasn't related to Morgan at all. Maybe it was a jealousy thing. They couldn't rule anyone out at this point.

Morgan hadn't said much after she hadn't been able to ID the perp, and Arrow was worried this could be the thing that pushed her over the edge. She'd been doing so well since she'd come back to Colorado Springs. She was eating well, looked healthier, and had been sleeping through the night. The last thing he wanted was for her nightmares to come back, or for her to step away from him out of some misguided need to protect him or some such bullshit.

Feeling helpless, and wanting to kill someone at the same time, Arrow kept her hand in his the entire way back to his apartment complex. He greeted Robert solemnly and held her against him as they rode up the elevator in silence.

Once they were safely inside his apartment, he asked, "What can I do to make this better, beautiful?"

"Hold me?" she asked.

"With pleasure." Arrow led her straight to their room and sat her on the bed. He gently took off her shoes and took hold of the bottom of her T-shirt. "Lift," he ordered softly.

She raised her arms above her head without protest and let him remove her shirt. He walked to the dresser and pulled out a tank top, knowing she liked to sleep in them. He pulled it over her head, then reached underneath to undo her bra. He'd seen her take it off from under her shirt enough to know how it was done. It was lying on the floor in seconds. "Lean back."

She did, and he unbuttoned her jeans and drew them down her legs, not even noticing what color panties she was wearing. His mind wasn't on sex. It was on trying to make her as relaxed as possible before comforting her.

He went back to the drawer and pulled out a pair of sweats. He pulled those up her legs and helped her lift her hips so he could settle them around her waist. Then he yanked off his own shirt and climbed into bed behind her, enfolding her in his arms.

She didn't cry, but held on to him so tightly he knew he'd have indentations from her fingers for hours. He didn't know what to say to make this better for her, so he said nothing, simply tried to make sure she knew how much he loved her by his actions.

An hour later, when he thought she was sound asleep, she said quietly, "I know she hasn't been behaving her best, and she's been annoying, but . . . I want my mom."

"Then you'll have her," Arrow said, kissing the top of her head.

She relaxed into him more, as if she'd been afraid of telling him what she wanted, probably since she knew he didn't care much for Ellie.

Arrow kicked himself. Every little girl needed her mother when she was feeling down. Morgan was no different. He'd get up and call her in a bit. He hoped she'd be able to take some time off and come visit. Surely for her daughter, she'd be able to arrange it.

⁓

Ellie Jernigan stared up at the third-floor apartment with hate in her heart.

Years and years ago, she'd been happy to have a little girl she could shape and mold. But because the courts insisted Carl have equal time with his daughter, she'd picked up too many of his habits and beliefs. Now, every time she looked at Morgan, she was reminded of her biggest mistake—marrying Carl Byrd.

Just thinking his name made her want to puke. Ellie had tried to teach her ex a lesson . . . by making Morgan disappear. And it had worked.

Carl had been a wreck. He'd been broken by his daughter's disappearance, just like Ellie wanted. But she'd known where Morgan was the entire time. Every time she saw an article or a TV show about the missing woman from Atlanta, she'd felt giddy inside. It was fun to know something no one else did. She'd made sure Morgan had been kept alive. *Ellie* was in control. She pulled the strings and made Carl dance to her tune.

But then Arrow had to ruin everything. She knew his finding Morgan had been an accident, a damn *lucky* accident, but it still pissed her off that the men she'd been paying down in the Dominican Republic were so incompetent they hadn't been able to prevent her daughter from leaving the country.

Now Morgan was back—and Carl was eating that shit up! He was more insufferable than ever. Every time she saw him on television, she wanted to strangle him. He was soaking up the limelight, and loved having all the attention on himself. She knew he was making money on Morgan's disappearance. He had to be. Her entire plan had backfired!

Yes, Carl had been devastated when she'd been gone, but the fact that he was actually *profiting* from and enjoying the aftermath was too much.

It was time to show Carl what it *really* meant to lose everything. He'd been upset when Morgan had disappeared, but that would be nothing compared to how he'd feel when she was *dead*.

Except Arrow kept getting in her way. She'd planned on poisoning Morgan. It had been perfect, actually. The ethylene glycol was undetectable in the orange juice that her daughter loved so much. She was going to get sicker and sicker, and no doctor would've been able to figure it out until it was too late and Morgan had already succumbed to whatever mysterious tropical illness she'd contracted while in captivity.

Everyone would have been devastated by her death—but Carl would've been destroyed. He'd found his daughter, the one he'd practically ignored while she was growing up, only to have her slip through his fingers.

But then Arrow had to go and convince her to come live with him in Colorado Springs, and Ellie had lost the upper hand. She'd been poisoning Morgan extremely slowly so as not to arouse suspicion, thinking she had all the time in the world. But it had been *too* slowly. After leaving, she'd obviously gotten better.

So now Arrow had to die as well.

Messing with him had been fun, but she was ready for the main show. For days, she'd hung around the stupid bar Arrow and his friends frequented, but when he didn't show, she got more and more pissed off. When the asshole bartender showed up, she took the chance to get her revenge on *him* too. It felt good to beat on him a bit, empowering . . . especially after he'd tried to make her feel bad about her own daughter and then kicked Ellie out of the bar. She'd hit him a few times, loving the rush of having someone so much bigger at her mercy. She made sure to keep her face away from the cameras—men thought they were so smart—then ran.

Fingering the ethylene glycol she'd obtained from a friend of a friend of a friend, Ellie tried to figure out what her next step should be. She knew Arrow and his friends would probably be even more vigilant now.

She needed to be able to get to Morgan. Carl had to pay for being a shitty husband, a shitty father, and a shitty person in general.

Her cell phone rang with an unknown number, and Ellie looked around to make sure no one could see her sitting in her car at the back of the parking lot of the complex, then cautiously answered it.

"Hello?"

"Hi. Ms. Jernigan? It's Archer Kane. Arrow. I'm sorry to be calling so late."

"What do you want?" Ellie asked in a harsh tone. She'd just been fantasizing about killing the man, and now she was supposed to be nice to him?

"Morgan needs you."

Ellie sat up straighter in her seat. "What?"

"She's had a tough few days, and she needs her mom. I was calling to see if you'd be able to take a few days off work and drive up here and stay for a bit."

Ellie almost cackled in delight. She'd never thought Morgan would be so weak as to ask for her mom, but was thrilled that she was playing right into her hands. "Oh no! My poor baby," she said in a sad tone she hoped she'd pulled off. "Is she okay? What happened?" she asked, playing dumb.

"Just a tough few days. Can you come?"

"I'll see what I can do," she told him. It wouldn't do to act too excited, especially not when Morgan had been blowing her off. The *bitch*. She had way too much of her father in her.

"I know she'll be glad to hear it. Oh, and she mentioned something about s'mores cookies that are to die for. Any chance I can convince you to make a batch to bring with you?"

Ellie smiled. A wide, evil smile that would've made the hair on the head of the most hardened criminal stand on end if he could see it. "Of course. My Morgan always loved her sugar."

"Thank you," Arrow said, the relief easy to hear in his tone. "I know things have been tough between you two. She loves you very much, and I know this will be just what she needs to feel more like herself."

"I kept trying to tell her that she needed to be home with her mother," Ellie said, not able to help herself. "I was surprised, after all she's been through, that she'd be thinking with her hormones instead of her head."

"Careful, Ellie," Arrow said in a deadly tone. "That was way out of line. I might have invited you up here, but I can just as easily uninvite you."

"I'm sorry," Ellie said immediately, trying to sound contrite. "You're right. I'm just so worried about her. I'll be there tomorrow afternoon. Is that okay?"

"Yeah, that should work. I think I'm going to see if her therapist can see her around one. I think she needs to talk to her as soon as possible. Her appointments are usually only about an hour."

"Maybe you shouldn't tell her I'm coming," Ellie said. "If you can get someone else to bring her home, I can come over around one thirty, and we can wait for her to arrive. It'll be a surprise."

"I could have Allye or Chloe pick her up," Arrow mused. "They've done it before."

"Perfect!" Ellie crowed. "She's going to be so surprised to see me."

"Thank you," Arrow said. "I'll see you tomorrow. Let me know if your plans change."

"I will," she assured him, then clicked off the phone.

The second the connection ended, she threw back her head and laughed. She giggled until her stomach hurt and she had to put down the bottle of poison before she dropped it. She'd met again with the people who supplied her with it before Morgan had left New Mexico, ruining her plans.

If her daughter had done what she'd asked, if she'd refused to have anything to do with her father, *none* of this would've happened. But she hadn't. And now Morgan was off the rails. Probably talking to Carl every damn day while cutting her *mother* out of her life.

Ellie wouldn't have it.

Both her daughter and Arrow would die. No more slow and steady. She could head down to Santo Domingo after it was done and hang out with the new friends she'd made over the last year.

But first, she had cookies to make . . . and taint. She had to play her cards exactly right in order to disable her daughter's guard dog—Arrow. Once she'd poisoned and incapacitated Arrow, she could make sure Morgan understood exactly what was going to happen, and why. The spoiled bitch would know just what she'd done to deserve *everything* that had happened to her.

Still smiling, Ellie Jernigan started the engine and pulled out of the parking lot. She needed to find a hotel with a full kitchen, then she'd go grocery shopping. Mommy dearest needed to make a special batch of cookies for her loving daughter and her boyfriend.

Chapter Eighteen

"Thanks for driving me over here," Morgan told Arrow. "I'm sure you have other things you need to be doing. Didn't you have an appointment with that guy who's trying to sell his house, to figure out why the sockets on one side of his home aren't working?"

"Yeah, but I've already rescheduled it. You're more important."

Morgan smiled at him. Arrow always made her feel wanted. He did a good job of putting her first in his life when he could, and when he couldn't, he somehow still managed to take care of her.

"Chloe is going to come and pick you up after your session. I have a quick meeting with the guys, and then I'll meet you at home. I have a surprise for you when you get home from seeing your therapist."

"You do? What is it?" Morgan asked.

"If I told you, it wouldn't be a surprise. But you're going to like it," Arrow told her confidently.

"If you arranged it, I know I will," she said with a smile. Then she bit her lip and said, "I'm sorry I lost it yesterday. I just can't believe my dad would have anything to do with my kidnapping. I mean, he'd have to be completely sadistic to do something like that."

"Don't be sorry," Arrow told her. "You're allowed to feel the way you feel, and it truly hasn't been that long since you were rescued. You've been doing extremely well; you have to cut yourself some slack. You aren't Superwoman."

"I know . . . and I guess that's what my therapist is going to say today. I'm just . . . disappointed in myself."

"You have *nothing* to be disappointed about," Arrow said sternly. "I'm going to make cheesy chicken tonight for dinner. Is that all right?"

Morgan smiled over at him. He was changing the subject again, but she appreciated it. "Sounds amazing."

Arrow pulled into the parking lot of the medical offices and turned to Morgan. "I'm proud of you, beautiful, but I'm also worried. I need you to take care of yourself. I just found you, and I don't want anything to happen to you. I love you and want to spend the rest of my life with you . . . so you need to do what the doctor says and give yourself a break. Okay?"

Morgan smiled wider. He didn't seem to care that she hadn't returned his words of love. She wanted to, but wanted to do so when she wasn't so vulnerable. When she was stronger. "Okay."

"Good. Now, come on. I'll walk you up."

"You don't have to do that," Morgan protested.

"Until we figure out who was behind your kidnapping, I do," Arrow countered. "Now, stay there until I come around."

Morgan rolled her eyes but did as he asked. It was a long way down from his truck, and she loved how he took great pains to help her each and every time. They walked hand in hand to the entrance of the building, and Arrow held the door open for her. He refused to just drop her off there, insisting on coming up with her to the fourth floor and her therapist's office.

"Remember that Chloe will be here to get you, so don't leave the office until she's here."

"I won't." And she wouldn't. Morgan wasn't stupid. The last thing she wanted was to be one of those too-stupid-to-live heroines in the romances she'd liked to watch a year ago.

"Love you," Arrow told her as he leaned down and kissed her.

While she wasn't ready to return the words, that didn't mean she couldn't show Arrow that she cared. She put her hand on the back of his neck, holding him to her as she plunged her tongue into his mouth. He immediately reciprocated. They made out in front of her therapist's door for a long moment until Arrow finally pulled back. He licked his lips, and even that was sexy.

"I'll see you later," she said softly.

"Yes, you will," Arrow returned. "God, you're beautiful," he said reverently, before getting himself together and stepping away from her. "Later."

Morgan stood outside the door and watched Arrow walk down the hall and disappear into the stairwell before she turned and headed inside for her appointment.

~

"I've watched this tape until I'm blue in the face, and nothing is clicking," Meat complained.

They were all at The Pit, and Noah was behind the bar. Dave had been discharged from the hospital with some bruises, a couple of stitches, and a cracked rib. He'd been very lucky in that whoever had attacked him had given up so quickly. Even the first blow he'd taken hadn't done much more than stun him. Dave was pissed he'd been ordered to stay off his feet for a week. He wanted to come back and work "his" bar, but Meat had promised retribution of the electronic sort if he dared show his face a minute before he was cleared by his doctor. What that meant, no one knew, but Dave wasn't stupid enough to test it.

"He was smart enough to keep his head down the entire time, as if he knew where the cameras were," Meat went on.

"He probably did," Gray agreed. "I mean, if he was smart, he would've cased the place before making his move."

"But if he was so smart, why attack Dave? We all agreed that he probably wasn't his main target. It doesn't make sense," Black added.

Arrow paced beside the table, too keyed up to sit and discuss this calmly.

"So it's not either of the Buswells," Ball mused. "They checked out and were seen on video surveillance entering and leaving their jobs yesterday."

"And Carl?" Arrow asked.

"Not him either," Ro said, piping up for the first time. "I personally spoke to the human resources director yesterday and convinced her to walk down to his office and see with her own eyes that he was there. He was. There is no way he could've gotten from Georgia to Colorado and back."

"He could've hired someone to do his dirty work," Gray said.

"Right, but I honestly don't think this is him," Arrow said.

Ro nodded. "I agree. Arrow might be biased since this is his woman's father, but I've studied the man in some of the old news clips, pleading for his daughter's safe return. He looks and sounds genuinely distraught."

"He could be a good actor," Ball said, playing devil's advocate.

"Maybe," Ro conceded, "but I don't think so. Pretty much every emotion is right there on his face for everyone to see. You saw him when he was here with his ex. He couldn't stand being in the same room with her."

"I suppose the same could be said about her mom," Arrow threw out.

"True. If we considered the fact that her dad could've hired someone, then I suppose we have to do the same with her mom," Black mused.

"Out of everyone involved, her mom's been the most concerned about her, though," Ball said.

"True, although that could be an act as well," Arrow said.

"I have serious doubts that a mother could do something as heinous as having her own daughter kidnapped. And for what reason? It doesn't make sense," Meat said. "But I get your point, Arrow. I'll see what I can dig up about her too."

Arrow nodded, and asked, "Have we had any luck looking into Sarah's and Karen's connections?"

"Nada," Meat said. "I mean, I looked into them, but those bikers are more interested in smoking dope and laying as many women as possible than a long-term kidnapping."

"Fuck," Arrow swore.

"We've upped surveillance around Morgan, just in case," Meat told the team. "Everyone needs to be more vigilant, especially you, Arrow. This might not have anything to do with your girlfriend, and everything to do with the Mountain Mercenaries. I know Gray and Ro's houses are covered, but the rest of us need to be on alert as well. The last thing any of us needs is an ambush."

Everyone nodded. Whoever had attacked Dave had seemed like an amateur, but even assholes got lucky . . . as evidenced by the fact the team still hadn't been able to track him down.

"Has anyone talked to Rex?" Arrow asked. "What does he think about this?"

"He's pissed," Black said. "I spoke to him last night. He was preparing a mission for the team, but after what happened to Dave, he said he's putting that on hold for the time being. He's also concerned about leaving Morgan vulnerable. If we all head out on a mission, she could be a sitting duck for whoever took her in the first place."

Arrow fisted his hands. Just the mere *thought* of Morgan being taken again was enough to make him want to kill someone. He knew he'd have to leave her alone at some point, but today wasn't that day. "Speaking of Morgan, I need to get going," he told his friends.

"How's she doing?" Ball asked.

"She's upset and frustrated. She thinks she should've recognized whoever attacked Dave. I dropped her off at her therapist's office before I came here. Then I'm going back to the apartment and meeting her mom."

"Ellie? She's here?" Black asked, his brows raised in surprise.

"She will be. I called her last night. I told you Morgan wasn't doing well. She said she missed her mom and wanted her." He shrugged. "So I got her for her."

Black, Ball, and Meat rolled their eyes, but Gray and Ro merely nodded. They understood. Arrow knew they'd do anything for Allye and Chloe as well. The others would figure it out . . . one of these days, when they met the women who were meant to be theirs.

"Anyway, Ellie is driving up from New Mexico right now and will meet me at the apartment. I thought I'd surprise Morgan."

"Chloe's picking her up from her therapy session, right?" Ro asked.

Arrow nodded. "Yeah. I called her this morning, and she said she was happy to do it."

"I was there," Ro said with a smile. "You should know, we didn't realize Ellie would be in town when we made plans, but Chloe is going to ask Morgan if you guys want to come over for dinner tonight." He shrugged. "We can do it some other time, though."

"Appreciate it. I'll see how things go. Morgan loves her mom, but I think she feels suffocated around her lately too. We might need the break."

"Her mom can come too," Ro offered.

"Now that's the sign of a true friend. She didn't exactly give the best impression the last time she was here, did she?" Arrow asked.

"Nope. But I try not to judge anyone until I've walked in their shoes," Ro said diplomatically.

"If anyone has any great epiphanies, make sure you call me," Meat said. "I know I'm missing something, and it's going to bother me until I figure it out."

Everyone agreed and headed out.

Meat called Arrow's name before he could leave.

"Yeah?"

"Stay on your toes," he said earnestly. "I don't know why, but just like when something's niggling at the back of your brain, something's telling *me* the shit's about to hit the fan."

"I'm not sure if I'm relieved I'm not the only one who feels that way, or if I'm pissed," Arrow told his friend.

"We're gonna figure this out," Meat said.

"I hope it's sooner rather than later," Arrow said.

"Me too. Later."

"Later." And with that, Arrow headed out of The Pit, nodding at Noah on his way out. He wasn't sure how long Ellie was going to stay, but if Morgan wanted her to spend the night at his apartment, he needed to grab some food to stock up, not to mention the ingredients for the cheesy chicken he'd promised to make.

He loved having Morgan in his apartment. Loved cooking for her. Loved hearing about her plans to get her bee business back up and running. Loved being able to talk to someone about his own job, even though being an electrician wasn't nearly as exciting as bees. Basically, he loved everything about sharing his space with her. His apartment was no longer so neat—his old drill sergeant would be appalled—but Arrow loved seeing her dirty clothes mixed up with his. Loved seeing her shoes in the middle of the floor. Even the blanket and pillow on the couch didn't bother him . . . because he knew they belonged to her.

Making sure to scope out his surroundings, and seeing nothing out of the ordinary, Arrow climbed into his truck and headed for the grocery store.

At one o'clock, Robert buzzed Arrow's apartment, letting him know an Ellie Jernigan was there and requesting permission to come up. Arrow told Robert she was good, and took a deep breath.

He didn't know Morgan's mom all that well, but considering how much she'd been pushing her daughter to go back to New Mexico, he was having a hard time liking her. Deciding that he needed to give her a fair shot, Arrow cracked his neck and waited for her to arrive.

A knock alerted him that Ellie was there, and he opened the door. Morgan's mom was still in great shape. He knew she was around fifty years old, but she could probably pass for someone in her late thirties. She was slender and obviously worked out to take care of herself. She had the same blonde hair and green eyes as her daughter, but had a few more wrinkles on her face.

She was wearing a pair of worn and comfortable-looking jeans with a long-sleeve black blouse. A large black purse hung off one elbow, and her hair was pulled into a low ponytail at the back of her neck. She smiled at him and held up a plate covered with aluminum foil when he opened the door.

"I come bearing cookies!" she said happily.

Arrow opened the door wide and gestured for her to come inside. The low heels she was wearing clicked on the floor as she entered his apartment. He closed and locked the door behind her, and followed her to the kitchen. She placed the plate on the counter and peeled back the foil.

"Looks good," Arrow told her.

The plate was overflowing with cookies. He could see the marshmallows oozing from the middle of every cookie, and each was drizzled with chocolate. There were chunks of what he assumed were graham crackers making the cookies lopsided and even more delicious looking.

"Have one," Ellie said, holding the plate out to him.

Arrow shook his head and held out a hand. "No, that's all right."

Morgan's mom pouted. "You don't want one?"

He didn't, but to be polite, Arrow said, "Okay, maybe just one."

His words made the frown disappear from Ellie's face as if by magic. "Yay! Here, take this one," she ordered, pointing at one of the biggest cookies on the plate. Arrow wasn't a huge fan of sugar, especially in its raw form, but he picked it up and smiled anyway.

"You want to go and sit while we wait for Morgan?"

"Sure. We can do that," Ellie said, not taking her eyes from the cookie in his hand.

Frowning, he asked, "Aren't you going to have one?"

Her eyes whipped up to his. "Oh no! I'm watching my weight, after all." She patted her flat belly. "But you look like you could handle more than one without any issue whatsoever." And with that, she reached out and put another cookie on a napkin sitting nearby and carried it over to the couch. She put it on the coffee table in front of her and smiled at Arrow.

Inwardly sighing, and hoping it wouldn't take Morgan long to get back from her appointment, Arrow took a bite of the overly sweet concoction in his hand and made his way to the couch next to Ellie.

He hadn't had a chance to introduce Morgan to his mom yet, but he was pretty sure she'd get along with his mother better than he got along with *hers*. Wanting to finish the cookie as soon as possible, he took another large bite and swallowed it almost without chewing.

Ellie looked so happy with his seeming enjoyment of the sweet treat, he couldn't regret eating it, even if he hadn't wanted it in the first place.

"So . . . tell me about yourself," Ellie said as she settled back against the couch, her purse on the floor at her feet. "I want to know everything about the man my daughter ditched her mom for."

It wasn't the best start to their conversation, but Arrow was determined to do everything he could to make the visit work. After all, if he was going to spend the rest of his life with Morgan, he'd have to put up with Ellie for a hell of a long time.

~

"I can't thank you enough for coming to get me," Morgan told Chloe as they walked down the hall toward the elevator.

"Anytime. How'd it go?"

"Good. Basically, I need to cut myself some slack and stop trying to pretend that nothing happened to me. I'm probably going to have triggers, things that remind me of what happened, for quite a while. And as long as I'm talking about them to someone, and not letting the stress build up inside, it's okay to have freak-outs now and then."

"Your therapist sounds smart," Chloe observed.

Morgan chuckled. "I would hope so."

Once they were inside the elevator, Chloe said, "I was going to invite you and Arrow to dinner tonight."

"You *were*? But not anymore?"

She smiled. "Nope. You have other plans."

"I do?"

"Yup."

"You're being awfully mysterious," Morgan mock complained. "Arrow said he had a surprise for me. I hate surprises."

"You want to know?"

Morgan turned to her friend. "Yes!"

"Too bad," Chloe said with a grin. "I'm not telling you."

"You suck," Morgan said with a pout.

Chloe laughed again and hooked her arm in Morgan's. "I know. Come on. Let's get you home."

"You know, I'll never get tired of hearing that."

"What?"

"Home. In regard to Arrow's apartment," Morgan explained.

"I know what you mean. I used to live in a mansion, but it never felt like a home to me. But the second I walked into Ro's house, I was comfortable. Though I could live in a cave with him, and it would still be home."

Morgan nodded. "I have a feeling Arrow feels bad that he only has an apartment when you and Allye have houses, but I honestly don't care. All I care about is that he's there with me."

"Have you told him that?" Chloe asked as they got into her car.

"Not really. He's told me that he loves me, though," Morgan admitted.

"Cool," Chloe breathed.

"I already talked to Allye about this, but you don't think it's too soon?"

"Nope. I'm all for the guys finding love. Arrow is awesome. A bit too straitlaced sometimes, but I have a feeling you can help loosen him up."

"The cans of food in his pantry were alphabetized," Morgan admitted.

"They were not!" Chloe exclaimed.

"Yup. And all the towels in his closet were stacked by color."

Chloe giggled. "That actually doesn't really surprise me when I think about it."

"I think it was the Marine in him," Morgan said. "Sometimes I feel as if I'm this hurricane that entered his world and is screwing everything up."

"Don't. If he didn't like it, he'd tell you. Has he said anything?"

"No."

"Then he doesn't care."

Morgan sighed. "I'm so happy that I'm afraid it's all going to disappear in a puff of smoke."

"And what did your therapist say about that?" Chloe asked with amazing insight.

"That I'm allowed to be happy. That I should take things one day at a time, which, incidentally, is what Arrow told me too."

"Well, there ya go," Chloe said.

"You want to come up?" Morgan asked after they'd arrived in the parking lot.

"Sure. But just because I was ordered by Arrow to make sure you made it all the way to the door."

Morgan rolled her eyes. "You can come in if you want."

"And ruin your surprise? I don't think so. Come on," Chloe ordered, gesturing toward the front lobby.

The two women walked through the lobby, said hello to Robert, then got in the elevator. They made small talk until they reached Arrow's door. Morgan pulled out the key he'd given her and put it in the lock.

"Thanks again for picking me up. One of these days I'm going to get a new driver's license and get my own vehicle."

"Whatever. I'm happy to help in the meantime," Chloe said. "Call me tomorrow, and we'll figure out when to do dinner."

"Okay, when are you—" Her question was cut off when the door opened.

Morgan stared in shock at the person who opened it.

"Mom! What are you doing here?"

"Hi, honey! Surprise!"

"Surprise," Chloe whispered from next to her.

Morgan could only stare at her mom in disbelief. If this was Arrow's surprise, it wasn't necessarily a good one. She might've said she wanted her mom the night before, but it had been a moment of weakness. Almost as soon as the words left her mouth, she'd realized that her mother wasn't the person who could make her feel better . . . it was the man whose arms she'd been lying in at that moment. Just being close to him gave her strength. Made her feel grounded.

But Arrow was a man of his word, and since she'd said she wanted her mom, Arrow had gotten her.

Taking a deep breath, Morgan decided to make the best of the situation. If Arrow had arranged it, she didn't want to make him feel bad.

"I'll call you later," she told Chloe with a smile, and turned to go inside.

Chapter Nineteen

Arrow didn't feel good at all. He had a raging headache, and his stomach was in knots. He felt queasy and nauseous. He'd known better than to eat one of Ellie's cookies when he wasn't used to that much sugar, and he'd eaten not only one, but half of a second as well.

Ellie had looked so pleased when he'd made the effort, though, and he really wanted to make a good impression on the woman. She was going to be his mother-in-law, hopefully, one day.

But he was so sick now, he was on the verge of excusing himself to go to the bathroom to throw up. Maybe that would make him feel better.

He heard Morgan at the door at the same time Ellie did.

"Don't get up. I'll get it," she said.

Arrow nodded, as he didn't think he could get up without hunching over. He watched as Ellie made her way across the room toward his front door . . .

And even though he was as miserable as he'd ever been, everything clicked in his brain.

He'd seen that walk before. Recently, in fact.

On the video he'd watched several times over.

No wonder the person on the tape had seemed familiar to him—it was Morgan's mother!

They'd been looking for a man, when they should've realized the perpetrator was a woman.

Her hips swayed as she walked, and she kept her head down, almost naturally.

He saw her open the door to Morgan, and he wanted to yell out, tell Morgan to run, but he had no idea what the woman would do to her daughter if he did. He didn't understand why Ellie would attack Dave—he was having a hard time thinking straight—but he knew he needed to play things as cool as possible.

Doing the only thing he could think of at the moment, he called out, "Chloe?"

The other woman stuck her head inside the apartment and said, "Yes?" She stared at him with a weird look on her face, and he couldn't blame her. It was rare that he didn't stand up when there was a woman around. Good manners had been bred into him by his mother, but he couldn't stand. He could barely move.

"Will you tell Ro that I'm having trouble with my fuse box? I'd appreciate his help with it as soon as possible."

"Um . . . okay. Yeah, I'll tell him."

"Thanks," Arrow mumbled, then hunched over on the couch, clutching his stomach.

He heard the door shut and female voices, but he couldn't look up to see what was going on.

"Arrow?"

He felt the cushion next to him dip and Morgan's hand on his knee, but he didn't look up. "I don't feel good." He could tell he was slurring his words, but he couldn't seem to control himself.

"What in the world is wrong? Mom? How long has he been like this?"

"Drunk? He started drinking when I got here."

"Arrow doesn't drink," Morgan said in shock.

"Well, he did today," Ellie said matter-of-factly.

"That doesn't make any sense," Morgan said. "I don't see any bottles."

"He already threw them away. He didn't want you to see them," her mom explained.

"Arrow? Are you drunk?" Morgan asked softly. She hadn't moved her hand from his knee, and he wanted to both grip it tightly and do something to make her leave the apartment.

"No," he managed to say. "Stomach hurts."

"I'm calling an ambulance," Morgan declared, standing up.

"I don't think so."

Arrow turned his head to see Ellie standing next to her daughter. With a gun pointed at her head.

Groaning, he shifted on the couch, but froze when Ellie said, "If you move, I'll shoot her."

He immediately stilled. He knew he needed to do something, but his stomach was cramping now, and he could feel a bit of drool on his chin. He had no idea what she'd poisoned him with, but whatever it had been was extremely effective. Arrow wanted to protect Morgan, but he couldn't make his muscles move.

"Mom, what in the world are you *doing*?" Morgan asked.

"Have a seat," Ellie said congenially. "We're going to sit and have a chat."

"He's hurting, Mom," Morgan said quietly. "I need to get him some help."

"No! I said, sit."

Slowly, Morgan once again sat on the couch next to Arrow, and he groaned when the motion made his stomach twist. He turned his head and vomited. Right there on his living room floor, in front of the woman he loved more than life itself. But he didn't feel even the least bit embarrassed. In fact, he wanted to do it again and again. His body wanted to purge whatever was inside it making him sick.

"Why don't you have a cookie, darling?" Ellie asked her daughter, nodding to the half Arrow hadn't eaten, which lay on the coffee table.

"I'm not hungry," Morgan replied.

"Eat. It," she ordered.

Moving slowly, Morgan picked up the s'mores cookie and nibbled at the end. Then she asked, "Why are you doing this?"

"Because I can," Ellie said. "Now, keep eating."

Suddenly, Arrow realized he was an idiot. "No. Don't!" he told Morgan.

"You shut up!" Ellie screeched at him. She'd gone from being calm and controlled to losing it in a second. "And *you*," she said, turning her wrath on Morgan. "Eat it!" She lunged forward and shoved the cookie into her daughter's face, smooshing chocolate and marshmallow all over her chin and cheeks.

Morgan struggled with her mom, and Arrow had never felt so helpless. It felt like his insides were being scraped out with a spoon. He'd thought he was tough, but whatever Ellie had put in the cookies felt as if it was eating him from the inside out.

He needed to help Morgan. Needed to protect her, but he was too weak to move. Too weak to be any kind of threat to her mom.

As the woman he loved fought her very own mother, he closed his eyes and prayed Chloe would relay his message to Ro sooner rather than later.

~

Morgan turned her face to the side as she struggled with her mother. She had no idea what was going on, but whatever it was, it was bad. Arrow hadn't moved from his hunched-over position on the couch, and she could hear moans coming from his throat. His throwing up had startled and scared her, but her mother acting like a psychopath was even more terrifying.

"Mom! Stop it!" she ordered, but it did no good. Ellie continued trying to shove bits of cookie into Morgan's mouth.

"Stop it? Did you stop seeing that cheating bastard of a father when I asked you to? No! Did you listen when I told you he was only using you to get back at me? *No!* You didn't! He should've stopped trying to see you. He discarded me like a piece of trash, and I warned him he'd pay, but *he* didn't listen to me either. And I made him pay! I bet he's sorry now!"

"Who's sorry? Dad?"

"Stop calling him that!" Ellie screeched, then abruptly straightened and hurried to the kitchen.

"Get out," Arrow mumbled from next to her. "She put something in the cookies. I only had one and a half. I can't move. Get out *now*."

"I can't leave you!" Morgan said, completely freaked out. It was as if she'd walked into the twilight zone.

"Leave!" Arrow ordered, but his voice was weak and unsteady.

"No one is leaving," Ellie scolded them. She was standing in front of them holding the plate of cookies she'd retrieved from the kitchen. "In fact, I think more cookies are in order. Look, they're your favorite, Morgan. S'mores. I made them just for you and your boyfriend."

"Mom, how'd you make Dad pay?" Morgan asked. She ignored the way Arrow gripped her thigh. She knew he wanted her to make a run for it, but she wasn't going to leave him there with her obviously unstable mother. He hadn't left her in Santo Domingo, so there was no way she was leaving him now. In the back of her mind, she knew it wasn't the same thing, but she didn't care.

"I took away the only thing he ever wanted from me."

Morgan stared at her mother in horror, knowing what she was going to say before she said it.

"His daughter. I took you away from him and watched in glee as he suffered. And it was *glorious*."

"Mom," Morgan whimpered. "It was you? *You* had me kidnapped?"

"Yup. And your father was beside himself. Boo-hooing to whoever would listen. I took you, and there was nothing *he* could do about it!"

"I was raped," Morgan whispered. "Beaten. Starved."

"All the better to make him feel guilty!" Ellie crowed.

"You don't even *care*?" Morgan asked in disbelief.

"That he felt bad? No way!"

"No, Mom, about *me*!" Morgan yelled. "I was in hell, and you did it to get back at *Dad*?"

"It worked too!" she bragged. "Until *this* asshole had to go and rescue you. Your father had the grand reunion he'd been praying to have for an entire year. He had you back, and that wasn't part of my plan. He got to be on TV. His name is known throughout the country now, and he got even richer than he was before as a result. His stupid company's stocks soared! That wasn't supposed to happen. He hadn't suffered enough!"

"What about *me*? Hadn't *I* suffered enough?"

Ellie waved her hand as if her daughter's words were unimportant. "But I decided to show him. His precious daughter was going to get sick. Reeeeally sick. No one would be able to figure out what from. Some tropical disease. But then you had to ruin *that* too by leaving and coming back up here! I had it all planned out. You'd slowly get sick from drinking my special blend of orange juice. But you always did have too much of your father in you. Ruining *everything*."

"That's why my stomach hurt and I had headaches?" Morgan asked, shaking her head. "You were poisoning me? With what?"

"My friends scored me some ethylene glycol. I could've just gotten some antifreeze from the store, but it's a weird green color. You might've noticed. I wanted the pure stuff. I was skeptical that it would work, but look at your boyfriend—I'd say it works just fine!" Ellie laughed.

Morgan turned to look at Arrow. He looked awful. And all because her *mom* had poisoned him. She could barely wrap her mind around what was happening.

"Why Arrow?" Morgan asked. "He didn't do *anything* to you."

"Oh yes, he did!" her mom countered. "First, he found you. Second, he was able to get you out of the Dominican Republic without being caught by my friends. Third, he convinced you to come back up here. And fourth . . . I just don't like him or his stupid friends."

Morgan clenched the hand that wasn't holding on to Arrow. She couldn't believe what she was hearing. She'd known her mom had been to the doctor often when Morgan was growing up, but she'd had no idea what for. Now she realized it had to be for some sort of personality disorder. There was no way her mother had been this psychotic her entire life and it hadn't been noticed.

"Mom . . . I didn't know you felt like that. I don't even like Dad. I was visiting him because I thought *you* wanted me to." Morgan tried to placate her mother. If she could get her to think she was on her side, maybe she'd have a chance of getting out of this alive. And getting Arrow to a doctor.

"Liar," Ellie said calmly. It was all the more scary because of the way she said it. "I know what you're doing. You're just trying to make me let down my guard. But it won't work. Don't you see, baby? You *have* to die to show your father that he can't make a fool out of me. He can't sleep with his secretary right under my nose and get away with it!"

"I didn't have anything to do with that," Morgan said softly, still trying to reason with her mother.

But there was no getting through to Ellie Jernigan. She was lost in the delusion her mind had created. "You need to eat these cookies, baby," she cooed. "They're your favorite. You won't even taste the poison."

"No," Morgan said. "I need to call the police and get Arrow some help."

"I'm afraid I can't let you do that," Ellie said with a sigh. Then she put the plate of cookies down on the table and reached for her purse on the floor. She was fiddling with it when Morgan looked at Arrow to see

241

if he had any bright ideas about what to do. She saw all his attention was on her mother.

His eyes widened—and that was enough for Morgan to look back at her mom just in time to see her lunge in her direction.

Surprised, Morgan let out a yell, but she was instantly on the floor with her mother on top of her. Ellie was holding a syringe to her throat and glaring at her. She must've pulled it out of her purse when Morgan had been distracted.

Morgan saw no emotion other than hate in her mother's glazed eyes.

"Get up," Ellie ordered.

Shaking, Morgan got to her feet, ever aware of the needle inches from her throat. She had no idea where the gun Ellie'd been holding earlier had gone. Maybe she'd left it in the kitchen when she went to get the cookies. Morgan desperately tried to think of what she could do. How she could distract her mom.

"Don't even think of doing something stupid," Ellie warned. "The second I jab you with this needle, you're dead. It's got undiluted ethylene glycol in it. Your kidneys will immediately begin to fail, you'll start to have seizures, and you'll puke your guts out. But it won't help."

"Mom, don't do this," Morgan begged, tears falling down her cheeks for the first time.

"Crying won't help either. Maybe *now* your father will regret what he did to me. He needs to repent! He'll *pay*. I'm *making* him pay!"

Just when Morgan was determined she had to attempt some sort of move, to fight her mom for the needle, the door to Arrow's apartment burst open and the Mountain Mercenaries rushed inside, weapons drawn.

❧

Arrow blinked, but his eyes were watering so much he couldn't clear them. His stomach continued to spasm, but he tried to ignore it and concentrate on what was going on around him.

Ellie Jernigan was obviously batshit crazy . . . or more likely off her meds. He didn't know if she was bipolar and hadn't been taking her medicine, or if she was truly just insane. At this point, it didn't matter. All that mattered was making sure Morgan was safe.

He had no idea how he was going to accomplish that, though. Ellie might be crazy, but she wasn't stupid. She'd planned well, poisoning him and taking him out of the equation before Morgan arrived home.

And he hadn't felt she was much of a threat until it was too late. Arrow wondered if there was anything in her past that would've pointed toward this possibility. While they'd looked into Morgan's mom, they obviously hadn't looked hard enough.

She'd been nurturing a grudge toward her ex her entire adult life, letting it fester and grow until it utterly consumed her, sucking her daughter down into the pit of hell with her.

Arrow knew he was in trouble. The ethylene glycol was making its way through his body, damaging his kidneys and wreaking havoc with alarming speed. She'd obviously put a lot of the stuff into the cookies, and he'd stupidly eaten one and a half of the damn things.

He jerked when Ellie tackled her daughter and they landed at his feet, inches from the contents of his stomach he'd vomited up earlier, but neither woman seemed to notice.

Arrow focused on the syringe Ellie was holding to her daughter's throat. If he weren't incapacitated, he'd be able to knock it away without any effort whatsoever, but he couldn't control his hands—they were shaking violently—and he didn't think he'd be able to even stand.

It felt as if he had knives in his lower abdomen, stabbing him from the inside out. He watched as Ellie forced Morgan to stand and taunted her with that damn needle at her throat.

The thought of Morgan feeling even a tenth of what he was feeling right now made adrenaline course through his body. No way did he want her to go through pain like this. She'd been through enough. More than enough.

Arrow had no plan in mind. He couldn't get his thoughts in order enough to make a plan. All he knew was that he had to get the needle away from the woman he loved. It was too close to her throat.

The second Arrow heard the crash of his door hitting the wall when it smashed open, he moved.

Painfully throwing himself from his crumpled position on the couch, he aimed for Morgan's torso. He'd never played football in school, but any coach would've been proud of the way he took her down. He heard the *umph* of a breath leaving her body as he grabbed her, but instead of loosening his grip, he tightened it.

His insides were screaming at him, but he twisted his body to land on his back on the floor, Morgan on top of him.

There was screaming around him, but the only thing Arrow was concerned about was protecting Morgan. With his last bit of energy, he rolled over, covering as much of her body as he could. If Ellie was going to stick someone with that damn poison needle of hers, it would be him. Not her daughter. Not the woman he loved more than life itself.

The last thing he remembered was Ellie screaming, *"No!"*

Then the unmistakable sound of a gunshot.

～

Morgan tried to take a deep breath, but Arrow had gone limp on top of her. He was extremely heavy, and it took all her strength to scoot out from under him. The adrenaline in her body was off the charts, and she didn't even spare a glance at her mother, who was lying motionless on the floor next to the couch.

She had heard the gunshot but hadn't even flinched, more concerned about Arrow.

"Help me!" she yelled, her voice wavering, as she tried to roll him over.

Then there were several hands helping her. Arrow lay on his back, his chest barely moving up and down. "She poisoned him!" she cried, not looking up. "With ethylene glycol. It was in the cookies! He had at least one. Maybe more."

"Scoot back," Ro told her, putting a hand on her arm.

Reluctantly, Morgan did as ordered, not taking her eyes from Arrow's chest. As long as she could see it moving, he was alive.

"Paramedics are on their way," Ball said.

"Police are about a minute and a half behind," Meat added.

Still, Morgan didn't look away from Arrow. He was pale, and even though he didn't have a mark on him, she knew things weren't good.

"Are you all right?" Ro asked, kneeling next to her and trying to turn her toward him.

She resisted and nodded quickly. "I'm fine."

"You didn't eat any?"

She shook her head.

"You've got chocolate on your face," Ro said gently, finally turning her head enough so she had to look at him.

"I had the tiniest nibble of one. Then she tried to shove one in my mouth, but I pressed my lips together. I'm fine," she repeated. "But Arrow's not."

"Black had to shoot your mother."

"I don't care! She was behind it! *All* of it."

"We know that now," Ro told her.

"How'd you know to come?" she asked, trying to keep her frantic mind off Arrow's still body.

"Arrow. He's the best electrician we know. There's no way he'd ask me to come over and help with a fuse box. Chloe called from the parking lot and relayed the message, and we immediately knew something was up. We rushed over here . . . and the rest you know."

"It was my *mom*," Morgan whispered, her voice breaking. "She didn't care that I was being hurt. She only wanted to make my dad suffer."

"Come 'ere," Ro said, pulling her into his embrace.

Morgan went willingly, needing the support. She angled her head so she could still see Arrow even as Ro knelt on the floor with her. He made sure to keep her turned so she could see the man she loved, and not her mother.

"He's going to be all right, isn't he?" she whispered, just as the paramedics rushed into the room.

"Yes," Ro said with no hesitation. "He's one tough Marine. He'll beat this."

"I love him," Morgan admitted softly. "I never told him, but I love him so damn much."

"He knows, love. He knows."

Ro helped Morgan to her feet while the paramedics got to work on Arrow. She couldn't do anything but watch as the love of her life was quickly bundled onto a backboard and rushed out of the room. She wanted to go with him, but Ro held her back. "He's in good hands. Let them get him to the hospital and start the antidote. We'll get you there as soon as possible."

Morgan wanted to protest. Wanted to demand to go with Arrow, but she took a deep breath and nodded. Someone would have to call his mom and sister. The police were entering the apartment now, even as the second set of paramedics worked on her mother. But with one look, Morgan knew it was too late for her.

Black was a damn good shot—and the hole in the middle of Ellie's forehead spoke for itself.

Morgan wanted to feel bad. Wanted to mourn her mother, but after learning what she had in the last half hour, it was impossible.

The woman lying on the floor wasn't her mother. She was a monster who Morgan had never known. Her mother had apparently died long ago.

Straightening her shoulders, she nodded at Ro and allowed him to guide her to a chair at Arrow's dining room table. He wrapped a blanket around her shoulders and went to assist his teammates.

A kind-looking police officer pulled out a chair next to her and said, "Can you tell me what happened?"

Morgan knew it was going to take longer than a few minutes to explain the events that had led up to her mother being dead on the floor, but she took a deep breath and began speaking. The sooner she got through this, the sooner she could get to Arrow's side.

Chapter Twenty

A week later, Morgan was sitting in the orange armchair a nurse had unearthed for her from somewhere in the hospital. She hadn't left Arrow's side except to shower or when one of his friends forced her to go get something to eat in the cafeteria.

The first two days had been touch-and-go. Arrow had been in the intensive care unit as doctors did what they could to counteract the ethylene glycol that had been coursing through his body. He had been intubated and had lain motionless, oblivious to everything going on around him.

After he'd been decontaminated, the next step was to prevent the poison from metabolizing further in his body. As well as administering the antidote, the doctors had put him on kidney dialysis to assist his body in cleansing itself.

It was a long and exhausting process, but the first time Arrow had opened his eyes and said her name, Morgan had cried.

Arrow was weak, and he still slept a lot, but he was no longer intubated, and she could tell he was getting stronger with every day that went by.

Hearing someone at the door, Morgan turned to look and saw that it was Black. She hadn't seen him since he and his teammates had stormed into Arrow's apartment like a pack of superheroes.

"Hi," she said softly, not wanting to wake Arrow.

"I can come back later," Black said, not meeting her eyes.

Morgan knew he'd been avoiding her, but she refused to let him do it anymore. "Get over here," she said as sternly as possible.

As if he were headed for the electric chair, Black sighed and shuffled over to her, sitting on the very edge of one of the other chairs in the room.

Deciding it was better to just get it out in the open, Morgan said, "Thank you for saving our lives."

Black snorted, but didn't otherwise comment.

"Seriously," Morgan pressed. "The cops said my mother had grabbed the gun she'd stashed in her waistband when you guys came in. She was bound and determined to see me dead. She would've shot me, and since Arrow was on top of me, protecting me, she would've killed him for sure. There's no way he could've lived through both the poisoning and a gunshot."

"I killed your *mom*," Black said softly.

"I know. Thank you."

At that, he looked up, and Morgan saw both the surprise and the guilt in his eyes. She reached for him and put a hand on his knee. "I'm sorry you had to do it in the first place, but I'm not sorry it was done. Black . . . the woman you shot was *not* my mother. I don't know what happened or how she became that way, but she was truly insane. You had to do it."

Black ran a hand over his head before saying, "When I was a Navy SEAL, I killed more than my fair share of bad guys. Even on missions for the Mountain Mercenaries, I've done what I've had to do . . . but I've spent the last few years protecting and saving women . . . not shooting them."

"She got what she deserved," Morgan said, her voice only hitching once. She knew she'd have to have more sessions with her therapist to put everything that had happened behind her, but at the moment, she was more concerned about making sure the amazing man in *front* of her didn't continue to beat himself up over what he'd done.

"I didn't even think," Black said, staring off into space. "I just reacted. She reached behind her, I saw the weapon, and I didn't even think about it."

"Good," Morgan said fervently.

That got his attention. Black turned to stare at her in disbelief.

"I love Arrow. More than I ever thought it would be possible to love someone. And knowing he's with you while he's on future missions makes me feel so much better. I want someone who can act without thinking when the shit hits the fan. I want someone like you to have his back.

"Black, I don't pretend to know what you've done and seen in your past, but you're good at what you do. She was going to kill me. Had already tried to kill both me and Arrow. You did what you had to do. If that had been a man, would you be beating yourself up like this? If it had been a stranger? No, you wouldn't. Bad guys aren't always strangers, and they don't wear black and cackle to let you know that they're the villain."

"I'm still sorry," he said.

"Me too," Morgan agreed. "But don't be sorry that you killed her. Be sorry that she didn't get the help she needed. Be sorry that she never got to know how great her hopefully future son-in-law is. Be sorry that her grandchildren will never know their grandmother. But do *not* be sorry for saving my life. Don't be sorry for ensuring I could start my life here without having to constantly look over my shoulder, wondering if whoever kidnapped me was going to do it again."

Black looked up and gave her a small smile. It wasn't exactly a full-blown grin, but he looked a lot more relaxed than he'd been when he'd arrived.

Moving without thought, Morgan stood and held out her arms. "I could use a hug."

Black moved quickly and had her in his embrace almost before she'd finished speaking. Morgan felt tiny with him, but not as much as when she was around a lot of his other teammates.

"Thank you," he whispered.

"No . . . thank *you*," she returned fiercely.

"Get your hands off my woman," Arrow said in a weak voice from the hospital bed next to them.

Morgan laughed when Black held her tighter and turned to face his friend. "You snooze, you lose," he quipped.

Arrow growled, and Morgan smiled even bigger. She pushed against Black. "Go get your own woman," she teased, happy that she and Arrow's friend seemed to be back on even ground. She hated that he'd felt even a second of guilt for firing the fatal shot.

Pulling her chair closer to the bed, Morgan sat and intertwined her fingers with Arrow's. "How do you feel?"

"Not bad," Arrow responded.

Morgan wanted to roll her eyes. She'd learned that Arrow had the unfortunate tendency to seriously downplay how he was feeling.

He lifted his hand to Black, and the other man took it in his own.

"Thanks for saving not only my life, but Morgan's as well," Arrow told him.

Black shook his hand, but said, "Fuck you. You would've done the same thing if you weren't taking a nap on the floor."

Arrow chuckled, and immediately winced at the movement. "I know I've been out of it, but I've heard bits and pieces of what happened. Can you elaborate?" he asked.

Black nodded and sat back down in the chair next to his bed. Morgan clasped Arrow's hand tighter and listened. She'd heard the entire story, so nothing Black could say would shock her, but every time she heard how awful her mom truly was, it was hard to understand how she'd gotten to that place in her life.

"Ellie Jernigan hired the men who drugged and kidnapped Morgan. They followed her to the bar that night and waited for their chance to grab her," Black said.

"And I made it really easy when I left early," Morgan said with a shake of her head.

"They would've gotten you one way or another," Black soothed. "Anyway, so she'd made contacts down in the Dominican Republic and had her daughter shipped down there. The plan was for them to just hold on to her until further notice."

"They didn't hurt me at first," Morgan added. "Rex and the others guessed that it was probably because they didn't want to risk my mom not paying them. But when they kept getting the money month after month, and weren't required to send any proof that I was okay or anything, they decided to take advantage of the situation and take what they wanted."

Morgan felt Arrow's hand tighten on hers, but he didn't interrupt.

"As you must have already guessed, the person on the video was Ellie," Black said. "She'd probably been waiting for *you* when Dave showed up. She didn't exactly have a lot of patience, and we think she just lost her temper. But she retained enough control to keep her face away from the cameras and to stop once Dave was down."

"How's Dave?" Arrow asked.

"He's fine. Back at work and bossing everyone around at The Pit," Black told him.

"Good. And yeah, when Ellie walked to the door in my apartment to meet Morgan and Chloe, I recognized her gait from the video," Arrow said. "That's why I thought the person looked familiar. But by then, I was already pretty much incapacitated. I did what I could to try to warn you guys."

"I can't believe I didn't recognize her. My own mother," Morgan said with another shake of her head.

"You thought it was a man, as did we," Black said. "And your mom was the last person you suspected."

Arrow lifted Morgan's hand and kissed the back of it, giving her silent support, as he always did.

"And Arrow, your message to us worked perfectly. Ellie had no idea what you'd said was a clue. Chloe was confused and immediately called Ro when she got back to her car, to pass on your strange message. He knew something was wrong, and we all converged on your apartment."

"Thank God," Morgan threw in. "I was clueless until it was too late."

"Anyway, Meat tracked Ellie's cell phone and found out she'd been in town for a few days. It was likely she who'd ordered the prostitute and slashed your tires."

"I thought as much," Arrow said.

"Right, so when you called and asked if she could visit Morgan, she was already in town. She checked into a hotel with a kitchen and made the cookies. Apparently, she'd brought the ethylene glycol with her in the hopes of getting it into her daughter somehow."

"Her plan was to poison me slowly when I was living with her," Morgan told Arrow. "She wanted to make it seem like I had some disease I caught when I was in captivity. That's why my stomach and head hurt when I first came back up to Colorado Springs. The dose had been small enough that my body had been able to process it. But over time, it would've built up enough that I wouldn't have been able to fight it off."

Arrow's teeth ground together, but he didn't comment.

"She put enough ethylene glycol in those cookies to kill someone within a couple hours," Black said.

"I didn't taste it at all," Arrow mused. "I don't usually eat anything that sweet, but I was trying to be polite. We hadn't exactly hit it off, and I felt bad about that. Have you seen your father?" Arrow asked Morgan, changing the subject.

"Of course. He flew out here the second he heard. And not surprisingly, he's been awesome in dealing with the press. They, of course, went apeshit when they heard what happened. I don't know what I would've done if it wasn't for him."

"I'm sorry we suspected him," Arrow told her.

Morgan waved off his apology. "He's not exactly a saint, and I'm not sure we'll ever be best friends or anything, but I do feel a lot better knowing he was honest in his worry for me and his sincere desire to find me when I disappeared."

"Lane and Lance Buswell were also completely innocent," Black said. "As are the rest of her friends."

"So you're truly free," Arrow said, not taking his eyes from Morgan.

"Looks that way."

"And that's my cue to leave," Black said as he stood. "Oh, and your mom and sister are here," he told Arrow.

His eyes widened. "They are?"

"Of course they are!" Morgan exclaimed. "You almost *died*. I called them the second I had the chance. They've been staying at a nearby hotel. I really like Kandi. She's so funny, and I've heard lots of stories about when you were younger."

Arrow groaned. "Figures. Half the things she says are lies. Don't believe her."

"That's exactly what she said you'd say," Morgan teased.

Black chuckled as he headed for the door. At the last minute, he turned and said to Morgan, "Thanks for being so understanding."

She rolled her eyes. "As if I could be anything else."

"You'd be surprised at how unforgiving people can be," Black said, then he was gone.

"Come here," Arrow said, tugging on her hand.

"I am here," Morgan replied.

"Here," Arrow insisted.

Morgan stood and sat on the edge of the bed, her hip touching Arrow's.

"You love me?" he asked, once she was settled.

Morgan knew she was blushing, but she didn't look away from him. "You heard that, huh?"

"Yeah. And it bears repeating. You know I love you. It almost killed me to not be able to protect you when your mom was going off. I've never felt so much pain as I did doubled over on my couch. But what *really* killed me was when your mom attacked you . . . and all I could do was sit there."

"But you did protect me," Morgan protested. "When it counted, you were there. I was frozen in fear . . . and confusion. I mean, it was my *mom* who was behind everything. I couldn't wrap my head around it, much less do anything about it when she grabbed me and was going to shove that needle in my neck."

"I love you, Morgan Byrd. I will spend the rest of my days doing whatever I can to protect you."

"I'm hoping that the days of me needing protecting are over," Morgan said dryly.

"I love you," Arrow repeated, and raised his eyebrows expectantly.

Morgan grinned. "I know."

"And? Do you have something to say to me in return?"

"Um . . . thanks?"

"Beautiful . . . ," Arrow said in the most threatening tone he could muster—which wasn't very scary, considering he was lying in a hospital bed with an IV in him and hooked up to various machines.

Morgan leaned over and took his face in her hands. "I love you, Archer Kane. More than I ever thought it was possible to love anyone. I don't want to see you like you were on your floor ever again. You scared the shit out of me."

"You won't," he vowed.

"You can't promise that," Morgan protested.

One hand moved and settled on her neck. The other he put on the small of her back. They were huddled together, their foreheads almost touching, when he whispered, "I promise you the world, beautiful. Happiness, laughter, friendship, and babies. Lots and lots of babies."

Morgan's breath hitched, and she stared at him.

"Will you marry me? I promise to love and cherish you for the rest of my life. I promise to be your friend as well as your lover. I'll do my best to make you laugh and never make you cry, unless they're happy tears. I'll live wherever you want to live, and we'll buy a big house with some land so you can have as many bees as you want. I'll go on vacations with you . . . except maybe not to the Caribbean. I love my job, but if it makes you feel safer, I'll quit today and concentrate on my electrician gig. I'll do whatever it takes for you to say yes."

"I . . . I want to marry you . . . but I'm scared that I'll never be able to be the woman you need in the bedroom," she admitted. "I want children, but I'm afraid I'll never be able to relax enough to make them with you."

"I told you once, and I'll say it as many times as you need to hear it to believe it. I love *you*, Morgan. Even if we never make love in the conventional way, even if all we ever do is cuddle and masturbate together, I want you exactly the way you are."

"Arrow," Morgan choked out.

"But I have to say, I believe that once you deal with everything, you're going to be able to do whatever you want to do . . . including making love to, and fucking, your husband. I'll never pressure you, you'll have all the control you want in the bedroom. I'll be on the bottom for the rest of my life if that's what you need."

Morgan had tears in her eyes, but she chuckled anyway. "You'll be my sex slave?"

"Hell yes. And if you think that's a negative, I'll just let you go on thinking that. Having you above me, riding me, getting off while I get to watch every single expression on your face and have your tits right there in front of me as you take me? Yeah . . . reeeeeal tough, beautiful."

This time, the laugh that escaped was genuine and heartfelt. "Then yes. Yes, I'll marry you."

Arrow lifted his head a fraction of an inch and covered her lips with his own. They were dry and cracked, but she'd never felt anything better in her entire life.

Epilogue

Four weeks later, Arrow was sitting on their new couch in their new apartment, watching a movie. He was as proud of Morgan as he could be. Finding out the truth behind her kidnapping had been cathartic. She had visited with her therapist every day for a week after he'd gotten out of the hospital and had been slowly tapering off the visits.

She was sleeping through the night, and they'd even had some pretty intense make-out sessions since then too.

Arrow hadn't pressured her for anything more than she was ready to give. It was fun getting to know who she was without fear hanging over her head.

He'd found a perfect piece of land in Black Forest, near Ro and Chloe, that he was planning on building a house on. It was going to be the ideal place to not only raise a family, but for Morgan to put up a beehive or two. She'd decided not to go full scale again, but just harvest enough honey for them and their friends instead.

She was researching what she wanted to do with the rest of her life, but for now, they were content to be alive and well.

"Arrow?" she asked as her fingers trailed up and down his arm, which was banded around her chest. She lay with her back to his front. She had on a tank top, as that was still her favorite thing to sleep in, and a pair of sleep shorts. He wore a pair of cotton lounging pants. He'd started sleeping in just his boxers and loved feeling her legs intertwined with his as she snuggled into him night after night.

"Yeah?" he responded.

She looked up at him. "Will you make love to me?"

He nearly choked.

He'd sat in on a session with her therapist, and they'd talked about the process of sexual healing. Arrow hadn't wanted to do anything that would give Morgan flashbacks or hurt her psyche further, and the therapist had told him to let Morgan take the lead, which he was already doing.

It looked like Morgan was definitely taking the lead at the moment.

Arrow looked into the eyes of the woman he loved and said, "We can do anything you want to do. But you know what your therapist said—if it gets to be too much, all you have to do is say the word, and we'll stop, or slow down, or switch things up. Okay?"

She nodded immediately. "I trust you."

And Arrow's stomach clenched. He'd never get tired of hearing those words from her. He almost liked them more than when she said she loved him. Almost.

"I bought condoms the other day. They're upstairs in the table next to the bed."

"I'm on birth control. And I'm clean," she responded.

Arrow wanted to take her bare more than he wanted his next breath. "I've never been with a woman without wearing a condom," he told her.

"I'd like to be your first," Morgan said without looking away from his gaze.

His heart sped up at the same time his cock swelled at her words. Without responding verbally, Arrow helped her stand and held her hand all the way to their bedroom. He shut the door and gestured to the bathroom. "Go on. I'll be here waiting."

Morgan nodded, stood on her tiptoes, and kissed him briefly on the lips before padding into the en suite bathroom.

Arrow took off his pants, but kept his boxers on and climbed under the covers. He fidgeted as he waited for Morgan, more nervous now than when he'd lost his virginity.

She entered the room thirty seconds later, and Arrow studied her face carefully as she made her way to the bed. He had thought she might be nervous, like he was, but all he saw was desire and anticipation on her face.

She smiled, and instead of getting under the covers next to him, she came around to his side and climbed onto the bed. Pulling the covers down, she straddled his stomach and braced herself on his chest. "This okay?"

"Hell yeah," he said with a smile. "I take it you're in charge?"

"You said I could be," she reminded him.

"And I meant it."

"Good," Morgan purred, then she sat up and in one quick movement pulled her tank top up and over her head.

"Shit," Arrow said, his dick immediately going hard at the sight in front of him. Morgan had regained much of the weight she'd lost while in captivity, and she was absolutely stunning. She had small, perky boobs that matched her slight frame perfectly.

Without thought, his hands moved to touch her—and he almost missed her slight flinch. Immediately, he put his hands over his head and gripped the sheet there.

"I'm sorry," she said, some of the desire dimming from her eyes.

"No. Don't be. Tell me what you want me to do so I don't accidentally trigger anything."

"Can you . . . leave your hands there," she said, changing her question to an order.

Arrow nodded. It was pure torture not to touch her, not to bring her down to him so he could suck on her small, hard nipples, but he did it.

Morgan shifted backward until she was straddling his thighs, and she moved with purpose as she grabbed his boxers and carefully but steadily pulled them down over his hips. She moved away just enough for him to kick them off, then settled back where she'd been.

Arrow felt vulnerable and just a little self-conscious as she stared at his rock-hard dick, but he'd also never been more turned on in his life. He hadn't been with that many women, but he'd always been the one to take control, to guide how things progressed. But there was something very exciting about letting Morgan dictate what happened in their bed.

She tentatively reached out and gripped his dick, and Arrow couldn't stop the deep inhalation at her touch. Her hand was smooth and warm, and felt like heaven wrapped around his shaft.

She began to slowly stroke him up and down, and Arrow moaned. "God, that feels good," he praised as she continued her movements. He loved the small smile that crossed her face and the way she seemed to gain confidence with every stroke.

Arrow's back arched a little, and he pushed his hips up into her as he begged, "Harder. Squeeze me a bit harder, beautiful."

Morgan's hand immediately tightened, and Arrow swore his eyes rolled back in his head. He felt a spurt of precome leak from the head of his dick, and as Morgan used that to lubricate him, the hand job she was giving him felt even better, if that was possible.

"I want to please you too," he said. "Tell me what to do. Can I touch you?"

Biting her lip, Morgan took a bit too long to respond for his liking, but eventually said, "Yes. But please be gentle. They . . . weren't."

Arrow understood. Now wasn't the time for anger, even though he felt it deep in his bones for the men who'd violated her. He slowly raised one hand, keeping the other above his head, and palmed her small breast. The nipple immediately puckered, as if anticipating his touch. His mouth salivated with the need to suck on her, but he forced himself to just use his hand to caress and tease her breast.

When Morgan closed her eyes and threw her head back, he said, "No, keep your eyes open and on me, beautiful. See who it is under you. Who's making you feel good."

She immediately looked down at him, desire swimming in her green eyes.

"That's it, beautiful. You're all flushed and pink for me." He tweaked her nipple and was rewarded by her quick inhalation and the press of her flesh harder into his palm. The hand on his dick had stopped, and she simply gripped him tightly now, but he couldn't complain. Not when she was allowing him to touch her as he was.

"Fuck, you're perfect," he said softly.

His words seemed to act as some sort of trigger, because she hunched her shoulders and pulled away from his touch.

"Shit, I'm sorry," Arrow apologized immediately, letting go of her and putting his hand back up and over his head.

He watched as Morgan took a deep breath, then shifted off his thighs.

Cursing himself for opening his big mouth, Arrow was prepared to soothe away whatever memories he'd invoked in her. But he was surprised when she pulled off her sleep shorts and climbed back onto his lap, naked as the day she was born.

"Morgan," he started to say, but she shook her head and interrupted him.

"I want this. I want you," she said fiercely. "I'm not perfect. Far from it. I'm scared, but I know it's *you* who's under me. They never took me like this. They were never gentle. I know who I'm with, but I'm not sure how this is gonna go." Her words were jumbled together and said quickly, as if she was trying to keep up the nerve to say them at all.

"That's right, you're with me—and I love you," Arrow said. "I'll never take anything you don't want to give me. And right now, you're in charge. Do whatever feels good."

She smiled down at him, and he was so proud of her for her courage. He'd never allowed himself to think about the aftermath the women the Mountain Mercenaries rescued went through. How hard it must be to resume their normal lives. But he did now, and he had more respect for them as a result.

She scooted up until she was hovering over his cock. He'd softened a bit when she'd gotten off him, but the second she reached down and stroked him again, he was just as hard as before.

Notching the head of his dick to her opening, she pressed down—and froze.

Arrow gritted his teeth together and stayed stock-still under her. He could feel her muscles clenching tightly, trying to keep him out of her body.

"Breathe, beautiful," he whispered.

She let out the breath she'd been holding, and it sounded almost like a sob.

"I . . . I can't."

"Then don't," Arrow told her immediately. "Lift up."

She did so quickly, and he wanted to cry at losing her warmth, but he didn't let one bit of the erotic pain cross his face.

"I want you so much, but . . . I *can't*," she said again, anguished.

"Do you trust me?" Arrow asked.

"Yes."

Her immediate answer soothed his pain and made him all the more determined to make this pleasurable for her. She'd been extremely brave, and he didn't want to let her courage go unrewarded.

Slowly, he lowered his hands and placed them on her hips. "Okay?"

She nodded, but he could tell she was still nervous.

Arrow urged her to drop down again, but this time her lower lips opened and rested on his dick. He moved a hand and smeared some of his precome on his shaft, lubricating himself. Then he slowly shifted her forward, then back. Then forward again. "Like this," he told her.

Sniffing once, Morgan nodded and moved her hips against him.

"That's it. Just like that," Arrow encouraged.

"This . . . feels good," she said with a shy smile.

"It's supposed to," he told her. "It feels amazing for me too." Then he slowly moved his thumb so it rested on her clit. He lazily rubbed the small bundle of nerves as she ground herself up and down his dick.

The longer she moved, the better it felt. His dick was constantly leaking now, helping to make her movements more fluid and smooth.

"I like this," she gasped in surprise.

He smiled up at her and kept his mouth shut this time. The last thing he was going to do was open his big mouth again.

The longer she rubbed against him, the wetter she got. She was riding his cock now as if he was inside her. Her hips undulated against him, caressing the sensitive skin on the underside of his cock. He could smell her arousal, and feel it against him. He continued to flick against her clit as she rubbed herself all over him.

Watching her chest flush and her nipples peak was hot as hell . . . not to mention the way her hips gyrated more and more frantically.

"I'm going to come, beautiful," he warned her.

"Okay," she breathed.

"Is that all right? I don't want to do anything that will startle you."

"Oh yeah," she said, her gaze dropping between her legs.

He could only imagine what she saw when she looked down at their bodies. Her hand, which had been resting on his chest, reached between them, and she lifted his dick, pressing it harder between her folds. He still wasn't penetrating her, but he could feel her pussy lips on either side of his shaft now.

"Fuck," he swore, tightening his grip on her hips.

"Come on me," Morgan ordered. "I want to see it."

As if her words were all he'd been waiting for, Arrow felt his orgasm move from his balls up his shaft until he was spurting all over his stomach, her hand, and her folds.

Wanting her to come with him, he pressed on her clit hard and fast. Morgan ground down on him, prolonging his orgasm, even as she exploded with her own pleasure.

She twitched and shook over him, her fluids mixing with his own. By the time they'd both come down from their orgasmic high, they were a mess. Arrow was soaked from his stomach to his balls and knew Morgan was just as wet.

But he couldn't bring himself to care.

She lowered herself down on top of him, keeping her legs spread over his crotch.

"I'm sorry," she murmured into his ear.

He couldn't believe what he was hearing. She was sorry? "For what?" he asked incredulously.

"For not being able to go through with it. For not being able to make love."

Arrow couldn't help it. He laughed.

He felt her stiffen above him, but he couldn't stop the laughter from escaping. When he had himself under control, he said, "I've never done anything *half* as intimate as what we just did together," he told her. "That was *definitely* making love."

"But you didn't . . . I couldn't . . ." Her voice trailed off before she could finish her thoughts.

But she didn't have to. Arrow knew what she was getting at. He pushed her up until he could look into her eyes. "It was perfect. Every second of what we just did blew my mind. There was only one thing missing."

She bit her lip, worry easy to see in her eyes. "What?"

"I haven't kissed you yet."

She breathed a sigh of relief. "I can fix that."

"I hoped you would."

Morgan leaned down and pressed her lips to his in a chaste kiss. But almost immediately, she changed it to a more carnal one, her tongue pressing against his lips, demanding entry and sweeping over his as soon as he opened for her.

They lay together, naked, sweaty, messy, and sated, and made out. Kissed as if they'd never kissed before in their lives.

When Morgan finally took her lips from his and rested her head on his shoulder, Arrow said, "We should get up and shower."

"Mmmmm."

"And put on some sleep clothes."

"Mm-hmm."

Arrow smiled and shut his mouth. He was sticky from their combined releases and knew he'd need to change the sheets, but if his woman wanted to lie on top of him and sleep, that's what she'd get to do.

He wasn't worried about what the future held for them. She'd come so far so fast that he knew she'd eventually wrestle her demons into submission. It didn't matter if it took one year or ten—she was more than anything he'd ever dreamed he'd have.

~

Black stood at the back of the room and watched the women and children with a smile on his face. The men on his team took turns coming to the women's shelter and spending time with the residents, to try to show them they didn't have to be afraid of all men. Many of them were there because they were homeless and trying to get back on their feet, but a vast majority had lived in tough situations where they were abused. Domestic violence seemed to be on the rise, and the shelter was a safe place for women from all walks of life.

Coming to the shelter was a tough assignment, especially if the kids cried when they first saw him and the women cowered away. But by the end of the evening, he could usually win over even the most frightened children and their moms.

Tonight, he'd colored pictures with the group. Then, after the kids were sent to the kitchen to participate in some sort of cooking lesson with the newly hired chef, he gave a short self-defense class to the women.

The children were now back, and everyone was oohing and aahing over the cookies they'd made during the last forty-five minutes or so.

"Excuse me. You're Lowell Lockard, right?"

Black turned in surprise to see who'd managed to approach him without his noticing.

The woman was the same height as he was, around five nine, and had blonde hair with the ends dyed light purple. She had dark-blue eyes that reminded him of a stormy ocean. She was full-figured and had the kind of hips he would die to put his hands on.

The thought startled him, even made him feel a little uncomfortable. He wasn't the kind of man who had intense feelings about women he'd just met. He cleared his throat before saying, "Yeah, that's me. Do I know you?"

"You probably don't remember me," she said, her voice low and husky. "I'm Harlow. Harlow Reese. We went to high school together. Well, you were a year older than me, but we both went to Roosevelt High."

Black blinked. "Harlow?"

She chuckled. "I know, I know. I look a lot different than I did sixteen years ago."

Now that he knew who she was, Black recognized her. She was right—she'd changed a lot since he was eighteen, but he could still see the teenager he'd known in her face. Back then, they'd both been in the yearbook club. He'd joined just to have something else to put on his résumé so he'd look good for recruiters, but she'd been doing it because she loved it. She was constantly taking pictures. She'd had a great eye for that sort of thing.

"Harlow Reese. I'll be damned," Black said slowly. "Your hair is longer . . . and more colorful, but of course I know you."

She blushed—and that was that.

Black was intrigued.

It had been a long time since he'd felt an immediate attraction to a woman like he felt right now. Too long. When he'd first become a SEAL, he'd slept with his share of women who'd trolled the bars looking for Navy guys to bag, but the emotionless encounters had gotten old really fast, and he'd become much more discriminating. Since joining the Mountain Mercenaries, his sex life had all but dried up. But there was something about the woman in front of him that piqued his interest.

"What are you doing here?" he asked. "Are you in trouble?" The thought of a man being abusive or stalking her was abhorrent.

She held up her hands and shook her head. "No, nothing like that. I'm the new chef. I was hired about two weeks ago."

Black relaxed a fraction. "If those cookies are any indication, they hired the right person for the job."

She smiled up at him. "Thanks. But cookies are easy. Getting the kids to eat their vegetables is way tougher. Can I ask you something?"

Black immediately nodded. "Of course."

Harlow looked around, as if she wanted to make sure she wouldn't be overheard, before asking, "You work at a gun range, right?"

"I not only work at one, I own it," Black told her.

"Oh. Well . . . um . . . I was wondering if you had any beginner gun-safety classes?"

Black narrowed his eyes, all his attention on the woman in front of him now. She no longer met his gaze and had her arms crossed defensively in front of her.

"Are you in trouble, Harl?" Black asked, using the nickname she'd used back in high school.

She shook her head. "No. I mean, I don't think so. I would just like to get more familiar with guns and how they work. You know . . . for my own protection."

Again, Black didn't like the sound of that. He gently took her elbow in his hand and lifted his chin to the director of the shelter. Loretta Royster was in her midsixties and not only was in charge of the non-profit organization but also owned the building. She waved at him and turned her attention back to a pair of children standing in front of her.

Black steered Harlow into the hallway and back toward the kitchen, where he assumed she'd come from. The appliances were as old as the building, but apparently that didn't matter, because the cookie he'd eaten earlier had been delicious.

Harlow pulled away from his touch and absently began to wipe down the already-clean counter, obviously trying to avoid looking at him while they talked.

"Harlow," Black said firmly. "Look at me."

She sighed, then met his gaze.

There was now a counter separating them, but Black could still feel the attraction arching between them. "To answer your question, yes, there are several beginner gun-safety classes offered at my gun range, but if you're in trouble, you can tell me. I can help."

She stared at him for a long time before saying, "I'm a big girl, Lowell. I can take care of myself."

"I don't doubt it," he replied. "But if you're in trouble, it could possibly affect the women and kids here. It's been a long time since I've seen you, but I don't think you've changed so much that you wouldn't care about that."

"Of course I care about that," she said heatedly. "The residents here are why I'm asking in the first place. I want to protect *them*."

The second the words were out of her mouth, she bit her lip and looked down at the counter in front of her.

Black's mind was racing with all the possibilities that could've made Harlow seek him out. "Tell me," he said gently.

Harlow sighed. "I've noticed some weird things happening around here. Loretta tries to act like they aren't a big deal, I think so she doesn't scare the residents. You know as well as I do how most women came to be here, that most don't have the best history when it comes to men. There have been some guys hanging around, harassing me when I come to work in the mornings. It's nothing I can't handle, but the last thing I want is them doing the same thing to the women and kids who reside here if they don't get a rise out of me."

"Are they exes of some of the residents?" Black asked.

"Loretta doesn't think so, but she's not sure."

"She needs to call the cops. Report them."

"She has. And I'm sure they'll deal with it, but in the meantime, I'd feel better if I could protect myself."

Black made a split-second decision. He took his wallet from his pocket and pulled out a business card. Grabbing a pen from a table nearby, he scribbled his cell phone number on the back, then held it out to Harlow. "Here's my card. You call me anytime, day or night, and I'll get you set up with a beginner's class. But more than that, if you ever feel scared or uneasy, let me know, and I'll come over and check things out."

She reached up and took the card from his hand, staring down at it for a beat before looking back up at him. "Okay . . . um, thanks."

"I mean it," Black said. "Call me."

Harlow pulled her hair back with one hand, then sighed, leaning on the counter. "Do you give your number to anyone who wants to learn how to use a gun?"

"No," he said succinctly.

"Then why me?" Harlow asked.

Black put his hands on the counter between them and leaned toward her. She didn't pull back, and it made his pulse speed up with anticipation. "Because I like your hair."

"You gave me your number because you like my *hair*?" she asked skeptically.

"That, and anyone who's more concerned about the people who live here than her own safety is someone I want to get to know better. Besides, we were friends once, right?" he asked.

"I'm not sure I would say we were friends," Harlow said with a small grin.

"Sure we were. We survived that yearbook club together, didn't we?"

She nodded. "Yeah. If you're serious, I'll call."

"I'm serious," Black said, willing her to read between the lines of what he was saying. He was interested in Harlow Reese. There was something about her that drew him in. If he had to use his job as an excuse for her to call him, he would. He'd teach her gun safety and how to shoot, but he hoped in the process he could convince her to go on a date and get to know him better as well.

Deciding he'd talk to Rex about the situation at the shelter, just in case, Black smiled at Harlow. "It's a date then."

She blushed again, but nodded.

Black straightened and smiled at her. "Don't wait to call, Harl. I'm looking forward to it." And with that, he winked at her and headed out of the kitchen. Suddenly, he was more than glad it had been his turn to volunteer at the shelter tonight.

He'd wait a few days for her to call, but if she didn't, he wasn't going to let this go. He knew where she worked—he'd just come up with an excuse to come back to the shelter so he could see her again. It had been a long time since he'd been as excited about a woman as he was right now.

Even though he'd known Harlow when they were kids, he didn't know anything about the woman she'd become. But he had a feeling when he did, she just might change his life.

About the Author

Susan Stoker is a *New York Times*, *USA Today*, and *Wall Street Journal* bestselling author. Her series include Badge of Honor: Texas Heroes, SEAL of Protection, Delta Force Heroes, and Mountain Mercenaries. Married to a retired Army noncommissioned officer, Stoker has lived all over the country—from Missouri and California to Colorado and Texas—and currently lives under the big skies of Tennessee. A true believer in happily ever after, Stoker enjoys writing novels in which romance turns to love. To learn more about the author and her work, visit her website, www.stokeraces.com, or find her on Facebook at www.facebook.com/authorsusanstoker.

Connect with Susan Online

SUSAN'S FACEBOOK PROFILE AND PAGE

www.facebook.com/authorsstoker

www.facebook.com/authorsusanstoker

FOLLOW SUSAN ON TWITTER

www.twitter.com/Susan_Stoker

FIND SUSAN'S BOOKS ON GOODREADS

www.goodreads.com/SusanStoker

EMAIL

Susan@StokerAces.com

WEBSITE

www.StokerAces.com